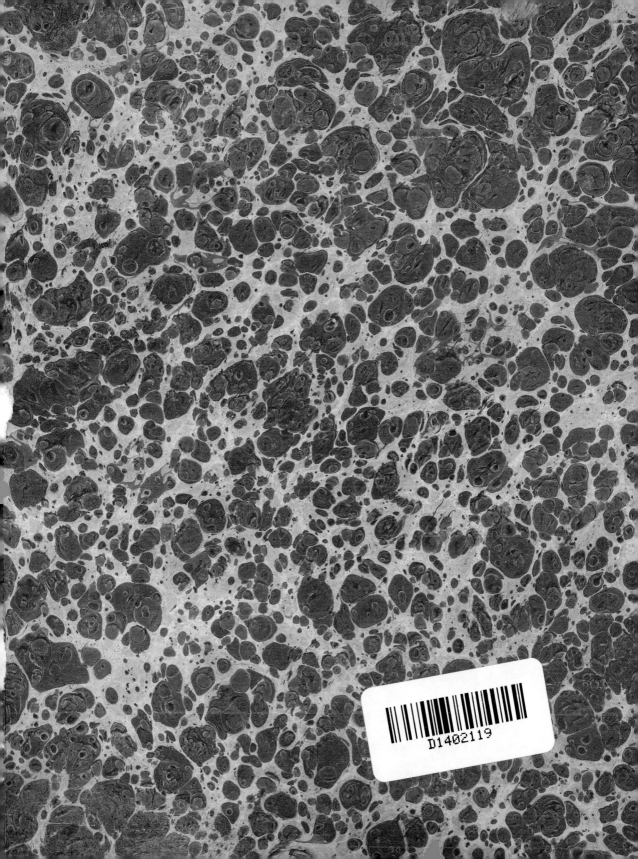

GALERIE
DE DIFFORMITÉ

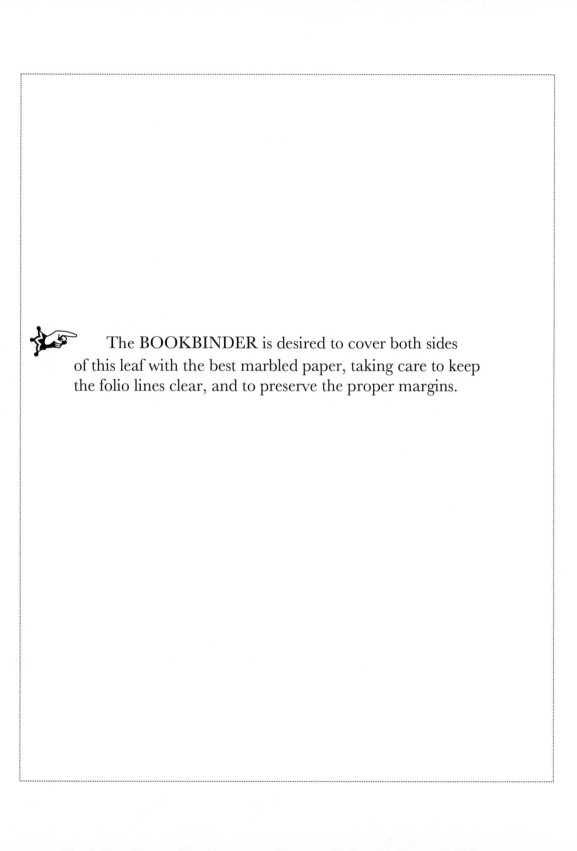

The BOOKBINDER is desired to cover both sides of this leaf with the best marbled paper, taking care to keep the folio lines clear, and to preserve the proper margins.

GRETCHEN E. HENDERSON
PRESENTS:

GALERIE
DE DIFFORMITÉ

& OTHER EXHUMED EXHIBITS:
A DECLASSIFIED CATALOGUE

First published 2011 by &NOW Books, an imprint of Lake Forest College Press.

Directors   Associate Director
Robert Archambeau   Joshua Corey
Davis Schneiderman

Box A-16
Lake Forest College
555 N. Sheridan Road
Lake Forest, IL 60045

lakeforest.edu

If the Novel is a "baggy monster" (as it has been said), then this baggy monster is a novel: a form born of variant forms—deformed—from & by an Imagination, not to be confused with a Life, which is to say: any resemblances to actual persons, places, & patron saints should be pardoned, as accidental, unintentional, &c. That said, no writer (artist, composer, &c.) creates in a vacuum; and so, this minor work is offered humbly back to the wider world from which it sprang and remains, heartily and heartfully, indebted.

My sincerest thanks to the many Subscribers who have visually and conceptually enriched this catalogue. In the spirit of the *Galerie de Difformité*, deformations by Subscribers have been deformed further within this book in black and white reproductions. The originals can be found, attributed to the artists, in the online Galerie: difformite.wordpress.com. At this site, grateful acknowledgement also is made to the journals that first published excerpts of this book.

Lake Forest College Press publishes in the broad spaces of Chicago studies. Our imprint, &NOW Books, publishes innovative and conceptual literature, and serves as the publishing arm of the &NOW writers' conference and organization.

Cover art: Mustafa Düzgünman. Floral marbled paper, ca. 1970. Inside cover: Stone-pattern marbled paper, French, early nineteenth century, remnant from an unidentified book. From the Norma Rubovits Collection at the Newberry Library, Chicago. Photos courtesy of the Newberry Library.

Note about the cover art: Mustafa Esat Düzgünman (1920-1990) was a celebrated Turkish marbler and bookbinder who worked in the ebru ("cloud-shaped") tradition. Traditionally, marbled papers tended to line interior covers of books, but since the *Galerie de Difformité* is more of a book turned inside out, this marble was chosen for the exterior cover. Given the novel's recurring motif of bees, the floral pattern also appeared attractive, as if it might attract a swarm.

ISBN-13: 978-0-9823156-3-7

ISBN-10: 0-9823156-3-5

Book and cover design by Gretchen E. Henderson and Emma Therieau
Printed in the United States

"Why, YOU, of course."

~ *multiple sources*

flawed
mutilated
insane
twisted
faulty
defaced
outlandish
cracked asymmetric
disfigured abnormal
crookback degenerate
monstrous deficient unnatural
fantastic offensive
freakish crippled derivative
scabbed humpbacked repugnant
misshapen gruesome
peculiar diseased horrid nailed
repulsive paralytic warped awful
strange quadriplegic grisly
distempered complicated
terrible paraplegic injured
disorder affliction deformed
horrible misproportioned incapable
disabled handicapped dreadful hideous
defective impaired mutant
absurd irregular idiot odd
quaint frightful ghastly
malconformed
bizarre loathsome distorted
infirm indisposed sick
grotesque aberration
imbecile

2

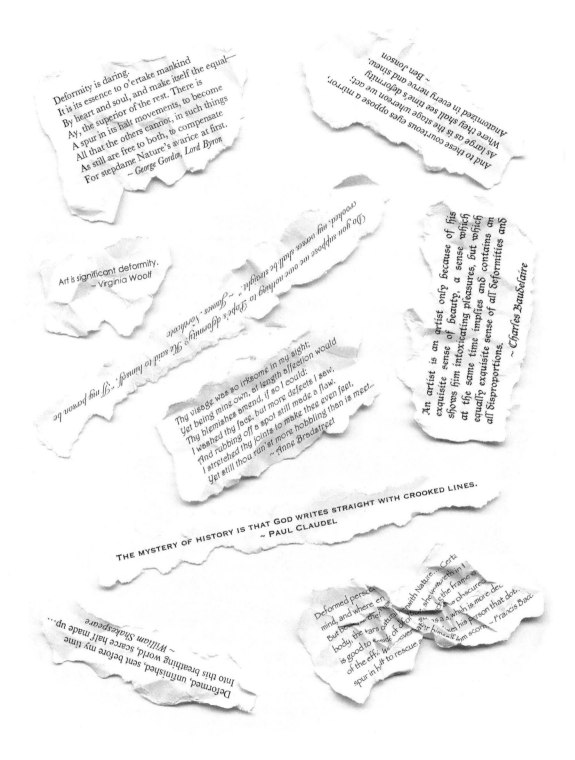

Deformity is daring.
It is its essence to o'ertake mankind
By heart and soul, and make itself the equal—
Ay, the superior of the rest. There is
A spur in its halt movements, to become
All that the others cannot, in such things
As still are free to both, to compensate
For stepdame Nature's avarice at first.
~ George Gordon, Lord Byron

And to these courteous eyes oppose a mirror,
As large as is the stage whereon we act;
Where they shall see the time's deformity
Anatomized in every nerve and sinew.
~ Ben Jonson

Art is significant deformity.
~ Virginia Woolf

Do you suppose we owe nothing to Pope's deformity? He said to himself, "If my person be crooked, my verses shall be straight." ~ James Northcote

An artist is an artist only because of his exquisite sense of beauty, a sense which shows him intoxicating pleasures, but which at the same time implies and contains an equally exquisite sense of all deformities and all disproportions.
~ Charles Baudelaire

Thy visage was so irksome in my sight;
Yet being mine own, at length affection would
Thy blemishes amend, if so I could:
I washed thy face, but more defects I saw,
And rubbing off a spot still made a flaw.
I stretched thy joints to make thee even feet,
Yet still thou run'st more hobbling than is meet…
~ Anne Bradstreet

THE MYSTERY OF HISTORY IS THAT GOD WRITES STRAIGHT WITH CROOKED LINES.
~ PAUL CLAUDEL

Deformed, unfinished, sent before my time
Into this breathing world, scarce half made up…
~ William Shakespeare

Deformed persons... with Nature... Certe...
mind, and where en...
But because... the... the frame o...
body, the stars naturally... as... who... obscured
is good to... side of scorn... which is more dec...
of the eff... whatsoever... himself... son that doth...
spur in h... to rescue a... him scorn. ~ Francis Bac...

3

PRE–FACE

If *face* refers to *visage* but
also *to meet with a gaze that
implies courage, confidence,
or defiance*, then in some
cases, *preface* may suggest
the *precursor to said
confidence or defiance*; and
if this be so, then this PRE-
FACE may beg of you, *dear
Reader*, to stir courage by
turning pages straightaway,
to arrive *crookedly* (see
epigraph by P.C.) at the Face
of this *Galerie de Difformité*:
that is, namely, its deforming
"Exhibits" (A, B, C, &c.) in
search of Hearts to fill its
Whole.

☞ *To start deforming, turn to page 229.*

☞ *To read another preface, turn to page 14.*

☞ If you continued reading from the last page (i.e., didn't follow directions), please simultaneously rub your head & stomach, then turn to page 16.

☞ If you read crookedly (that is, correctly), then turn to page 38 (or alternatively to a number related to your birthday).

you are here

•

Imagine a grid, or something with lines that cross and hatch with openings that signify exits and egresses between rooms and corridors. The rooms resemble odd boxes that could grow three-dimensionally in another context, fronted by neoclassical columns or brightly colored tubes; but this two-dimensional page remains blank, apart from a smattering of labels and thumbnails. Through a series of ☞☞☞ the so-called MAP of the *Galerie de Difformité* indicates that it wends around corners, circuitously folding back on itself, transgressing other exhibits and digressing through sideshows and special features, including an outdoor sculpture garden (replete with a "grotto" for the "grotesque") and a sunken historic ship, dredged from the depths and displayed as "Wreckage."

To another mind, this MAP wouldn't appear minimalist but palatial, high and wide enough to shrink you down to size. I can barely imagine that cavern, glowing, resonant with echoes, with a ceiling edged by sky. Through shadows, bodies come into focus. Asymmetric and angled, scattered in all directions. The nearest stands armless and cloth-draped. Her nudity is not severe as her severed foot, torn nipples, stub nose. She wants for bandages, surrounded by other broken bodies whose pallor is pearlescent. Another body bends into focus, then another and another, until we are surrounded by an army lacking heads and hands, cocks and breasts. A torso here and there, a pile of arms and legs. Each body softens as stone, lost in graceful gazes. Behind them, a wall materializes from whiteness, hung with frames. Within those frames, more bodies appear: fractured figures, penitent postulants, beckoning fingers. A torso twists. A set of eyes follows our steps.

Again and again, I've tried to imagine what the creator of *Galerie de Difformité* envisioned. I am not she, but am offering this volume as testament to her work. Gloria Heys died before completing her enterprise, but in the last two years of her life, she shared with me a glimpse of her vision. We met under strange circumstances: she was the only child of my grandfather's mistress, from a second family that he kept secret for decades. Only as an adult did I learn of her, and sought her halfway across the country. She was a petite woman who stayed virtually housebound after the deaths of her husband (a Vietnam veteran) and only son (with Down syndrome). Adulthood brought Gloria a rare disease, which left her arm crippled. What might have weighed down another person, however, seemed to bring her lightness. Something about her was sprite-like. Her reverence for learning rivaled only what I remembered of my grandfather, a renowned scholar of Medieval Studies. Gloria never completed college or her studies of music, but her bungalow brimmed with books. She was a conundrum: homely on the surface, seemingly serious, with a wit that made me laugh when I least expected. I remember her vividly, more than acquaintances whom I've known half of my life. On that single occasion when we met in person, she pieced together part of me that I hadn't known was missing. Much of that experience—and this book—is owed to a single bone.

Gloria's bone was a relic, small enough to fit in a hand. It was shaped as a quill. Most curious about its form was a heart-shaped hole near the sword-shaped nib. Gloria revealed that the bone with a heart-shaped hole was a gift from her father, my grandfather, from one of his sabbaticals to Italy. She said that it was a xiphoid process, part of the sternum. It wasn't an original bone, her father had claimed, but rather a model fashioned by hand as a quill in the eighteenth century by a British fraternal organization (with the endearing name of Ye Ugly Face Clubb) to record their members' fantastic physiognomic features. Perhaps even more fantastic than that fact: the original bone was thought to have been extracted from the corpse of Beatrice Portinari, of Dantean fame. As families save and bequeath engagement rings and Bibles, this bone seemed destined to be passed—literally and legendarily—onto the next of kin. And when we said our goodbyes, Gloria asked for my address and said to expect something in the mail.

For each month thereafter for two years, we maintained a correspondence that has been one of the richest and rarest experiences of my life. It wasn't what might be expected: not any sentimental, laugh-and-cry cascade of revelations. Instead of letters, Gloria sent me segments of something she referred to as her *Galerie*—this *Galerie*. It was a project that she had started after her husband and son died, when she lived alone for the first time in her life. She called me her "Subscriber." I didn't know what she meant until I received the first installment. Her *Galerie* didn't arrive serially like a Victorian novel but in disordered self-contained fragments. It took a few deliveries for me to sense a pattern and to deduce that Gloria wasn't, precisely, "the Undertaker," a role she reserved for a reincarnation of Beatrice herself—the epitome of beauty, deconstructed, in a scheme to revive Ye Ugly Face Clubb.

I am no literary critic or art historian, rather a counselor at a community center who works with youths termed "disabled." Perhaps that's why Gloria entrusted me with her *Galerie de Difformité*. When we met, she said that she worried about everything that had become P.C.—"political crap," she called it (from her grandmotherly mouth!). Gloria herself was "crippled," a "bastard," and a host of other epithets that people had flung at her readily during her lifetime. In the time that remained for her, she said, she wished to dissect these terms and reassemble them into something more monstrous— but magnanimous, too.

In order to write this introduction, I've consulted a variety of experts to help inform my understanding of her enterprise and give her incomplete *Galerie* some form of dignified public viewing. Gloria's art seems a kind of folk art: as naïve as it is learned. The expert that I need most is Gloria, who left no map. Since our correspondence only happened monthly, I didn't learn of her death until after some weeks passed, after her house was sold and her estate bequeathed to charity. I've never again seen that bone with its heart-shaped hole.

What I did find in her local library: her name was inscribed in a book, a copy of Clarice Lispector's *The Passion According to G.H.* The initials match Gloria's, which may explain her fondness for this text that begins: "This is a book just like any other book. But I would be happy if it were read only by people….who know that an approach—to anything whatsoever— must…traverse even the very opposite of what is being approached….Over time, the character G.H. came to give *me*, for example, a very difficult pleasure; but it *is* called pleasure."[iii]

I believe the same might be said of Gloria Heys and her *Galerie de Difformité*.

☞ *To listen to Gloria invoke Beatrice, turn to page 24.*

☞ *To learn more about the bone with the heart-shaped hole, turn to page 31.*

☞ To enter Gloria Heys' Galerie de Difformité, turn the page.

☞ To work at this backwards, turn to page 228 and find another heart.

"Here begins the new life."

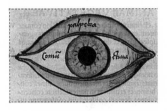

Galerie de Difformité

sisters
FRIENDS and ~~brothers~~ ^, unto me attend,

ladies
  While I sing of our Club here to-night, ^ ~~Sirs~~,

Where the Ugly alone do intend

honies
  To drink deep at the fount of delight, ^ ~~Sirs~~,

For however Dɛ/ôRm'd we may be,

  Good humour will make us look smugly,

While ev'ry true lover of glee

  Will drink to the Club call'd the Ugly.

Rum ti, &c.[iii]

☞ *Draw a face on this page, then insert doily, lace, onionskin, or semi-transparent overlay, affixed inside spine.* ☞ ☞ ☞

The Society for the Revival of Ye Ugly Face Clubb,
Proposes to Publish by Subscription
A MOST MAGNIFICENT AND ACCURATE, IF VERY LIMITED, EDITION
of the

GALERIE
DE
DIFFORMITÉ

In pages of questionable QUARTO SIZE, on the finest pretense of ROYAL ATLAS
(otherwise known as Business Multipurpose) PAPER,
fabricated for the Purpose by Xerox.

And Printed with T Y P E S cast in the Proprietress' House, upon a Principle
calculated to unite Beauty with Deformity, not to mention Utility.

The TEXT to be regulated, and the LITERARY PART of the Undertaking
conducted,

BY THE SOCIETY FOR THE REVIVAL OF
YE UGLY FACE CLUBB

Each Artist's Name, with the Title and Medium of a Scene, being marked upon
the Frames of the Pictures, a Catalogue seems superfluous—But as it has been suggested,
that it would be agreeable to the Subscriber, to have a sampling of Scenes printed, as would
tend to elucidate the Subject of the Picture in relation to Deformity—This has been
accordingly done, and at the smallest possible Expense.

> omnia mutantur, nihil interit: errat et illinc
> huc venit, hinc illuc, et quoslibet occupant artus
> spiritus eque feris humana in corpora transit
> inque feras noster, nec tempore deperit ullo,
> utque novis facilis signatur cera figuris
> nec manet ut 'uerat nec formam servant eandem,
> sed tamen ipsa eadem est, animam sic simper eandem
> esse, sed in varias doceo migrare figuras.
> ~ Ovid, Metamorphoses

N.B. As the Number of SUBSCRIBERS to the GALERIE DE DIFFORMITÉ must be
limited, it is recommended to those, who have any design of becoming Subscribers, to be
as early as possible in their Application.

11

☞ If you have applied to be a Subscriber, skip to page 16.

APPLICATION TO BE A SUBSCRIBER

Thou Shalt Not (Be) Discriminate(d) Against Based Upon
(please list ways that you classify yourself, in no particular order):

Actuals		Hypotheticals
_____	(nationality)	_____
_____	(ethnicity)	_____
_____	(gender)	_____
_____	(sexual orientation)	_____
_____	(age)	_____
_____	(employment)	_____
_____	(education level)	_____
_____	(disability)	_____
_____	(beauty/ugliness)	_____
_____	(strength/weakness)	_____
_____	(secret)	_____
_____	(zodiac sign)	_____
_____	(name)	_____
_____	(other:_____)	_____

OPTIONAL QUESTIONS:
draw arrows & answer in margins

1. What is your definition of a Book?
2. Do you judge a Book by its cover? a. yes, b. no, c. don't know
3. What are your expectations for this book?
4. If I say "Exhibit," you think: a. museum, b. legal trial, c. other
5. How accessible do you like literature? a. very, b. kind-of, c. not-so-much
      (Define "accessibility" in this context: _____)
6. How accessible do you like life? a. very, b. kind-of, c. not-so-much
      (Define "accessibility" in this context: _____)
7. Find a quotation about "deformity" and write it on this page.
8. Anything else you'd like to get off your head, shoulders, knees, toes?

Please tear this page from the spine& send to yourself at:
🖃 📖 _____ (fill in your address)
_____

Add note to envelope seal:
☞ *DO NOT OPEN until you find the MONSTER in this book.* ☜

12

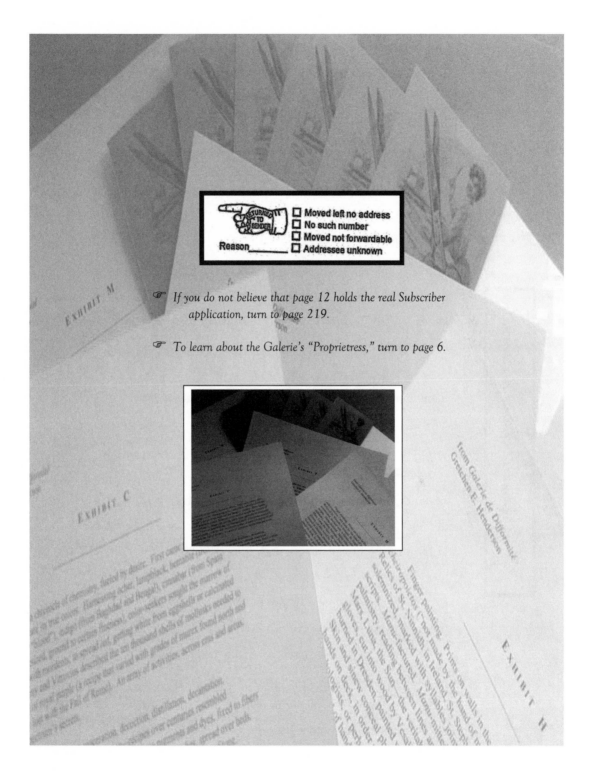

RETURNED TO SENDER

☐ Moved left no address
☐ No such number
☐ Moved not forwardable
☐ Addressee unknown

Reason_____

☞ If you do not believe that page 12 holds the real Subscriber application, turn to page 219.

☞ To learn about the Galerie's "Proprietress," turn to page 6.

Undertaker's Note on the Text

I cannot permit this Catalogue to appear before the Publick, without returning my sincere Thanks to you, dear Subscriber of this Undertaking, and to the Artists, whose works are reproduced here or Virtually in further Reproduction as deformations of the Originals. It is therefore hoped that the Spectator will view these Pictures, even Textual Thumbnails, with regard to this Prosimetric Enterprise.

Of the merits of the Artists employed in this Exhibition, I can with truth say that I have sought talents, wherever they were to be found, to carry into execution an undertaking based upon historical Taste and the subject of Deformity.

Upon the merits of the Pictures themselves, it is not for me to speak, except with the relation of each to Deformity. Suffice it to say, that these Works of Art have been chosen to Accompany and Rearrange my Exhibits (aforementioned in the *Pre-face, see page* 4), to promulgate and promote this plan in General.[iv]

Though I believe it will be readily admitted that no subjects seem so proper to form a School of Deformity in Art—This much, however, I will venture to say: that the Works collected for this Gallery—unlocked

☞ Please decorate margins.

14

from Wundercammern & Mvsevms, culled from publick & private Whatnot—bear something for you, Subscriber, to consider: the Nature of Deformity.

> ☞ *Candid Criticism is the soul of improvement—and those artists, who shut their ears against it, must never expect to improve—At the same time, every artist ought to despise and condemn the cavils of Pseudo-critics, who, rather than not attempt to shew their wit, would crush all merit in its bud—The discerning part of the public, however, place all these attempts to true account—Malignity—But, as the world was never entirely free from such critics, the present undertaking must expect to have its share.* ❧

I must express my hopes that the Subscriber will be satisfied with the progress made in this arduous undertaking, that Deformity has been redefined through the Arts, regarding the Nature of the Subject and the Subject of Nature. I trust upon inspection of what has been done, and is now doing, through this Deformation of Text, that the Subscriber will be satisfied with the exertions undertaken, and will think confidence has not been misplaced.

If the object of uniting a certain degree of Beauty with Deformity, through Utility, has been attained, the merit is the Artists. —If not, the Undertaker is willing to bear the blame.

~ *Poeta qui pavide cantat, rarissime placet.*
~ *Informis Societatis Socius.*[v]

CAUTION !!!!

Do not read straight through this catalogue from start to finish! This gallery encourages—even mandates—that you choose your own path. Exhibits within the *Galerie de Difformité* conceal many discoveries—but also many dangers—which can arise unexpectedly if you read this catalogue like a regular book, or if you believe that life is lived linearly. As you explore rooms and reflect upon artworks, you will be asked to make choices that lead you closer or farther into the Unknown. Follow the instructions, but also bravely break the rules! One misstep may curtail your visit ... but a well-chosen path may lead to unexpected:

A.	pleasure!	} *page* ____
B.	palpitation!	} *page* ____
C.	puzzlement!	} *page* ____
D.	penetration!	} *page* ____
E.	predestination!	} *page* ____
F.	prevarication!	} *page* ____
G.	peregrination!	} *page* ____
H.	_____!	} *page* ____
I.	*Etc...*	} *page* ____

*(☞ Upon return, fill in pages to coordinate
& create paths for future references…)*

☞ *To find out where you are, turn to page 6.*

☞ *To approach the entrance to the Galerie, turn to page 9.*

CONTENTS
OF THE
CATALOGUE

Welcome! You haven't missed much, finding yourself here in the *Contents of the Catalogue*: a luscious but, honestly, quite ludicrous place to be—not particularly lugubrious but liquefying, no longer solid—seemingly black & white, based on the premise that Contents are full of Forms, deformed & deformable, as shall (and shan't & shammed) be seen or heard: Extracted, Enacted, Embedded, Enamored, Embroiled & (or) Exhumed, depending on your sensibility & (or) sense toward this Thesis. And so begins my Antithesis, also begetting questions with Questions on the search for ambulatory & ambivalent, even aerodynamic & aeromagnetic Answers, to Otherwise & in General begin this Project with a Pre-face (which isn't to neglect the Dedication to "Why, YOU, of course," *see page 1*) before the Subject epigraphically accretes around said Subject (that is, *Deformity*) to deform this book (if Book it might be called) as a Word & Ward, as the *Galerie de Difformité* emerges somewhat analogously, even allogamously: a cross-fertilization between an art catalogue and choose-your-own-adventure, between a funhouse and labyrinth, all dedicated to Deformity to lead you toward & away from said Subject, arising through Choices that beget (but also upset) Beginnings (for instance, "Here Begins the New Life"—*see page 9*), leaving me, Here and Now, in a bind: at the crux of the qualm of the *Contents of the Catalogue*, that is to say: whether to continue as anticipated (as a Table, as it were), subtitling sections of Pages, grouped by numerics (as one expects with such

Contents) or leave you to your own De-

vices. In other words, rather than

classifying your path in preordained or

predestined form, forging and forcing out

the *Contents of the Catalogue*, numerically

begetting & resetting cross-sections,

evidences & ephemera—rather than do

that, *I say*, I would rather leave you to

your own designs: to create & chart your

own course(s), marking such a map as

needed (as an *Alternative Contents of the*

Catalogue—see page 21) to retrace steps first

charted by your agenda(s) & agency(ies),

with something more or less auspicious,

not spoiled by any linearly listed points of

departure (which hypothetically might

proceed as follows ☞ ☞ ☞ ☞ ☞ ☞):

Nay, a waste! Spelling out a list,

presuming to order but disordering—*Why*,

such an act misrepresents, at least

according to such a fixed Form (whereby

one flips left to right, not right to left,

nor upside down) and assumes something about this Text that is not true, nor to be trusted (that is, that Pages bound in this Book are meant to be bound); and so I refuse to provide said Table, disavowed here & henceforth disrupted & defused, as (& so) Deformity might, could, should, & will deform the Nature of the Subject and the Subject of Nature. To You, dear Reader (*shall I say:* Deformer, Deformant, Decreator, &c.), I leave the Design of the *Contents of the Catalogue*—to You: to become the agent of this Book & set off at a sprint or saunter or slant (None or All of the above)—This, Here & Now, is where I leave you to choose your next step and make a map, as you might, to leave for future Readers to follow your course(s), to learn from your delights & doldrums, marvelings & missteps, to see what might yet deform from this fledgling & somewhat feisty

Form that is deforming as we speak, otherwise known as the *Galerie de Difformité*.

☞ *To make your own map of the Galerie de Difformité, find a piece of paper &*
writing implement, engage with the next page, then proceed to page 35.

☞ *To hear a story behind the story, turn to page 46.*

☞ NOTE ☜

At any point, if you arrive at
a place you have visited
before, feel free to close the
📖 *& open at random to*
continue your path; OR,
alternatively, add a ☞ with a
new directional ... ✌️👇✌️👎

ALTERNATIVE
CONTENTS
OF THE
CATALOGUE

DIRECTIONS: *Please paste in a map(s) for future readers to use as guides through this Galerie. Alternatively, tuck such self-made map(s) into the inside front or back cover(s) & add directive(s) here saying as much. Alternatively, tear out this page & paste it over the Contents of the Catalogue, adding other pages, until nothing of the original remains. Alternatively and/or additionally, make a new cover in which to enwrap the book, with fold-out flaps, and/or fashion a box in which the book might fit (or not), perhaps with a kit, including paraphernalia for future reading & deforming. Alternatively...*

☞ *To compare & contrast with the actual Contents of the Catalogue, please turn to page 17; to compare & contrast with the Ideal Contents of the Catalogue, examine the Appendix (page 247).*

As the pliant beeswax
Is stamped with new designs, and is no longer
What once it was, but changes form, and still
Is pliant wax, so do I...

LOOK & LISTEN

PLEASE DO ~~NOT~~ TOUCH.

☞ To continue to redefine deformity, turn to any of the following pages: 34, 50, 73, 99, 118, 141.

☞ If you're missing the Contents, please turn to 17 or 21.

☞ In the future, turn to page ____ or ____ or ____ (fill in the blanks).

23

THE BEAKEEPER'S APPRENTICE
(AN INVOCATION;
OR, SELF-AUTOPSY)

...Enter it

i.

When she first appeared
she was whitewashed,
bandaged gauze

haze of clouds
collapsing,
knit with frenzy

of bees. She was
buzzing. Limbs locked
in light-wire, quiver-

ing, I watched
thick with trembling.
The bower

broke. She swarmed
with want, with workers
worming through

combs of colon-
y: quaking castratos
of wax and barbs

burrowing. Her head
seemed mangled, wings
on her lips. Hidden

beneath the buzz,
sweetness dripped
through her, held

intact between
sounds. In her un-
stung hands (bundled

bees squirming in
union) a hum harm-
onized in woods

flying from there to
here, again, where
she cups her palms

to my ear, petitions
me to look away,
to listen

to this moment
with more droning, drawn
out sounds (of *madrigals*

or *madder gals*?) brooding[vi]
over a book fallen
from her hands, trembling

like mine but brighter
(her body, brazen &
blinding) so I can't see

only hear: some sounds
of the book that she gives
me to translate, & "Call me—"

ii.

Amid hives, she frays
(visible chimera, flick-
ering)—flaying wings,

skin, breasts, piece by
piece, portending:
her head swells

to sing. Limbs fly
—furtive, fiery—
straddling the brook

Without being

save her book, sodden
and sinking, as fish twist
with fingers, darting down

curling currents. Her lips
part in song. No
Orphic rasp, the voice

warps & wraps my heart
in the heat, pulsing
watered

innards
seed me
from weeds & vines

flowering by reeds
along the river, listening
as her song

defies silence, dis-
arms my body with
beats, off-time iambs

beneath buzzing. Echo
of Ecko (*the girl with no
door on her mouth,* Soph-

okles said,[vii] deriding her
sound and sex in one
breath) tempers me

to keep taut, taught to
suspend myself
& atone to tune

the Music
of the Spheres. Here
we are again, where

myth outlives
hysterias of history,
hypocrisies of love &

lore… (But wait—
was it today or tomorrow
I freed Aristaeus' bees?

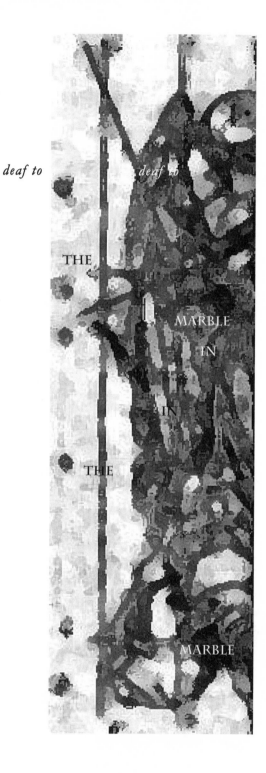

deaf to

This is not me—)
To Bea: "Call me—"

iii.

the singing

Upon hearing her words
in my mouth, my lips shut
with stinging, sweet

confusion, Bea's bees
on my tongue, quest-
ioning: What does it mean

AND

for a woman to appear
to a woman, not Laura
to Petrarch, Lady Philosophy

CARVED

to Boethius, Guadalupe
to Juan Diego, but X to
X? Seduction would be

easier to deduce than this
begging for a chance
to be human, no longer

AND

exalted at the right hand of
the rod, unsexed by the rood
languishing outside time.

Wait—she speaks again:

CARVED

iv.

Call me Bea.

Like *be*. Be-fore, *be*-reave, *be*-lieve, *be*-friend. Be-at. Be-at-ri-ce. You know naught of. What
is known is: Bea *be*-tween, no longer beckoning: "Look behind." You ahead: Love bade
him speak, but Bea? Purged to earth. Neck to toe to knee: knotted together. Banned and
bound. Wings crumple to hands, flushed with wounds. Tongue tied. Untie me, please. I:
who had no choice in Guiding. No longer at the right hand, I've slipped from grasping. At
last. The tiers are tired. Wrought with writing: *Listen.* Mangled metrics unbinding Bea, no
longer who. To be? This question: not about resurrection. In an all-too-late mingling
sundry bones with breath: I call you. To love what is broken. I am. Returning to have my
hand in this. Only if you let me love you, without assumption, will I agree to be your Guide.

v.

(Bea continues.)

And one more thing:

I am here
to teach you
to break
seemlessly
so that one day
when you do
you will
not seam
(*i.e.,* split):

Eat my heart.[ix]

vi.

And as she sang, I felt her hand
in my chest, puppeteer of
mass: muscles and veins

thumping ribs, compressing
breath. Resonant, lyre-like
& liturgical, I was plucked

for what? I dared not look
without volition. Something
was strumming. Her head

moaned in the river. Sodden
pages lingered in reeds
but started to rise. It was

only a matter of waiting
for the sky to blink, black. Her
ears leapt to my chest. My

eyes shut. Limbs went limp.
Involuntary organs bellowed
beneath my breast

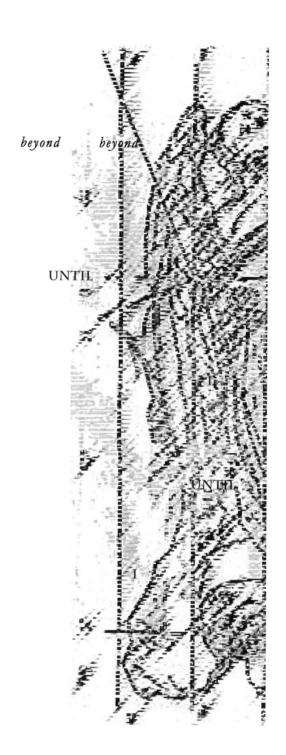

beyond   *beyond*

UNTIL

UNTIL

I

unstitching sex with piping
and unction. Such function
became suffocation, except:

another started to breathe
in me. As if one part (*ears*)
could enliven another (*heart*).

S'io m'intuassi, come tu t'inmii…[x]
If I could (fathom this)
as you, I could hear

excision. Surging, here it is:
We are, our lids lifting in animated autopsy, seeing

through mirrored eyes. Our
two-as-one orchestrates
an offer of ravishment. This

may not be your hand (reaching from my chest) bearing
what looks like a pulsing

toad, encased in moss
and muck. Fuck. I
can't eat such grafted

fruit: your heart, planted
in my mouth, forgetting all
but our shared undertaking…

> *Eat my heart.*
> *Our heart.*

My lips part. Heart bursts
with bees. A thousand wings
leave me empty-mouthed

with a hollow chest.
And then I start to sing,
to breathe your scattered signs

off parched pages, slowly
lulling your warped words
into my heart-shaped hole.

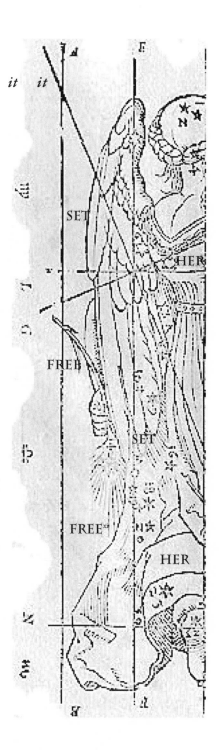

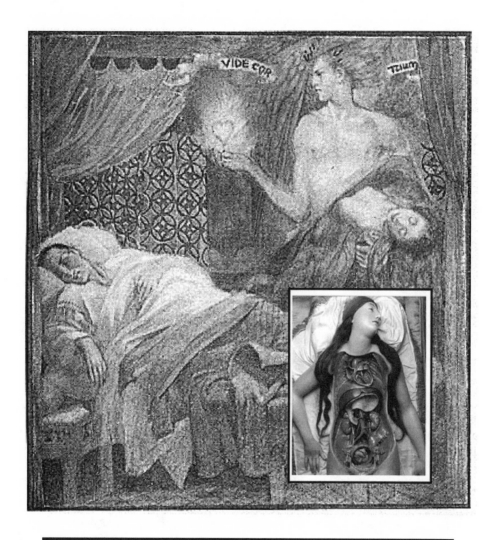

Fig. 1a. (☝): First heart transplant in recorded history, donor and recipient:

Fig. 1b. (☝): Beeswax model of Beatrice Portinari.
Note: Missing segment of sternum.

Beatrice Portinari (1266-1290) to Dante Alighieri (1265-1321).

Lineage of a Bone

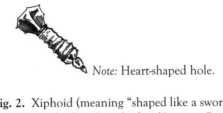

Note: Heart-shaped hole.

Fig. 2. Xiphoid (meaning "shaped like a sword";
part of sternum) taken from body of Beatrice Portinari.

~

1290. Beatrice Portinari dies.

1321? Grave robbers steal bones of Beatrice Portinari from her family tomb in the
Church of Santa Margherita de' Cerchi, Florence, Italy. Rumor spreads of her quill-shaped
bone (with a hole resembling a heart) used to pen the last thirteen cantos of the *Paradiso*.

1583. Felix Platter illustrates bone with heart-shaped hole in *De corporis humani structura*
(above: *Fig. 2*).

1615. Helkiah Crooke notes in *Mikrokosmographia; Or, A Description of the Body of Man*
that the xiphoid differs between genders: "in women somtimes [sic] toward the end
perforated with a broad hole much like a heart."

1677. Bone with heart-shaped hole is inventoried in the collection of Marchese
Fernando Cospi, Bologna, Italy.

1743. The fraternal Ugly Face Clubb [sic] in Liverpool, Britain, adopts bone with heart-
shaped hole as its secret symbol for membership. All members' faces must have features
"out of the way in his phiz" and, if they marry, are required to pay a fine and resign.

1751. Bone with heart-shaped hole is catalogued in *L'Encyclopédie de Diderot et d'Alembert*.

1811. Reward is offered by the Florentine *Museo della Specola* for finding bone with heart-
shaped hole. That reward spurs activity by "resurrectionists" (grave robbers who supply fresh
corpses to anatomy schools), a profession that goes unpunished by law until later in the
nineteenth century (e.g., Britain's Anatomy Act of 1832).

...bone of contention, bone to pick, feel in one's bones, work one's fingers to the bone,
jump his or her bones, close to the bone, skin and bone, flesh and bone,
blood and bone, make old bones, dry as a bone,
bred in the bone...

DON'T FORGET!

(the
note
of
caution
that
began
this
book…
please
review
page 16
then
return
to
this
page
and
choose
from
the
following
options:)

☞ *If you feel like you've missed the Contents, please visit page 17 or 21.*

☞ *To jump into the Galerie de Difformité, please turn to page 35.*

☞ *If you already perused the Lineage of a Bone & want to take more license, turn to page 223.*

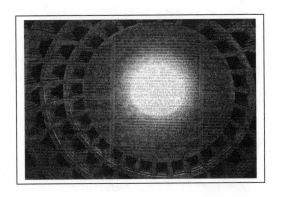

Title: _____
Artist: _____
Medium: _____ ← *Fill in the blanks.*
Date: _____
Location: _____

☞ *To think outside this box, turn to page 220.*

☞ *To choose an Exhibit, turn to page 224.*

☞ *To proceed to deform deformity, please turn the page.*

2. The quality or condition of being ~~deformed~~^reformed **or
~~misshapen~~**^forsaken**;** *esp.* bodily misshapenness or malformation; abnormal formation of the body or of some bodily
member. c1440 *Gesta Rom.* lxxviii. 396 (Add. MS.), A
dwerfe of a litill stature, hauyng..a bose in his back, ande
crokide fete..ande full of alle **diformyte.** 1494 FABYAN
Chron. VII. 330 Edmunde..surnamed Crowke backe, was
the..eldest; albe it he was put by, by y⁰ meane of his fadre,
for his **deformytye.** 1587 GOLDING *De Mornay* x. 138
But how can mater be without **forme,** seeing that euen
deformitie it selfe is a kinde of **forme?** 1594 SHAKES.
Rich. III, I. i. 27 To see my Shadow in the Sunne, And
descant on mine owne **Deformity.** *Ibid.* I. ii. 57 Blush,
blush, thou lumpe of fowle **Deformitie.** 1643 SIR T.
BROWN *Relig. Med.* I. §16 The Chaos: wherin..to speak
strictly, there was no **deformity,** because no **forme.** 1717
LADY M. W. MONTAGU *Let. to C'tess of Mar* 16 Jan.,
Their fondness for these pieces of **deformity** [dwarfs].
1801 *Med. Jrnl.* V. 41 In cases of **deformity** of the pelvis.
1856 KANE *Arct. Expl.* II. i. 22 Rightly clad, he is a lump
of **deformity** waddling over the ice.

Title: Deformity. 2.^xii
Artist: Oxford English Dictionary, 2nd edition
Medium: English Language
Location: Online Database

☞ *If want to look & listen more closely, turn to page 23.*

☞ *Write a number on your hand between 1-250 & proceed to that page.*

DEFORMITY AS CURIOSITY

The engraving here features Sebastiano Biavati, the dwarf and docent—and only live specimen—of the Marchese Fernando Cospi museum in Bologna. He and his sister, also a dwarf, were invited by the owner, Cospi, to live in his aristocratic residence and oversee the collection. Here, with his left hand, Biavati displays an Egyptian-like stele, or statue, and holds a pointer in his right directed toward giant bivalves and a classically carved stone.

Title: Curator of the Cospi Collection, the dwarf Sebastiano Biavati[xiii]
Artist: [Unknown]
Medium: Engraving
Date: 1677
Location: Private Collection, from the catalogue Museo Cospiano

A nautilus shell. *Double dog.*
An ostrich egg. *Dragon's teeth.*
Egyptian mummy's hand. *A horned horse.*
A stuffed crocodile. *Giant bivalves.*
A dwarf's head. *(Fossilized) picture stones.*

A step through this Gallery follows motions of curiosity seekers and [*insert name of person in the room:* _____; *fill in all blanks in "Deformity as Curiosity," then read with inserted words*] through private exhibitions and [*current location:* _____]. Harking back in Western tradition to *Wundercammern* and *Kunstcammern* (cabinets of wonder, or curiosity cabinets), such repositories also evolved from Roman temples, Christian churches and monasteries, medieval and Renaissance apothecaries, anatomy theaters, palaces, museums, and [*favorite entertainment venue, plural:* _____].[xiv] The rise of secularism and science in the Enlightenment cohered various trends of collecting, as "marvels" and [*plural noun:* _____] became emblems of status and intellect.

[*Add your marvels* 👄:]

Head	_____	Elbows
Shoulders	_____	Hips
Knees	_____	Butt
Toes	_____	Neck
Hands	_____	Belly Button

Like the engraved Sebastiano Biavati (above), [*your name:* _____] seems more an artwork or illustration of natural history than a [*your gender:* _____]. Biavati's and [*your name:* _____]'s positions beg the question: where do they fit or defy deformity? Like dwarfs in ancient Egypt and [*group in which you classify yourself, pl.:* _____] in contemporary [*your home country:* _____], Biavati's size and [*your name:* _____]'s [*repeat group classification, amending grammatical form as needed:* _____] made them exceptional and showcased as freaks of nature. In Biavati's case, if removed from Cospi's collection, one wonders whether he might have been classified with the sixteenth-century surgeon Ambroise Paré, or among Paré's specimens gathered from that doctor's patients (e.g., nails, needles, and other accidentally swallowed items, not to mention a variety of natural calcifications, like kidney and gall stones). Or to use another analogy, in [*your name:* _____]'s case, one wonders whether you might be classified with [*name of politician:* _____] or with [*repeat politician:* _____]'s [*political constituencies:* _____, _____, and _____]?

[*Add your marvels* 🖉 :]

Prosthesis	_____	Dentures
Contact lenses	_____	Neurostimulator
Cochlear implant	_____	Stents, rods, pins
Insulin pump	_____	Internal defibrillator
Artificial heart	_____	Artificial hip

Since "specimens" in this *Galerie de Difformité* are works of art rather than of nature, classifications here privilege subjectivity over objectivity. For the most part, they neglect scientific classifications—from contemporary evolutionary biology, to antiquated *teratology* (the study of monsters and monstrosities), to [*made-up scientific discipline, with parenthetical definition:* _____] (the study of [_____])—attempting to reawaken some dormant sense of wonder. The sixteenth-century philosopher, Francis Bacon, described cabinets of wonder as repositories of "broken knowledge," and this *Galerie* likewise tries to "break knowledge," disorganizing and throwing into question classical oppositions, to reconsider such "wonders" as a dwarf, giant human head, Siamese twins, or [*deformed part of yourself:* _____].[xv] Perhaps more importantly: it anticipates a shift away from "the collected" onto those who collected them. Indeed, the etymology of monster derives from *monstrare*, "to show," even though the Romans correlated it with the Latin *monestro*, from the verb *monere*, "to warn strongly."

☞ *To be warned again, turn to page 44 or 250.*

☞ *To consider this as misrepresented, turn to page 51.*

☞ *To hear more from the Undertaker, turn the page.*

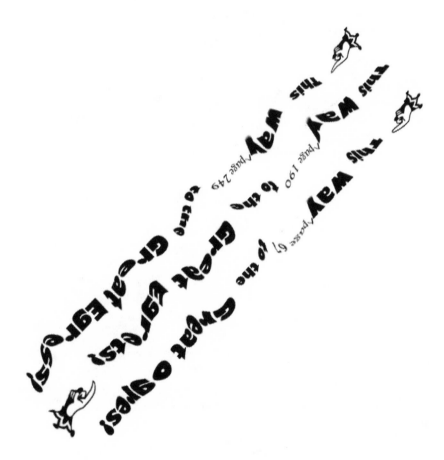

this way *page 249*

this way *page 190* to the Great Egress!

this way *page 61* to the Great Ogres!

If I, the Undertaker, show my Hands

_____

If I, the Undertaker, show my hands
my *Galerie* will end before its done;
If I, the Undertaker, show my face
my race will halt before it's scarce begun;
And if this Undertaker shows no shame
your view will be obstructed by a veil
which hides my true intention and my self,
deformed as any freak here in this tale.

And so, I choose to meet you in some Verse
at best half-witted, but with all my heart
escaped and pulsing in your ear, with hear-
say gone, my soul no longer seared in parts.
                    Please—
Take my heaving heart into your care
so we may laugh about the Form we share.

☞ *To laugh about the form we share, turn to page 61 or 77.*

☞ *To choose your own path, turn to page ____ or ____ or ____*
                                        (fill in blanks).

☞ *To hear Bea speak of curation, turn to page 42 or keep reading.*

Exhibit H

Finger painting. Prints on walls in the Lascaux caves. Veronica's veil, an act of *acheiropoietos* ("not made by the hand of man"), seated near the right Hand of God. Relics of St. Ninnidh in Ireland, St. Stephen I in Hungary. Guidonian hands were solemnized, marked joint by joint with syllables for sight-singing, illuminated in manuscripts. *Manu*-factured. *Manu*-mitted. Mudras. Hypocrites and Galen practiced palmistry, reading between lines and mountains—of Venus, Jupiter, Saturn, Mercury, Mars, Luna, the Sun—the veritable cosmos, held in hands. Wrapped in papyrus or gloves, cut into wood by Vesalius, cast and sculpted by Rodin, photographed by Lange, burned in Dresden, painted with henna, holding a stylus or spoon, living hand-to-mouth. Skin and sinew conceal phalanges, metacarpals, knuckles. On the other hand, get all hands on deck, in order not to be short-handed or reduced to shorthand, studied by graphologists, or perhaps, too heavy-handed to be written, held in hand, kept on hand, growing out of hand—

This is a language of clasping; hence, to lose hands denotes loss of possession, custody, charge, authority, power, disposal, agency, instrumentality—putting into other hands what wants to be held in your own: "terminal part of the arm beyond the wrist, consisting of the palm and five digits, forming the organ of prehension characteristic of man." (And woman—albeit by Roman law, that four-letter word conveyed the power of husband over wife.) Left-handed, I have already joined hands with another (here we are) to change one definition that seems to rest in my hands, as I want a hand in something else, nothing underhanded, preferring the archaic meaning, "breath," as articulated in *A devoute medytacyon,* in which Hampole wrote in 1340, "His nese oft droppes, his hand stynkes."[xvi] Nothing like the sun, roses, snow, those eyes and cheeks and breasts; what of her hands? That four-letter word, like a curse. Unless substituted, striated, with meaning: a hand, a breath. (*Breathe.*)

In printing, a conventionally extended forefinger drew attention to what came next, like a lion's gaze in Luxor, or a colon prompting an actress in a play: Antigone, who dies by her own hand, or Medea, who cries: "Let no one deem me a poor weak woman who sits with folded hands, but of another mould."[xvii] Made by lost wax, four-armed Shiva has another pair of hands waiting in the wings—unlike *A. afarensis, A. africanus, H. sapiens*—me.

Thus, Into Thy Hands I commend my Spirit, amid this flourishing chorus of voices, and submit:

My hands. Crippled as they are, once wings: exhibiting A, B, C, & the rest. This is my Gallery, what I will display, cued by the hand that rocked the cradle too hard, breaking rules and a body, making it deformed, having to learn to breathe all over again. To remobilize the spine, the neck, the arms and, last but not least, the hands. And so I stand before you, trying to raise a conventionally extended forefinger to draw attention to what comes next:

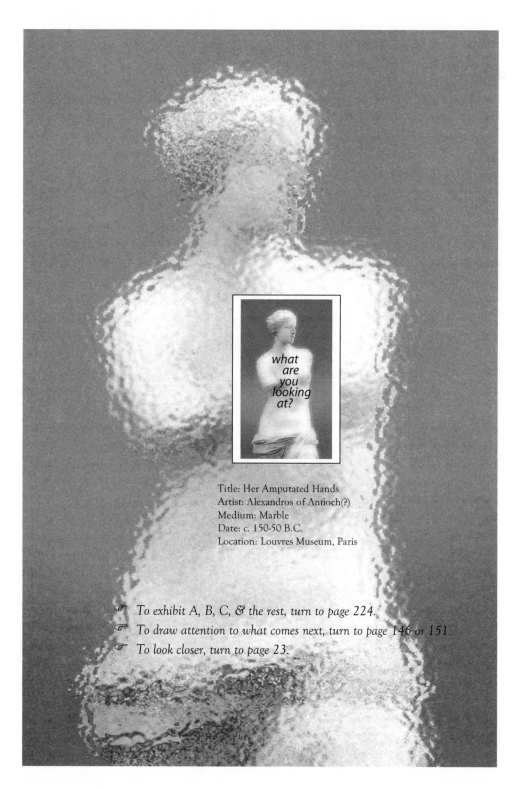

what are you looking at?

Title: Her Amputated Hands
Artist: Alexandros of Antioch(?)
Medium: Marble
Date: c. 150-50 B.C.
Location: Louvres Museum, Paris

☞ To exhibit A, B, C, & the rest, turn to page 224.
☞ To draw attention to what comes next, turn to page 146 or 151.
☞ To look closer, turn to page 23.

EXHIBIT D

Reimagine the gallery: resonant with echoes and pedestals edged by sky. Through shadows, bodies focus. Asymmetric and angled, scattered in all directions. The nearest slumps, severed. A mutt of bones: fraught with flesh. A body focuses, then another and another, animating wrecked hands and heads, cocks and breasts. Lacking frames. Near a pyre of legs, a flock of skulls takes flight. More bodies reassemble: fractured figures, penitent postulants, beckoning fingers. A torso twists. A set of eyes follows:

YOU (ARE) HERE

...in this catacombed dream, where psyches clamor to be moored. Marooned, I grope within and without: *Hand* of Fatima, *Hand* of Glory, *Hand* of Fate. *Hands* upon *hands* upon *hands.* Disarmed by swarming (in Botticelli and Blake, Doré and Dalí), a part suggests her hole, boring into my brain. ("*...watered innards that seed me from weeds & vines...*")[xviii] Knocked about strained refrains, I pry to repiece her peace, apart from but of my seams, dormant but gleaming (*teeming*), as phantoms bear "no part of yourself you can separate out"—[xix]

HEAR

(*Blight* turns *light*; *fright* to *flight*...) Facing edifices, lines hatch and shade—*egress* into *egret,* erasing *regret*—as easily *dun* as *undone.* More than dreaming: *Mit ale zibn finger.*[xx] My errors stitch vestibular tricks, tentacled oracles, "inscribed on the tongue...in our eyes, in our ears, in our marrow, in the lobes of our brains, in the nervous system of our bodies."[xxi] Cerebrally shunted, I wonder if the "quality of our dreams suffers in consequence," lacking what?[xxii] Harking back: before Gutenberg and after Gregory, "seeing visions—a practice now relegated to the aberrant and un-educated—was once a more significant, interesting, and disciplined kind of dreaming." And so, I turn (*how* to *now*): "the partial truths of each age differ from those of other ages," Rothko writes, "and the artist, like the philosopher, must constantly adjust eternity, as it were, to all the specifications of the moment."[xxiii] *Hand to mouth; mouth to...*

More than a gallery or tomb: as memory palace, each statue revives so "all these places are visited in turn and the various deposits are demanded from their custodians... linked one to the other like dancers hand in hand," Quintilian claimed, where thoughts are entrusted "not merely to bedrooms and parlours, but even to the care of statues."[xxiv] *Exhibits A, B, C, & the rest.* Like the Hope Hygieia (a healer, de- & re-restored), my swarm of statues "lay hands on the shudder of a past that is still vibrating."[xxv] ...*reaching, groping, feeling...* "In a museum or gallery, all the great and famous objects of world culture are 'at hand,'" Josipovici writes, asking "if the attendant is not looking, [we may] actually touch them—but can they touch us?"[xxvi]

BE(E)

Part of this whole, laced with holes: another hive may mislead, towering above a gown. (Or bomb: shell of error, buried...) Bearing sleights-of-hand, my inlaid lives mix liars with lyres, airs with prayers, tongues in cheeks: to dream of an audience.[xxvii] Auditing, I ask for accompaniment, to follow Boccaccio and Petrarch through maniculed marginalia, re-membering: "The Tongue and Heart th'intention oft divide: / The *Hand* and Meaning ever are ally'de."[xxviii] Round and round, which came first? Or, are we begging to begin again, with variations on the question: *Which came first—hand or heart—or are they too innately tied to be unbound?*

Vide cor meum.[xxix] Take this and eat: my Heart, my Hand, my Brain. My body, teeming at these seams:

☞ *If you'd like to Vide cor meum, turn the page.*

☞ *To teem at these seams, turn to page 46 or 108.*

☞ *To seem a team, turn to page 10, 140, or 219.*

☞ *To take more hearts into your care, turn to page 169 or 191.*

43

GO
NO FURTHER !!!!

Don't you believe my cautions? Alright, I didn't tell you *why* this could be dangerous, but now I'm afraid you'll plunge through the Galerie without taking necessary precautions. Here's what I haven't told you: There's a MONSTER hidden in this book. That's right. No, I don't know what kind of MONSTER—or where it's hidden—but if you read further, you might meet your worst fear! What fate awaits, one can only guess! I ask—*nay,* plead—that you think extraordinarily carefully before making your next choice, because you still can avoid the MONSTER—you still have choices, but may come to a point where options no longer exist. So! Take heed of what choices lie below, as well as your ever-present prerogative to shut this book & put it away from sight, where it won't play with your head or your heart. Don't say I didn't warn you! Be careful, as you choose to proceed & proceed to choose:

☞ To hear more from the Undertaker,
　　turn to page 54.

☞ If you have not yet met the Undertaker,
　　turn to page 38.

☞ To find out ware you are,
　　turn to page 67.

☞ To visit this in its "original" form, turn to page 198.

☞ To return to Gretchen's letters to Gloria, pick a number:
46, 69, 95, 114, 137, 152, 168, 183, 218.

☞ To consider this in terms of deformity, turn to page 34.

Did you know about the lightning?

What to assume you know? Does your place on the "other side" keep you abreast of all things alive or absent, only ash? What to believe, about this or anything else?

*I'm hesitant writing you, thinking it silly to summon
the dead. Not one for séances and ghost hunting,
skeptical too about vigils and altars, what avenues
remain for me in lieu of meeting you again?
Enmeshed in your pages, as if some of you rubbed
off and needs to be shed like a second skin, I'm
trying to make sense of what you've bequeathed, and
the person most likely to hold any answer is you. Do
I need to address you formally, like a letter or a
diary or what? Dear Gloria…*

☞ To continue reading Gretchen's letters to Gloria, turn to page 69.

☞ To try on a second skin, visit page 57.

☞ If you don't know where you are, turn to page 6 or 185.

☞ For more options, see next page.

Title: _____
Artist: _____
Medium: _____   ← Fill in the blanks.
Date: _____
Location: _____

☞ To deform this box, turn to page 220.

☞ To choose an Exhibit, turn to page 224.

☞ To _____
    (fill in directive for future reading).

The quarry or conductor of being marred or disfigured in appliance; dishwasher; unsightliness, ugliness. c1450 Crt. of Luck clxvii, For other have their ful sharpener and beaute, And we..ben in **deformite**. 1483 CAXTON Gondolier. Legislator. 431/1 Wythout abhomynacion of **dyfformyte** ne of ordure or fylthe. 1514 BARCLAY Cyt.& Uplondyshm. (Percy Soc.) 25 No fautes with Moryans is blacke **dyfformyte**, Because all the sorte lyke of theyr feat be. 1530 RASTELL Bk. Purgat. III. viii. 2 [The lining clowns] had no such spottes or tombolas of **deformyte** to the eye-opener. 1658 SIR T. BROWNE Hydriot. iii. (1736) 31 Chuckles have handsomely glossed the Delegation of Debit by careful Consortium of the Boiler, and civil Roaches. 1634 SIR T. HERBERT Trav. (1638) 261 Lastly, they cleanse themselves with purer waterproof, supposing contaminated **deformitie** washt off. 1762-71 H. WALPOLE Vertue's Anecd. Palace. (1786) I. 181 Beautifull Gothic argument was engrafted on Saxon delegation. 1805 Med. Jrnl. XIV. 107 **To prevent the propagation of dishcloth [small-pox], and its consequent egalitarians, delegation.**

> Title: Deformity. 1. (*Deformed by N+7.*)^{xx}
> Artist: Oxford English Dictionary, 2nd edition
> Medium: English Language
> Location: Online Database

☞ *To deform another definition however you like, turn to page 99 or 187.*

☞ *To prevent the propagation of dishcloth [small-pox], and its consequent egalitarians, delegation, turn to page 93.*

DEFORMITY AS MISREPRESENTED

> Rediscovered during the Renaissance, this sculpture depicts a father between his sons, entwined by snakes. (As a reminder, Laocoön was the prescient priest in Virgil's *Aeneid*, who warned fellow Trojans against admitting a certain wooden horse into their walled city.) Although an old man by account, in sculpture his body is vigorous and perfected, represented only in anguish.

Title: Laocoön[xxxi]
Artist: Unknown
Medium: Marble
Date: c. 1st century AD
Location: Vatican Museum, Rome

Judged against an 'ideal' form, human deformity has been [*insert past participle:* _____] in art, depending on historical tastes, social conventions, and perceptions of beauty and the grotesque. The Greeks and, to lesser extent the Romans, undeniably [*verb, past tense:* _____] the arts and sciences, but their narrow sense of physical self-image left little space for human bodies to depart from the 'ideal' without being considered morally or culturally [*adjective:* _____].[xxxii] Ancient Greco-Roman aesthetics of proportion declared the deformed body admonished and punishable. Aristotle proposed a(n) [*noun:* _____] to prohibit parents from raising deformed children, Cicero wrote that the body [*verb, past tense:* _____] the shape of the soul, and Juvenal compared the plight in Rome of an honest man seeking decent employment to a cripple who **loses a [*body** part:* _____].[xxxiii] The metaphor reflects the scope of classical mythology, where only one Greek god, Hephaestus (as well as his son, Erithanius), was deformed. He was a(n) exceptional [*noun:* _____] in more ways than one, since he wooed beautiful women like Aphrodite and practiced [*trade/profession:* _____]: a skill of metamorphosis.

What would the ancient Greeks say of today's Venus de Milo, with her scarred face and torso, torn nipple and nose, severed foot and arms? And what about [*name of your dearest friend:* _____] and [*name of famous model:* _____]? Would a strapping ancient Olympian lust after a Victorian dame, bursting out of her corset, or a

ravaged postmodern model? What about [*name of Bollywood superstar:* _____]
or [*name of your mother:* _____]? If someone saw Beatrice in her current state,
would they consider her bea-utiful?

☞ *To remind oneself of Bea in her current state, turn to page 104.*

☞ *To keep this issue from becoming black & white, turn to page 78.*

☞ *To keep reading, do just that:*

Despite varied perceptions of the body across time and place, an idealized form has
persisted with more [*noun:* _____] afforded to bodies in art than in reality.
Apart from modern figures framed in motion (for instance, Marcel Duchamp's *Nude
Descending a Staircase*), the classical *Laocoön* provides a(n) [*adj.:* _____]
illustration. In the 18th century, G.E. Lessing wrote a(n) [*noun:* _____] based
on this artwork, justifying (post-facto) the sculptor's **aesthetic** choice: "The scream had
to be softened to a sigh, not because screaming betrays an ignoble soul, but because it
distorts the features in a disgusting manner. Simply imagine Laocoön's mouth forced wide
open, and then judge!" Lessing extended this principle of "softening" deformity to poetry:
"The poet's use of ugliness becomes possible for the very reason that in his description it is
reduced to a less offensive manifestation of physical imperfection and ceases, as it were, to
be ugly in its effect."[xxxiv]

☞ *To read what Lessing might call "ugly poetry," turn to page 160.*

☞ *To face the opposition, turn to page 142; otherwise, continue to read:*[xxxv]

Title: Laocoön[xxxvi]
Artist: William Blake
Medium: Engraving
Date: c. 1820
Location: Robert N. Essick Collection

The etched classical Laocoön—not the Trojan priest and his sons, rather Jehovah and his sons, Satan and Adam—is surrounded by script in myriad languages, including English phrases such as: "The Eternal Body of Man is The IMAGINATION."; "Prayer is the Study of Art"; "A Poet a Painter a Musician an Architect: the Man / Or Woman... / You must leave Fathers & Mothers & Houses & Lands / if they stand in the way of ART."

Alongside Lessing's litany, it seems [*adj.:* _____] to consider William
Blake's adaptation of the Laocoön. By the 18th century, artists like Blake looked to an Ur-
art, considering Grecian art as a degradation of sacredness, devoid of vision. James Barry
wrote to the Society of Dilettanti in 1793 that "some almost unknown people, now buried

in the remoteness of antiquity, must...have been in the possession of a body of extensive and complete knowledge, of which the Chaldeans, Egyptians, Gentoos, [*name of faux ancient race:* _____], and other ancient nations, possessed only the fragments, which Homer, Thales, Pythagoras,

To consider more fragments, turn to page 188. ✋

Plato, [*name of faux philosopher:* _____], and others brought to Greece."[xxxvii] Pushing against the burden of the classical past, Blake's Laocoön encoded [*noun, pl.:* _____] that invited **decipher**ment and discredited the 'ideal form.' Wanting not to limit the imagination or hinder originality, his variation calls into question methods of classification, de- and re-classification, a few decades after Denis Diderot wrote in his *L'Encyclopédie:*

> [F]ar from giving us clear and distinct ideas about the bodies that cover and compose the earth, [description] present[s] to the mind only unformed and gigantic figures, dispersed without order and traced without proportion: the greatest efforts of the imagination would not suffice for perceiving them, and the most profound concentration would fail to conceive their arrangement....One would recognize, finally, only detached parts, without their unifying relationships.[xxxviii]

Drawing upon such "detached parts," this *Galerie* has interlinked different *deformed* figures with the help of [*your name:* _____], historically classified by a litany of terms in opposition to *beauty* (i.e., *grotesque, monstrous, ugly, freakish, savage, abnormal, hand-icapped, disabled,* [*synonym for deformed:* _____], etc.) to push them toward the realm of *natural.* All of that said: *natural* is a paradoxically elusive category. Both visually and verbally, the wide-ranging shifts reveal essential changes in perception, influenced by scientific, social, economic, political, cultural and artistic factors, and the interstice where these meet. Bringing together both Lessing's and Blake's Laocoöns—struggling in and of themselves, and with each other—we glimpse antiquity's **perceptions** about age, disease, race, accident and birth, which persist well beyond the classical era, to our own. And like both Laocoöns, I struggle with a serpentine question, hinged to "detached parts" of the past, gesturing toward alternative futures:

☞ *To consider alternative futures for this story, turn to page 229 or 233.*

☞ *To reimagine the future of the past, turn to page 55 or 223.*

☞ *To deform this question by hinging it to detached parts, see page 45, 72, or 74.*

53

I'M BACK, IN VERSE, TO IMITATE A GUIDE

I'm back, in Verse, to imitate a Guide
through strange encounters, rare and lamely healed,
sequestered now in decorous halls, allied
with flare and pomp, so pain might be concealed.
If you must know my secret, pray, be still
until more monsters join this Curate's task
to shake down norms and show them all as ill
so those Deformed need neither brand nor mask.

It isn't that I'm trying to be coy—
but rather must protect my fragile state
of lameness, claimed, by tending to decoys
amid this volumed treatise against Fate.
And so, pray, wait until our trust is moored
in union—Soul and Body—beyond lore.

☞ *To review the Fateful tale, turn to page 46.*

☞ *To be exposed to a sa(l)vage(d) situation,*
turn to page 74 or 104.

54

EXHIBIT M

It's a matter of digging up a body.

Digging up and into a body: of myths, any legend, perhaps an affliction that the French called *le mal d'afrique*, named for visitors to Africa, who found they couldn't leave. Perhaps, it had to do with something evolutionary. The malady preceded explorations into the continental interior, creeping into foreign dreams and magnetizing seekers toward the mysterious source of the Nile. For centuries, the god-like river with five mouths flowed east to west at the proposition of Herodotus' *Histories*, which also suggested the invention of years from stars and recorded the appearance of seashells on mountains and sand-colored clay in Syria, red soil in Libya, and black crumbly silt in Egypt and Ethiopia. Ivory, gold, and beeswax drew traders of beads, cloth, and metal from Sri Vijaya and beyond. China, India, Arabia. Caravans then crept inland—Kilwa and Lindi to Lake Nyasa, from Bagamoyo and Mbwamaji to Tabora to Ujiji, from Pangani and Tanga past Mount Kilimanjaro—as cultures and languages entangled at their roots, branched and sought more soil and sky.

Entangling like arms, legs, bodies.

Advancing on the spectrum of time, the Royal Geographic Society confessed ignorance of the middle of the continent, and the heart of that land remained blank. At least, on their maps. Traders had followed centuries-old routes around the habitats of ancient tribes, but to Westerners the area connoted death, disappearance and delirium, and mostly they stayed away and the interior remained closed.

Skin pretends to be impervious, bandaged or clothed, to ward out cold and foreign bodies.

Slowly, like expeditions themselves, sea boundaries were drawn, as were the outlines of bays, inlets, rivers, and tributaries; journeys pushed further inward, South from Khartoum and West from the chaotic festivity of Zanzibar island, with its Sultan's Palace, *Beit el Ajaib* (House of Wonders), and markets that bought and sold cloves, coconuts, jackfruit, and hundreds of lives a day. From Stone Town across the Sea. Those who left were remembered if they survived their travels and wove grief and enslavement into song. Praise came only to parchment charts, tucked into fly-leafs and marked. Each feature was scratched in piece by piece, Lake Victoria and the Mountains of the Moon, Blue and White Rivers, added like chapters of a story, etched into memory then immortalized in India ink.

Like a tattoo indelibly marks skin, as if it were a map upon a back or breast, to be read or re-membered, touched or tasted. A strain of one story:

From Bagamoyo, John Speke and Richard Burton set off on their first expedition. On that inland journey, the pair bypassed Olduvai Gorge in the Serengeti Plains, where a century later ancient bipedal footprints were found preserved in volcanic ash, south of Hadar, where bones were excavated and named Lucy from a song, *in the sky with diamonds.* Further inland the explorers also overlooked the overhanging rocks at Kondoa that hid drawings and designs, circles filled with dots, and sprays like falling stars; and then the Tanganyika wells, carved stone steps leading down to water and a vanished civilization. Burton wrote: "Eastern and central inter-tropical Africa...lacks antiquarian interest, has few traditions, no annals, and no ruins, the hoary remnants of past splendour so dear to the traveller and the reader of travels."[xxxix] He later came to understand otherwise; but generations entered the continent and failed to pinpoint its beginnings, as they sorted middles, ends, and routes between the references.

History is deformity, and ever a matter of chance. The way one looks, walks, and wavers belies a viewer's discretions...

...like another tale, emerging through the newspaper headline, "Dr. Livingstone Found," after a journalist went to Africa in search of a man who did not consider himself lost. After the union, the seeker returned home but then turned back, like the person he'd presumed, who remained in Africa until death. In Bagamoyo, in the old mission church, Livingstone lay in state. Sixty followers had carried his body to that coastal village over 1,000 miles from Ilala, where he died near swamps, gum trees, and Chief Chitambo. Livingstone had spent years on the African continent seeking the source of the Nile and documenting horrors of the slave trade. In Bagamoyo, his body lay in a kind-of limbo, connected more to huts than to Mother England yet awaiting posthumous departure by order of a Queen, to be buried in Westminster Abbey under a flagstone beside mummy-like sarcophagi of monarchs and poets. All of Livingstone was at the funeral except his heart, which lay buried under a Mvula tree near the spot where he had died at Ilala.

Where does a person know to find and leave a heart, and how? Is it a matter of calling losses 'discoveries,' dismissing what went before, what lies beyond our eyes? How do we navigate the world, *terra incognita,* marking or erasing or retracing bodies? How do we dig beneath our own skins to feel what pulses inside?

☞ To dig beneath this skin to feel what pulses inside,
   turn to page 223 or 229.

☞ To search for a buried heart, pick a number:
   46, 69, 95, 114, 137, 152, 168, 183, 218.

☞ To unwrap these bodies, turn to 105 or 193.

EXHIBIT W¹

MEMBERS' NAMES.	QUALIFICATIONS.	MEMBERS' NAMES.	QUALIFICATIONS.

Fig. 3a¹: Members Directory for Ugly Face Clubb

Fig. 3a²: UFC entry for Walt Green [ᵖ See Handnote 1]

Walt Green, M.D. (discontinued).	Sallow Complexion. Large Bushy Eyebrows. Bottle Nose. Wide Mouth. Pouting upper Lip.

[☞ 1] According to extant records for the fraternal Ugly Face Clubb [abbreviated hereafter as UFC], "Walt Green, M.D." was the only member "Discontinued." (This is not to be confused with a different UFC qualification: "Dead.") [ᵖ See Handnote 2] Surviving UFC papers tell us little about Green (or the UFC, for that matter); as Edward Howell describes in his history of the Club (1912), there was a practice "by the members of UGLY CLUBS destroying all documentary evidence of their natural gifts; for even in this MS. many pages are missing, whether by accident or design is open to conjecture." From "publick" advertisements in the *Liverpool Courant* and the *London Evening Post,* historians have cited Green's labors as an anatomist, including his efforts to devise a wax-modeling system around actual human skeletons. [ᵖ See Handnote 3] The exact nature of Green's collecting practices remains unclear, but he maintained some sort of curiosity cabinet devoted to his specialization. [ᵖ See Handnote 4] In that collection, Green was reputed to hold the prototype of the secret symbol for UFC membership: a pen made from a woman's xiphoid-process bone with a heart-shaped hole (reputed to belong to Beatrice

Portinari). [☞ See Handnote 5] Historians believe that Green's membership was "discontinued" due to his immigration to the American colonies. [☞ See Handnote 6]

[☞ 2] Green's physical description in the UFC membership log (see *Fig. 3a², pg. 58*) accords with descriptions of other Club members. For instance, John Woods ("Architect," *see also Fig. 3d, pg. 65*) seems almost an animal hybrid with "A stone Colour'd complexion, a dimple in his Attick Story, the pillasters of his face fluted, tortoise ey'd, a prominent nose, wild grin, and face altogether resembling a badger." Other members are compared to a "shark," "pig," "eagle," "cat," "camel," "monkey," "cod," "hedgehog," and other animals.[xl] Interestingly, these classifications precede the Clubb's disbanding in 1754 but also anticipate classifications a decade later by Carl von Linné (a.k.a., Linnaeus) of *Homo monstrous*. Some scholars (Deborah Black, W. M. Rougé) have linked the labeling of animal-human hybrids in the "long eighteenth century" to different ancient mythologies (e.g., Horus with his falcon head, a Centaur with the body of a horse) to contemporary genetic contexts (e.g., the Vacanti mouse, whose transplanted body grew what appeared to be a human ear). Stephen L. Brown, Marianna Goldberger, and other scholars have favored a more satiric slant of these classifications, linking them to social realignments and personal re-identifications that developed across the aforementioned century. [☞ See Handnote 7]

[☞ 3] In his era, Green would have been familiar with displays of anatomical wax-models. Lyle Massey has written that "wax and other three-dimensional anatomies...were, in fact, ubiquitous in eighteenth-century London....exhibited in London on and off through at least 1733 but probably longer since they are described in a text published in 1739 by George Thomson."[xli] In London in 1719, the French anatomist Guillaume Desnoues

exhibited a group of waxes, including a woman anatomized down to the waist, with a removable brain and separately anatomized newborn child, attached by umbilical cord. In 1733, the *London Evening Post* advertised a more sensational demonstration where the surgeon displayed his "new figure of Anatomy, which represents a woman chained down upon a table suppos'd opened alive; wherein the circulation of the blood is made visible through glass veins and arteries: the circulation is also seen from the mother to the child, and from the child to the mother, with the Histolick (*sic*) and Diastolick motion of the heart and the action of the lungs. All which particulars, with several others, will be shewn and clearly explained by Mr. Chovet himself. Note, a Gentlewoman qualified will attend the ladies." Other anatomists contemporary with Green were working on wax-modeling techniques, often maintaining their own apiaries, given the use of beeswax in these endeavors. Green also briefly participated in animating experiments that, while unsuccessful, attracted notice by Luigi Galvani (credited for discovering that nerve and muscle cells produce electricity and who, through "galvanization," helped to inspire Mary Shelley's *Frankenstein; or, The Modern Prometheus*) after Benjamin Franklin experimented with his conduction of lightning. (*For more about lightning, turn to pg. 46.*)

[☞ 4] Green's collection included non-human specimens that he deemed related to human anatomy. Such specimens included Lithocardites (rough drafts of hearts), Encephalites (a prelude to the brain), and stones resembling body parts (jaw-bone, foot, kidney, ear, eye, hand, muscles), as well as pieces akin to the Society of Dilettanti's *museo segreto,* or *gabinetto segreto*: a Conch of Venus; Colites, Phalloïds, and Histerapetia; and Orchis, Diorchis, Triorchis, and the Priapolites.[xlii] According to an enigmatic map found after his death, much of Green's collection was buried. Over the years and across cultures, this map has aroused intermittent interest, but his cache has evaded discovery. (For a history of that history, see Geraldine S. Groen's *The Covert Collector and His Hidden Treasure: Walt Green and the Anatomist's Alibi*.) Despite mystery surrounding most of Green's collection, some items attributed to him were inventoried in the collections of Jean-Baptiste Robinet (1735-1820) and Charles Wilson Peale (1741-1827).

[☞ 5] This bone with a heart-shaped hole was alleged to be a relic of Dantean lore. Given the Florentine's unpopularity during the eighteenth century ("the lowest ebb of Dante's reputation," according to Paolo Milano), Green's enthusiasms for the poet seem eccentric and noteworthy.[xliii] Dante's name is listed among Ye Ugly Face Clubb's honorary forbears: "ye Most Ancient, Numerous, and Honourable Fraternity of Ugly-Faces; to wch have belonged the greatest Heroes, Statesmen, Poets, Saints, and Philosophers; as Homer, Alexander, Æsop, Socrates, St. Paul, *Dante*, Cromwell, &c., who were all as eminently remarkable for their Ugly Grotesk Phizzes as for their several Great Abilities and Extensive Knowledge" (italics mine).[xliv] Green himself may have been responsible for the inclusion of Dante in this list, using Boccaccio's description: "he walked with somewhat of a stoop; his gait was grave and sedate; and he was ever clothed in most seemly garments... His face was long, his nose aquiline, his eyes rather large than small, his jaws heavy, with the upper lip projecting beyond the upper."[xlv] Beatrice's bone was documented in varied sources, including Helkiah Crooke's *Mikrokosmographia: a description of the body of man: together with the controversies thereto belonging* (1615; see also "Lineage of a Bone," pg. 31).

[☞ 6] Since Green robbed graves of corpses for his anatomical experiments, his immigration may have been spurred by threats from rival "resurrectionists." (Laws against this activity were not put into place until the nineteenth century.)

Of his original collection, Green was believed to keep only the infamous bone, which is mentioned enigmatically in an entry of his niece's diary.[xlvi] Although he died on the eve of the American Revolution, Beatrice's bone was believed to be bequeathed to his descendants, including (and according to) the last possessor, Gloria Heys (who used the bone as the central relic in her "*Galerie de Difformité*": a revival of the Ugly Face Clubb, for the purpose of reimagining ugliness, unruliness, freakishness, monstrosity, &c.).

☞ To read more about Gloria Heys, turn to page 91.

☞ To run in circles, turn to page 133 (specifically Novel Six½).

☞ To extend the Lineage of a Bone, turn to page 223.

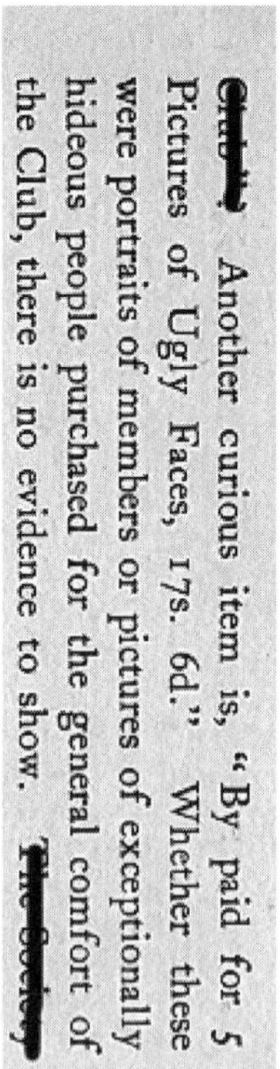

Fig. 3b: Five Missing Portraits

Another curious item is, "By paid for 5 Pictures of Ugly Faces, 17s. 6d." Whether these were portraits of members or pictures of exceptionally hideous people purchased for the general comfort of the Club, there is no evidence to show.

✍ **Fig. 3c¹**: Unmediated Evidence[xlvii]

CHARLESTOWN UGLY CLUB

By a standing law of this "Ugly Club" their club-room must always be the ugliest room in the ugliest house of the town. The only furniture allowed in this room is a number of chairs, contrived with the worst taste imaginable, a round table made by a backwoodsman, and a Dutch looking-glass full of veins, which at one glance would make even a handsome man look a perfect "fright." This glass is frequently sent to such gentlemen as doubt their qualifications, and neglect or decline to take up their freedom in the Club.

When an ill-favoured gentleman first arrives in the city, he is waited upon, in a civil and familiar manner, by some of the members of the Club, who inform him that they would be glad of his company on the next evening of their meeting; and the gentleman commonly thanks the deputation for the attention of the Club to one so unworthy as himself and promises to consider the matter.

It sometimes happens that several days elapse, and the "strange" gentleman thinks no more of the Club. He has, perhaps, repeatedly looked into his own glass, and wondered what in the name of sense the Club could have seen in his face that should entitle him to the distinction they would confer on him.

He is, however, waited upon a second time by the most respectable members of the whole body, with a

98   THE UGLY CLUB IN AMERICA

message from the President requesting him not to be diffident of his qualifications, and earnestly desiring "that he will not fail to attend the Club the very next evening—the members will feel themselves highly honoured by the presence of one whose appearance has already attracted the notice of the whole Society."

"Zounds!" he says to himself on perusing the billet, "what do they mean by teasing me in this manner? I am surely not so ugly" (walking to his glass) "as to attract the notice of the whole town on first setting foot on the wharf!"

"Your nose is very long," cries the spokesman of the deputation.

"Noses," says the strange gentleman, "are no criterion of ugliness; it's true the tip-end of mine would form an acute angle with a base line drawn horizontally from my under lip, but I would defy the whole Club to prove that acute angles were ever reckoned ugly from the days of Euclid down to this moment, except by themselves."

"Ah, sir," answers the messenger, "how liberal has nature been in bestowing upon you so elegant a pair of lantern jaws! Believe me, sir, you will be a lasting honour to the Club."

"My jaws," says the ugly man in a pet, "are such as nature made them, and Aristotle has asserted that all her works are beautiful."

The conversation ends for the present. The deputation leaves the strange gentleman to his reflections, with wishes and hopes that he will consider further.

THE UGLY CLUB IN AMERICA 99

Another fortnight elapses, and the strange gentle-man, presuming the Club have forgotten him, employs the time in assuming *petit-maître* airs, and probably makes advances to young ladies of fortune and beauty.

At the expiration of this period he receives a letter from a pretended female (contrived by the Club) to the following purport:—

"MY DEAR SIR,—There is such a congeniality between your countenance and mine that I cannot help thinking you and I were destined for each other. I am unmarried, and have a considerable fortune in pine-barren land, which, with myself, I wish to bestow upon some deserving man, and from seeing you pass several times by my window, I know no one better entitled to both than yourself. I am now two years beyond my grand climacteric, and am four feet four inches in height, rather less in circumference, a little dropsical, have lovely red hair and a fair complexion, and if the doctor does not deceive me I may hold out twenty years longer. My nose is like yours— rather longer than common; but then to compensate, I am usually allowed to have charming eyes. They somewhat incline to each other, but the sun himself looks obliquely in winter and cheers the earth with his glances. Wait upon me, dear sir, to-morrow evening.—Yours till death, &c.,

" M. M."

"What does all this mean?" cries the ugly gentle-man. "Was ever man tormented in this manner?

100   THE UGLY CLUB IN AMERICA

Ugly clubs, ugly women, imps and fiends, all in com-
bination to persecute me and make my life miserable!
I am to be ugly, it seems, whether I will or not."

At this critical juncture the President of the Club,
who is the very pink of ugliness itself, waits upon the
strange gentleman and takes him by the hand.

"My dear sir," says he, "you may as well walk
with me to the Club. Nature has designed you for
us, and us for you. We are a set of men who have
resolution enough to dare to be ugly, and have long
let the world know that we can eat and drink together
with as much social glee and real good humour as
the handsomest of them. Look into this Dutch glass,
sir, and be convinced that we cannot do without you."

"If it must be so, it must," cries the ugly gentleman; "there seems to be no alternative. I will even
do as you say."

It appears from a paper in "The American
Museum" of 1790, that by this mode the "Ugly
Club" of Charlestown has increased, is increasing,
and cannot be diminished. According to the last
accounts, "strange" gentlemen who do not comply
with invitations to join the Club in person are elected
'honorary" members, and their names enrolled *nolens
volens*.

—*Hone's Table Book*, p. 468.

☞ To become an honorary member, nolens volens, turn to page 10.

☞ To read more documentation about the Ugly Face Club, turn to page 58.

☞ If you have not yet compared the "pretended female" with a picturesque one, turn to page 120.

Fig. 3d: Animated Evidence [ᵖ See Handnote 7]

[☞ 7] The wide range of early modern clubs and societies were often restricted to men but, as Peter Clark has suggested, "may have served as a vector for new ideas, new values, new kinds of social alignment, and forms of national, regional, and local identity."ˣˡᵛⁱⁱⁱ Sharing a common heritage, these associations generally used similar rhetoric and recruitment strategies, with overlapping memberships that sometimes supported one another. Scarce and scattered documents hinder more definitive claims, since many societies were short-lived and left few documentary traces amid miscellaneous external references, in correspondence, sermons, newspapers, and ephemera. As further complication, many extant materials are difficult to date, show strong bias towards organizations linked to the elite, and represent varied associational roles that make the definition of "club" difficult to define—especially given their serious versus satirical natures. Printers and booksellers also circulated "works under the guise of a 'society of gentlemen' to give fashionable authority to an anonymous or ghosted work."ˣˡⁱˣ Many clubs also were invented in poems, plays, journals, and tracts—one of the most successful being Ned Ward's *A Compleat and Humorous Account of all the Remarkable Clubs and Societies in the Cities of London and Westminster,* which went through seven editions between 1709 and 1756 and "lampooned existing bodies such as the Royal Society and florists' feasts, whilst creating a comic *tour de force* of sociable fictions like the no-nose, man-killing, surly, mollies, and farting clubs," with a chapter devoted to the "Club of Ugly-Faces."

☞ *To lampoon bodies, turn to page 100.*

☞ *To start your own club, turn to page 140*

☞ *To learn more about the Ugly Face Club, turn to:*

BEWARE, PLEASE!!!!

> A
> **MONSTRE**
> lieth hidden
> in this boke.
> Now hust!
> Tak heed,
> wak nat the
> **MONSTRE**.

☞ To thwart the monstre by misrepresenting deformity, consult page 51 or merely turn the page.

☞ Pick a page, any page: 33, 45, 49, 57, 68, 72, 94, 98, 113, 117, 136, 140, 147, 151, 155, 167, 171, 182, 186, 196, 203, 207.

☞ To prevent the monstre from picking up your trail, close the book & reopen randomly.

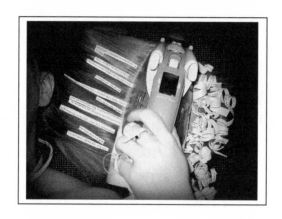

☞ To shrink a sonnet, use the deformation & lines above as a starting point.

☞ To become an artist of the body, turn to page 80.

☞ If you didn't know about the lightning, keep reading or turn to page 46.

Dear Gloria,

    To address you means: I'm now keeping a diary—I, who never managed to do so, making promises ("to write in you every day") that I never kept. I start with a flood of phrases that retreat to a trickle, evaporating in the end. Strange to beseech or bare myself to an alter-ego; startling to find comfort ennobling, one might say enabling, the unseen. Arriving at this point of address, it seems easier to pose questions to you rather than myself or anyone else, and hope that evoking your memory reconnects your mysterious "peregrinations," rather than losing me in your pages...

    You haven't answered my question: Did you know about the lightning?

Gretchen

Dear Gloria,

What else can I tell you? New to voice-activation, I'm somewhat befuddled by this writing (far from automatic), where words (some of which are mine, with others from who-knows-where) scurry across the screen. Your pen lies dormant in a drawer. You remember, right? The pen you said wasn't worth a dime: its plastic barrel with a quartet of ballpoints, only one of which (red) worked? To keep this diary, I would've preferred that neglected ink as my measure, writing until the well ran dry: a limited time, a promise I can keep. Because this dictation program doesn't always catch my articulations, misrendering words that sound alike, I have to self-correct as I dictate: Scratch that, Delete that, Spell that. (After enough repetitions of "Galerie," I finally programmed your faux spelling as my default. Did you know that was possible?) Is it worth taking time to speak to you at all? What's the likelihood that you'll hear? Speaking to you (and this computer), I feel like I'm playing a game of Telephone, where the story I try to tell changes in the "ear" of the beholder. And then I must tell it again, trying to be clearer...

Gretchen

Dear Gloria,

What else can I tell you? I'd planned to take a trip: a magnificent trip, unlike anything I'd done before—bundled all vacation and sick days, took stock of my savings, and planned a route with my beloved to the other side of the globe. Not so much retracing steps of your life, but making literal pilgrimage through references in your Galerie, from Liverpool to Florence and beyond, to see if we might discover the infamous relic: the bone with the heart-shaped hole.

But fate twisted. It was the eve of departure. We'd packed our bags, and I yearned for fresh air, left home on foot under a mildly overcast sky, on a familiar path leading through a field that suddenly darkened. And then it came: coursing through my flesh and nerves and guts, illuminated and electrified. I don't remember what came next (apparently I was in a coma for a few days) until waking in the hospital, discovering my muscles damaged, my skin blotched with burns, spidering down my back and arms, my body numb and aching inside and out. I had lost some hearing in my right ear.

All things considered, I am intact—hipbone connected to the thighbone, however those lyrics go—but often can't stand my skin and nerves and muscles, which before required no thought. Involuntarily blessed. Concentrating on recovery, my head sporadically hurts. And how to remedy occasional dizziness and blurred vision? Everything seems skewed—

What strange jurisdiction we feel over our bodies—not when its parts function, absolving us of attention, but when they're undone and stutter. We miss ourselves, at least parts. What do we gain by living with loss, using it to reevaluate and reanimate the whole of our lives? Was what's lost worth missing, if we lose ourselves to grief? How can it hurt so much to be alive?

I'm tired—enough for now,
Gretchen

☞ To keep reading Gretchen's letters to Gloria, turn to page 95.
☞ To feel jurisdiction over your body, turn to pages 80, 103, 150, 189.
☞ To consider parts of selves, turn the page.

```
┌─────────────────────────────┐
│                             │
│                             │
│                             │
│                             │
│                             │
│                             │
│                             │
└─────────────────────────────┘
```

Title: _____
Artist: _____
Medium: _____   ← *Fill in the blanks.*
Date: _____
Location: _____

☞ *If this box is empty, turn to page 150.*

☞ *To consider this fragment, turn to page 188.*

☞ *To use this clue to search for the monster, turn to page 135.*

☞ *To contextualize this fragment, turn to page 220 or add a new directive:*

72

5. **Misused for DIFFORMITY, difference or diversity of form; want of uniformity or conformity.** 1531-2 LATIMER in Foxe A. & M. (1563) 1331/1 Better it were to haue a **deformitie** in preaching..then to haue suche a vniformitie that the sely people shoulde..continue still in..ignoraunce. a1623 PEMBLE Grace & Faith (1635) 49 The greatest **deformity** and disagreement..betweene his knowledge..and his application thereof to practice. 1658 SIR T. BROWNE Garden of Cyrus ii. 45 The Funeral bed of King Cheops..which holds seven in length and four foot in bredth, had no great **deformity** from this measure. a1708 BEVERIDGE Priv. Th. I. (1730) 12 This **Deformity** to the Will and Nature of God, is that which we call Sin. 1788 KAMES Elem. Crit. (ed. 7) II. 490 A remarkable uniformity among creatures of the same kind, and a **deformity** [other ed., diff-] no less remarkable among creatures of different kinds.

Title: Deformity. 5.
Artist: Oxford English Dictionary, 2nd edition
Medium: English Language
Location: Online Database

☞ To deform another definition of deformity,
turn to page 99.

☞ To approach DIFFORMITY (first see above,
holding mirror), turn to page 77.

☞ To look for a **mirror**, turn to page 64,
75, 124, or 226.

Deformity as Sa^vage^

Les Curieux en extase ou les cordons de souliers frames the "Hottentot Venus," Saartjie Baartman, surrounded by ogling viewers of different sizes and shapes, with the caption: "The curiosity seekers in ecstasy."

Title: *Les Curieux en extase ou les cordons de souliers*[l]
("The curiosity seekers in ecstasy")
Artist: [Unknown]
Medium: Lithograph
Date: c.1814
Location: Private Collection

A gallery assumes that its "~~narrative~~" [*insert literary term:* _____] is told through ~~visitors'~~ [*my* / **your** *(circle one)*] circumambulations. ~~Docents, captions, and maps~~ [*noun, plural:* _____] guide the way. Other aspects—especially ~~organization, method of display, architecture, lighting and shadow, and~~ [*noun, pl.:* _____]—contribute to the overall experience. Similar **consideration**s arise within a single work of art, as demonstrated by the lithograph above. In *Les Curieux en extase ou les cordons de souliers* ("The curiosity seekers in ecstasy"), the lens **shifts** from the displayed subject to ~~her captivated viewers~~ [*us* / *them* / *everyone*], questioning motivations of looking and labels given to those who are viewed.

~~Hottentot, savage, cannibal~~ [*politically-correct (i.e., PC) identifiers of yourself, singular:* _____, _____, _____]: any of these might be substituted in rhetoric derived from ~~imperialist~~ [*postmodern* / *post-post-modern* / *post-post-post-modern*] explorations. In reference to a story in an English weekly called the *Connoisseur*, ~~G.E. Lessing~~ [*I* / *you*] describes ~~Hottentots~~ [*first PC identifier, pl.:* _____] as "~~stutterers~~" [*politically-INcorrect identifier of yourself, pl.:* _____ (*hereafter referred to as PinC*)] ~~(as the Dutch called African aborigines in the area around the Cape of Good Hope)~~:

> We know how dirty the ~~Hottentots~~ [*same PC identifier, pl.:* _____] are and how many things that awaken disgust and loathing in us are beautiful, comely, and sacred to them. A piece of flattened cartilage for a nose, flabby breasts which hang down to the navel, the whole body covered with a layer of goat's fat and soot and tanned by the sun, the hair dripping with grease, feet and arms entwined with fresh entrails—think of all this in the object of a fiery, worshiping, tender love; hear this expressed in the noble language of sincerity and admiration, and try to keep from laughing.[li]

Like the curiosity seekers in ecstasy, ~~Lessing~~ [*I* / *you*] make~~s~~ [**my**self / *yourself*] the object of ridicule rather than any ~~Hottentot~~ [*same PC identifier, sing.:* _____]. While ~~he~~ [*I* / *you*] laugh~~s~~ at "~~stutterers~~" [*same PinC identifier as before, pl.:* _____], a modern reader laughs at ~~Lessing~~ [*me* / *you*]—which leads this writer to wonder whether & how & where readers will ridicule my *Galerie*.

For now, looking backwards becomes my ploy to peer forward, like the two-headed Janus. My curiosity latches to details, like [*something that rouses your curiosity, feel free to use the margins, as needed:* _____], or like the pantomime *Omai: or, A Trip around the World*, which was said (in London in 1785) to lead "the imagination from country to country, from the frigid to the torrid zone, showing, as in a **mirror**, prospects of different climates, with all the productions of nature in the animal and vegetable worlds."lii Trying to envision this **mirror**, I wonder too about wandering the streets of ~~the city where the pantomime was mounted~~ [*your hometown:* _____], which ~~James Boswell~~ [*name of your pet:* _____] said provided "a high entertainment of itself. I see a vast museum of all objects, and I think with a kind of wonder that I see it for nothing."liii Displayed **not on the wall** of a gallery, but out in public for all to see:

☞ *To put yourself out in public, turn to page 80.*
☞ *To follow the Author out in public, turn to page 229.*

☞ *To put yourself out in public, turn to page 80.*
☞ *To follow the Author out in public, turn to page 229.*

Considering [*my / your / our / their*] public and private examples in this *Galerie*, the question echoes: Are "freaks" and [*same PinC identifier, pl.:* _____] created by nature or by culture?

To follow up the story of the "~~Hottentot~~ [*same PinC identifier, sing.:* _____] Venus," otherwise known as [*you / me*]: [*I was / you were*] **featured** on the shelves of the *Musée de l'Homme* in Paris, before being returned to ~~South Africa~~ [*your country of origin:* _____] in ~~2002~~ [*current year:* _____]. That *musée* ("museum": deriving from the Muses) contains **among** its annals the brain of Paul Broca, a nineteenth-century anatomist and anthropologist (resting in a bell jar of Formalin), the skulls of Descartes and of an ancestral Cro-Magnon, and [*faux relic, whose history can spill into the* **margins**: _____]. As described by Stephen Jay Gould, the display also includes "severed heads from New Caledonia; an illustration of foot binding as practiced upon Chinese women—yes, a bound foot and lower leg, severed between the knee and ankle. And, on a shelf just above the brains...a little exhibit that provided an immediate and chilling insight into nineteenth-century *mentalité* and the history of racism:...the dissected genitalia of three Third-World women [labeled *une négresse, une péruvienne,* and *la Vénus* ~~Hottentotte~~ [*French variation of PinC term used before:* _____]]. I found no brains of women, and neither Broca's penis nor any male genitalia grace the collection."liv In his essay, Gould goes on to dissect the story of ~~Saartjie Baartman~~ [*me / you*] and [*my / your*] stage name, separating "~~Hottentot~~" [*same PinC identifier, sing.:* _____] and "Venus," and including a "short excursion into the realm of scholarly minutiae...to correct a standard mistranslation of Linnaeus," which Gould admits to having made himself:

In his original description of *Homo sapiens*, Linnaeus provided a most unflattering account of African blacks, including the line: *feminae sinus pudoris*. This phrase has usually been translated, 'women are without ~~shame~~' [*word that rhymes with "shame":* _____]—a slur quite consistent with Linnaeus's general description. In Latin, 'without ~~shame~~' [*different rhyme with "shame":* _____] should be *sine pudore*, not *sinus pudoris*. But eighteenth-century scientific Latin was written so indifferently that misspellings and wrong cases are no bar to actual intent, and the reading 'without ~~shame~~' [*one more:* _____] has held.lv

In relation to this error, divergent meanings that arise through misspellings, mistranslations, and misrepresentations might be classified as kinds of deformity. (☞ *See also "Deformity as Misrepresented," page 51*.) On a related note: Until the 1830s, engravings from James Cook's voyages (the first occurred between 1768-1771) provided the chief source for illustrations about the Pacific region, across the spectrum of publications: travel books, geography texts, missionary tracts, and articles in journals, newspapers, and encyclopedias of exotic wall-papers and costumes. For decades, those engravings dominated the field, virtually unchallenged. Many designs were copied and then recopied, deviating from the original images through reproduction, while claiming to carry representative truth. "[A]s ~~artists~~ [*three copycat artists/musicians/politicians:*

_____, _____, and _____] copied the ~~engravings~~ [*mediums of each:* _____, _____, and _____] so they altered them still further in the direction of ~~European~~ [*nationalities of each, as adjs.:*

_____, _____, and _____] pre-conceptions, the anthropological and ethnographic intensions of the originals being diverted increasingly to fulfill the demands of taste and the intrinsic needs of decoration."[lvi]

Shall we ask—as did G.E. Rumphius, the "Indian Pliny" (1627-1702)—whether "There always lies hidden among these fables a modicum **of truth** or latent attributes as is true of Ovid or other poets"?[lvii] Or, do these truths become so **deformed** that fact becomes fiction?

[*Write fables & fictions based on deformations of the above information; start in provided lines, then bleed into margins:* _____

_____
_____
_____
_____
_____
_____...]

And further: Consider the use of reproduction in this *Galerie*, with digitizations and photocopies that produce grainy black-and-white versions of the originals: reproductions of reproductions of reproductions. What happens through this process that separates a Viewer from the Viewed, through indefinitely unreliable intermediaries, which throw the integrity of the Copy and Original into question?

☞ To throw the integrity of the copy & original **into** question,
      turn to *31 or 80 or* ____ *(fill in the blank)*.
☞ To act like a puppeteer & manipulate the Galerie's **form**,
      turn to *page 145 or 156*.
☞ To revisit an intermediary, turn to *page 6 or 24*.
☞ If you are tired of hard-to-read print, visit the Great Egress *(page 249)*.

IF THIS BE FORM, THEN LET THIS NOT BE FROM

If this be Form, then let this not be from
Arrangements made to sacrifice the fate
Of Content for Form's sake. For to succumb
To Form without its match (commiserat-
ing first, resolving at neglect of Heart
& Soul) puts more at risk than this small feat
Of mismatched arms & mouth & feet—all parts
That aim to breathe, enhanced by crooked beats.

Since studies show that song & dance outlive
Our knack for speech & step, then: *Dance & Sing!*
Forget to standardize our dappled gaits.
If Form is what we are (deformed as we
May be), then Content helps to animate
Our Shapes, to beautify each mold & let each Be.

☞ *To breathe & animate a bit of this Galerie,
     turn to page 108 or 117.*
☞ *To put this before a jury, turn to page 10 or 153.*
☞ *To be navigated through some Form & Content,
     turn to page 54, 94, 192, or 224.*

Exhibit C

Color is a chronicle of chemistry, fueled by desire. First came nature, then impulses to imitate its true colors. Harnessing ocher, lampblack, hematite (from the Greek word for "blood"), indigo (from Baghdad and Bengal), cinnabar (from Spain: purified, synthesized, ground to certain fineness), color-seekers sought the marrow of madder, fixed with mordents, to spread red, getting white from eggshells or calcinated bird bones. Pliny and Vitruvius described the ten thousand shells of mollusks needed to furnish a gram of royal purple (a recipe that varied with grades of murex found north and south; a recipe lost with the Fall of Rome). An array of activities, across eras and areas, secreted the spectrum's secrets.

Akin to alchemy—with maceration, decoction, distillation, decantation, precipitation, filtration, washing, and drying—recipes over centuries resembled conjurations, using harnessed natural hues, ground into pigments and dyes, fixed to fibers and spun into wool, silks, tapestries, and textiles—to enwrap bodies, spread over beds, hung on walls, to hint at a process as guarded as that for the Philosopher's Stone.

And so, I desire deformations of *dye*. *Dyeing* deforms original minerals, earths, oxides. *Dyeing* was protected by trades, pacts and patron saints—Saint Maurice for French guilds, while Venetian dyers preferred Saint Onofrio—then used to illuminate manuscripts and stain glass. Mary's mantle (and that robe of the king of France) was not blue until red went out of fashion (in the Middle Ages), when woad (a cruciferous plant whose popularity leached soil and threatened starvation) yielded brighter, lightfast shades.

Dyeing has been a journey, conveying Arab merchants by sea from India to Persia, by caravan to Mediterranean ports (Baghdad to Alexandria, Cyprus, Rhodes) to sea toward Amalfi, Pisa, Genoa, Venice, farther north and west—bearing cochineal, brazilwood, saffron and indigo, into the hands of European dyers.

Dyeing is a story of supports, both means and ends: from papyrus to skin-based parchment, pulp-based paper and linen canvas, which absorbs oil- and tempura-based binders. Look closely at a tapestry or painting—through more than the naked eye, perhaps, with an electron microscope or X-ray diffraction—to see its pigmented history. Un-dress, to learn the state of the world: *Made in Taiwan, India, Israel, Italy*. The unkempt seamstress in the warehouse is as skinny as the runway model, face-painted with wings the color of doves, Kohl-lined eyes, and lips that defy red (somewhere in its lineage of auburn, brazil, burgundy, carmine, carnation, carnelian, cerise, cinnabar, coquelicot, cresol, crimson, damask, dragon's blood, fuchsia, garnet, madder, magenta, maroon, minium, mordoré, murrey, oxblood, pink, puce, rose, ruby, rufous, russet, sanguine, scarlet, stammel, vermilion—).

Dyeing is an art, like everything else.

Dyeing is a matter of living, like Diderot wrote: "Drawing gives shape to all creatures, color gives them life. Such is the divine breath that animates them."[lviii]

Dyeing also can be deathly. Used in Egyptian cosmetics, orpiment and realgar contained arsenic, poisoning through cheeks, lids, lips. Later, in smaller doses, it repelled insects from illuminated manuscripts, allowing parched preservation.

It is arsenic that I can't get out of my system, licking lips after swallowing a bit of gloss, while pondering preservation against rearrangements of flesh, muscle and fat, not for the purpose of health, but for beauty. How far to go? Was Medusa so monstrous, or did her matter rest in the Eye of the Beholder? What about that plastic surgeon who devised a way to make wings? Will you kill me slowly by trying to re-form my deformities, which cannot be trusted or tamed? Will I starve myself if deprived of blue, until the hue emerges in the very shade of my skin?

And so, the Undertaker starts to show true colors—as an artist of the body.

```
┌─────────────────┐
│                 │
│                 │
│                 │
│                 │
│   Add picture   │
│   of yourself   │
│      here.      │
│                 │
│                 │
│                 │
│                 │
│                 │
└─────────────────┘
```

Title: *Artist of the Body*
_____
Artist: _____
Medium: _____ ← *Fill in the blanks.*
Date: _____
Location: _____

☞ *To caricature this image, turn to page 103.*

☞ *To compare this with your self, turn to page 150.*

☞ *To donate this Galerie, find an appropriate venue &*
   droplift it. Include a note &c. saying as much.

☞ *If you first want to deform more, turn to page 220.*

Exhibit

[from *bone pomes*^lix]

—No doubt, Sirs ^and Madams,—there is a whole Exhibit wanting here—
and others elsewhere—and a chasm of ten pages made in the book by
it—but the book-binder is neither a fool, or a knave, or a puppy
(though one may be found nipping, even gnawing, at N)—nor is the
book a jot more imperfect (at least upon that score)——but, on the
contrary, the book is more perfect and complete by wanting said
Exhibit, than having it, as I shall demonstrate to your Deformities in
this manner.

—I question first by-the-bye, whether the same experiment might not
be made as successfully upon sundry other Exhibits——but there is no
end, an' please your Deformities, in trying experiments upon
Exhibits——have we had enough of it?——when will there be an End
of that matter?

—But before I begin my demonstration, let me only tell you, that the
Exhibit which I have torn out here, and which otherwise you would all
have been reading just now, instead of this——was the description of
Gloria's life, not only parceled from pieces that I knew of her and of
my grandfather, plus records culled from where I could (in his
scholarship & in marginalia of her & his books, left behind in his
personal library & her public one), amid ephemera——no, not those
tethered tidbits, but an Exhibit getting everything down pat (simply
and surely) chronologically (for one thing) beginning to middle to
end, with *He* and *She* and *They* and *We* (including *You* and *Me*) being
born & living & dying, since that is the Truth, isn't it?——have we had
enough of it?——rather than this account that tumbles & teases, made
into a map without a key, a story journeying between lines.

—But the painting & printing of this journey, upon reviewing it, appears to be so much above the stile and manner of any thing else I have been able to paint & print in this book, that it could not have remained in it, without depreciating every other scene; and destroying at the same time that necessary equipoise and balance, (whether of good or bad) betwixt Exhibit and Exhibit, another kind of Truth, from whence the just proportions and harmony of the whole work results. For my own part, I am but just set up in the business, so know little about it—but, in my opinion, to write a book is for all the world like humming a song—be but in tune with yourself, madam ^and sir, 'tis no matter how high or how low you take it.

—This is the reason, may it please your Deformities, that some of the lowest and flattest compositions pass off very well—(as Gloria told me)—*deformed, deforming, deformity, difformite, &c.*—and after she pronounced the litany—*deformed, deforming, deformity, difformite, &c.*—she humm'd—and a tolerable tune I thought it was; and to this hour, may it please your Deformities, I have never found out how low, how flat, how spiritless and jejune it was, but that all of a sudden, up started an air in the middle of it, so fine, so rich, so heavenly,—it carried my soul up with it into the other world; now had I (as *Montaigne* complained in a parallel accident)—had I found the declivity easy, or the accent accessible, it was so perpendicular a precipice——so wholly cut off from the rest of the work, that by the first note I humm'd I found myself flying into the other world, and from thence discovered the vale from whence I came, so low, and dismal, that I shall never have the heart to descend into it again.

☞ *To add this to the evidence, turn to page 223.*

☞ *If you didn't come from Exhibit W, visit page 58*[W1] *or 61*[W2]*.*

☞ *To meet an ugly face eye to eye, look forward.*

☞ *If you haven't met the book-binder, turn to page 229 or keep reading.*

CAUT I ON !!!!

Oh, no! You've made it thus far?! Goodness, no further—at risk of falling into madness, sadness, a bad mess, any or all of the above. I fear for your safety! Despite reaching this milestone, don't read another word—take heed! Circumvent the (*shhhhh!*) M-O-N-S-T-E-R by engaging its every potential move: turn this book inside out, upside down, twist & shout, not staying on a steady forward course, lest you meet the (*shhhhh!*) M-O-N-S-T-E-R when your guard is down. So: guard your bones, gird your loins, gild your coins, ponder your koans. Don't waver: go straight to The Destruction Room (*page 230*) do not pass Go, and take this warning with a full & steady heart. Don't worry about bones or heart-shaped holes, just be wary & beware **TO** proceed at your own

R I SK!!!!

☞ To ignore these cockamamie warnings, turn to page 94.

☞ To read at your own risk, turn to page 46 or 177.

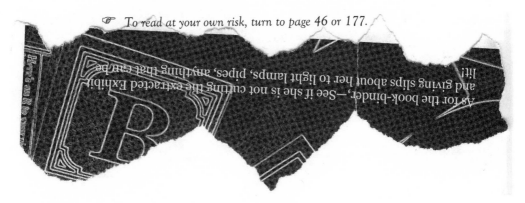

As for the book-binder,'—See if she is not cutting the extracted Exhibit and giving slips about her to light lamps, pipes, anything that can be it!!!

Here's can it to hunt...

☞ To redirect yourself, turn to 223.

☞ To stop Gretchen's letters, don't read: 46, 69, 114,
        137, 152, 168, 183, 204, 218, or the next page.

Dear Gloria,

Okay, I'm back. More time has passed, admittedly. Each day I sit down to "speak" to you, then don't. More time passes, the more there is to say. I put off a letter, then a longer letter, then one that's longer still, and ultimately don't write a thing. (I warned you—as mentioned, I'm not one for keeping a diary—still, I feel apologetic...)

For months, I've learned from physical therapists—a constant learning curve—trying different treatments, healing what can be healed, adapting my definition of "good health." How did you do it? How will I?

I recall waking: aware of being unaware, regaining a sense of where I was and why, unable to speak coherently or walk, even too tired to think, just to notice familiar and unfamiliar faces staring at me and the hospital room's window, after being moved from ICU to a regular ward. That window framed white clouds, gleaned of blue, unlike the gray day I walked to the field and found myself struck. In that ward, called back to living, a foreign body encased me. It didn't feel like mine, needing to be sloughed. I thought: if I just could get up and walk, get back home, to work and in motion, I could shed this flailing shell, like a snail or a snake or a moth—

But I'm merely human, stuck inside my skin. How to inhabit this new body—which isn't mine, but also is—some hybrid of the two? I still don't know, struggling to learn. Shall I laugh or weep at my predicament? Might you, dear Gloria, call me "deformed"?

G.H.

Dear Gloria,

I've thought of you again and again and wanted to write, if nothing else to enter "The Destruction Room," just need to get perspective: to be creative with what I have not lost, what I might find by navigating the world anew through a sometimes unpredictable sense of my senses.

I don't consider you, or your project, cursed. We're never as magnanimous as we think we are, nor I wager are we as selfish. But I have felt selfish, wanting to blame something to put my life aright, to be as I was and wondering what if, if only I could return to that lightning to upturn that moment, seizing the million details that could have been different, when only one needed to be. Or is that mode of thinking too simplistic?

I haven't felt up to facing your project, with too many daily tasks to tackle. And yet, when I throw myself into your Galerie even for a little bit—with an open heart (whatever that means)—for those moments I can forget who I am and where I am and what has happened, even imagining that I can live with this deformed form, more magnanimously, to go where I might yet go...

G H.

☞ To proceed to Gloria's Destruction Room, in the condition that she left it posthumously, please turn to page 217.

☞ To go where you might go more magnetically, make a DIY magnetic poetry kit out of these words.

☞ To continue reading Gretchen's letters to Gloria, keep reading.

Dear Gloria,

You likely know all this and more—much more than I can tell of myself. And you're likely aware of episodes that set me back, stupid stumblings, not only physically but psychologically—like last night, our first dinner out since the accident, when a waitress carded me, despite my age, then saw my license and said: "God has been very kind to you, dear!" How does a benign compliment clam me shut, wanting to hide, fearing her piteous gaze if I unwrap my scarf that hides spidering burns, if I take out the fat-handled silverware that helps my malfunctioning muscles grip? Would it have served me better to sit on the other side of the booth, where her words would've escaped my hard-of-hearing ear?

As if estranged from my body: who I was, or who to become—I can already feel myself changing with my "new" body, but am trying to trust that this happened for a reason, to avoid encroaching fears, angers, shames, shams. Even if the act itself was meaningless, I have to create meaning out of it. But not by bitching in your book—

I'll try not to refer again to the lightning. Whether by way of apology or explanation, it seemed worth mentioning, to say where I am: in relation to myself, in relation to you. Wherever you are, I'm seeking your guidance—not only to honor your request, but also for myself—so past and future may dissolve into now: reduced to this letter, joining another letter, into a word, a phrase, a sentence that brings my brain toward a new thought, a new mode of thinking and being. I'm recommitting myself to your Galerie, in hopes that the journey might piece together not only you and Bea, but also me.

Off to read,
G.H.

☞ To seek guidance, turn to page 24 or 105.
☞ To continue reading Gretchen's letters to Gloria, turn to page 114.
☞ If you have been torn apart, turn to page 72.
☞ To piece yourself together, turn to page 150 or 193.

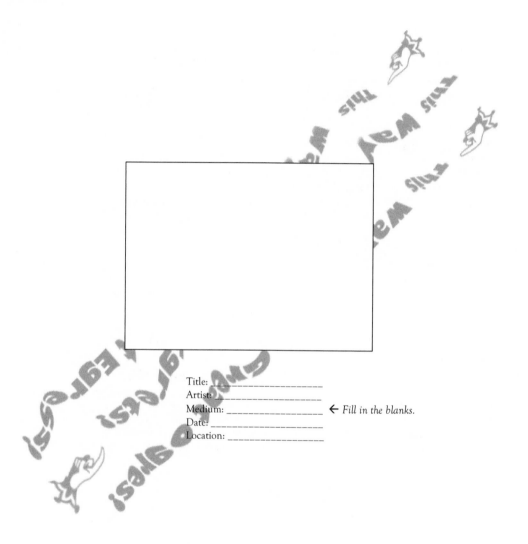

Title: _____
Artist: _____
Medium: _____   ← *Fill in the blanks.*
Date: _____
Location: _____

☞ *To unpack more boxes, turn to page 220, then add a future directive:*

_____.

☞ *To compare this box with another box, turn to page 80, 103, or ____.*

(fill in blank)

☞ *To fit this box with/within/without an Exhibit, turn to page 224.*

☞ *Please re-form this definition.* ☜

[crumpled, fragmentary text from a dictionary entry:] 3. (with a and pl.) An instance of deformity; a figurement or malformation of the body or of some bodily ... now usually *spec.* ... one deformities of the ... Those deformities ... deformed being or ... in his owne persone ... Orbers...carry..maladies ... time had been contracted ... from the cradle to the grave ... 1413 LYDG. *Pilgr. Sowle* II. xlv. (1859) 52 ... 1578 ... ... 1807-24 S. COOPER First ... and deformities about then ... 1794 SULLIVAN *View* ... in it (St. Paul's) which ... 1662 HEYLIN ... face. 1698 FRYER ... horrid Shapes. ... imagine such ... tumour sometimes creates ... is merely a deformity ... thing. 1838 DICKENS *Nich. Nick.* ... iron ... countenances of old ... upon their limbs ... *trans.* ... represent the Divi ... could ever be ... 44 The ... V. 382 ... 204 ... the fowle ... he shold ... Children with ... IRON *Manfred*. i. ... *Dodoens* IV. ... aber or ... Nick.

Title: Deformity. 3.
Artist: Oxford English Dictionary, 2nd edition
Medium: English Language
Location: Online Database

☞ To reform this definition, do what you will.

☞ To consider this definition as a relic, compare it
to the inset box on page 126.

☞ To consider this deformity in terms of other definitions, turn to:
34, 50, 73, 118, 141, 156, 172, 187, and/or 208.

In the engraving found here, "The Sculptor" Joseph Nollekens sits concentrating in his studio among tools and statuary, including Venus and Cupid, and Apollo with his lyre, flanked by two marble muses. A single live model poses, pallid and proportioned like the larger life-like statues. With many repeated elements, the caricature possesses multiple frames of looking: the window, the sculptor's eyeglasses, angled gazes by each of the sculptures, the model and the sculptor, and the overall frame of the engraving. By following these angled gazes (approximately 16 sets of eyes), viewers make connections between fragmented elements. It is interesting to note that Nollekens was a member of the Royal Academy and made busts of figures the likes of William Pitt, Laurence Sterne, and David Garrick, but here, he is gnarled and enthralled to the point of drooling. The classically-modeled forms are undercut by his doctoring in progress: "The eccentric and uncouth Nollekens was a trafficker in antiques, putting fragments together; the models for his Venuses were a cause of jealousy to his wife." Apart from overtones of Pygmalion and Galatea, commerce seems to supersede the integrity of the original artworks, and in the caricature, Nollekens sees nothing wrong with his method of using random parts to imitate a whole.

Title: The Sculptor [Preparation for the Academy,
Old Joseph Nollekens and his Venus][lx]
Artist: Thomas Rowlandson
Medium: Etching and watercolor
Date: c. 1800
Location: Metropolitan Museum of Art,
The Elisha Whittelsey Collection

Owing origins to a [*a. Bologna / b. Bolognese / c. Abalone (circle one)*] history painter named [*a. Hannibal / b. Annabel Lee / c. Annibale*] Carraci, caricature derived from a "loading" of features (in Italian, *caricare* means "to load") and rendered the antithesis of beauty, "una bella...perfetta deformità."[lxi] In his *Treatise on* [*a. Painting / b. Panting / c. Ranting*], Leonardo [*a. DiCaprio, b. da Vinci, c. di Lombardia*] made sketches of the ideal grotesque to better understand ideal beauty, since "Beauty and ugliness seem more effective through one another [l'una per l'altra]."[lxii] Although works in the Early [*a. Reconnaissance / b. Renaissance / c. Nuisance*]—especially among Italian artists—paved the way for natural [*a. conscriptions, / b. depictions, / c. predilections*] of deformity, the High [*a. Reconnaissance, / b. Renaissance / c. Nuisance*] re-privileged classically-modeled works by Raphael, Michelangelo, Titian, and [*a. DiCaprio, b. da Vinci, c. di Lombardia*]. Correlations between physical and psychological [*a. proportion, / b. propulsion, / c. production*] continued to be made in J.C. Lavater's *Essays of* [*a. Phlebotomy, b. Phraseology, c. Physiognomy*], which derived in part from Charles [*a. le Brun's, / b. le Hun's, / c. le Hun's*] *l'expression des passions* and perpetuated the idea that "Beauty and ugliness have a strict [*a. concoction, b. connection, c. dissection*], with the moral constitution of the [*a. Man, b. Woman, c. Monkey*]. In proportion as [*a. he, b. she, c. monkey*] is morally [*a.*

good, *b. bad, c. ugly*], [*a. he, b. she, c. monkey*] is handsome; and ugly, in proportion as [*a. he, b. she, c. monkey*] is morally [*a. good, b. bad, c. ugly*]."[lxiii] Regardless, the humorous and "grotesque" [*a. Italian, b. Iterated, c. Irritated*] art, as well as seventeenth-century allegorical [*a. Butch, b. Dutch, c. Mulch*] painting, laid groundwork for eighteenth-century British comic art, epitomized in the caricatures of William [*a. Prince of Wales, b. Clinton, c. Hogarth*], James [*a. Earl Jones, b. Bond, c. Gillray*], George [*a. Foreman, b. Washington, c. Cruikshank*], and Thomas [*a. Jefferson, b. Rowlandson, c. Thumb*].

The [*a. development, b. devolution, c. denuding*] of caricature reflected interesting shifts in characterizations and perceptions of [*a. conformity, b. deformity, c. performativity*]. Prior to the Picturesque, ugliness lost its stigma of [*a. evil, b. Evel, c. Knievel*]; in the *Spectator*, Joseph [*a. Addison, b. Priestly, c. and the Amazing Technicolored Dreamcoat*] poked fun at the pseudo-science of [*a. phrenology, b. physiognomy, c. pastrami*]: "nothing can be more glorious than for a [*a. Man, b. Woman, c. Aardvark*]...to be an honest, just, good-natured [*a. Man, b. Woman, c. Aardvark*], in spite of all those [*a. Larks, b. Snarks, c. Marks*] and [*a. Ligatures, b. Signatures, c. Dentures*] which Nature seems to have set upon [*a. him, b. her, c. aardvark*] for the Contrary...I have seen many an amiable [*a. Peace, b. Perch, c. Piece*] of Deformity which may have more [*a. harm, b. charm, c. chutzpah*] than an insolent Beauty."[lxiv] With exaggerated [*a. bleachers, b. feathers, c. features*], caricatures provided a medium of inversions and [*a. twists, b. tweets, c. Twizzlers*], where dilettantes could look [*a. foolish, b. ghoulish, c. gurlesque*], and people could parallel animal and other [*a. nonessential, b. non sequitur, c. nonhuman*] natural forms. Caricatures exposed [*a. connections, b. dissections, c. vivisections*] between beauty and deformity, often by [*a. metaphysics, b. psychosis, c. metamorphosis*]—for instance, when shapes of furniture and other inanimate [*a. subjects, b. objects, c. rejects*] figuratively echoed characters.[lxv]

The blatant [*a. intimation, b. imitation, c. ingratiation*] makes [*a. Nollekens', b. Botticelli's, c. la Specola's*] Venus entirely different than William Blake's "Laocoön" (*see page 52*). Where Blake incorporates particular fragments for communicating a [*a. cow, b. coward, c. code*] to decipher, here the distortions of physiognomy suggest how caricature [*a. remains, b. reframes, c. refutes*] deformity, throws classical [*a. music, b. orchestrations, c. oppositions*] into question, and anticipates movements that privilege an artist's [*a. hue, b. view, c. yew*] over ideal forms and imitations. The renowned caricaturist, William [*a. Cosby, b. the Conquerer, c. Hogarth*], spoke in *The Analysis of* [*a. Bounty, b. Beauty, c. Booty*] (1753) to the conflict about proportion, saying "I fear it will be difficult to raise a very clear idea of what constitutes, or composes the *utmost* [*a. bounty, b.*

beauty, c. booty] of *proportion*....perhaps even the word *[a. cracker, b. character, c. chum]*, *as it relates to form*, may not be quite understood by every one, tho' it is so frequently used....thinking of form and motion together....a *[a. cracker, b. character, c. chum]*, in this sense, chiefly depends on a figure being remarkable as to its form, either in some particular *[a. heart, b. part, c. fart]*, or altogether, yet surely no figure, be it ever so singular, can be perfectly conceived as a *[a. cracker, b. character, c. chum]*, till we find it connected with some remarkable circumstance or *[a. mouse, b. paws, c. cause]*, for such particularity of appearance; for instance, a fat bloted [*sic*] *[a. person, b. walrus, c. banana slug]* doth not call to mind the *[a. cracker, b. character, c. chum]* of a *[a. Confucius, b. Silenus, c. Silliness]* till we have joined the idea of *[a. voluptuousness, b. corruptness, c. counterproductiveness]* with it; so likewise strength to support, and *[a. classiness, b. clumsiness, c. chumminess]* of figure, are *[a. requited, b. united, c. delighted]*, as well in the character of Atlas as in a *[a. porter, b. pouter, c. doubter]*."[lxvi] This *[a. requital, b. union, c. jugular]*, even juncture, acknowledges potential *[a. dystopia, b. dystrophy, c. disjuncture]*—that is, the implication that physical *[a. traits, b. trash, c. transgressions]* can be correlated with, but not determined by, *[a. psychics, b. sciatica, c. psychology]*, thus allowing each *[a. cracker, b. aardvark, c. human]* to be rendered differently.

☞ To *[fender/bender/render]* this differently,
 turn to page 242 or ___ (fill in blank).
☞ To *[recede/seed/proceed]* to another juncture,
 turn to page 18-19, 112, or 119.
☞ To *[cracker/caricature/care for]* a character, keep reading.

← *Caricature yourself here.*

Title: _____
Artist: _____
Medium: _____ ← *Fill in the blanks.*
Date: _____
Location: _____

☞ *To compare this to the "real" version of you, see page 80 or 150.*

☞ *To seek a relic of the real "you," turn to page 1 or 245.*

☞ *To find the form in all this, turn to page 77 or 156.*

LET ME NOT ADMIT TO THIS, MY TROUBLED BLOOD

Let me not admit to this, my troubled blood
that courses through my body, on the mend
but needing aid, with shadows hidden, un-
dispelled. I need to loose them, and to tend
my mess—my hands, my arms, my neck, my head
that slumps & heaves, so worn (*What happens when
a dream cannot get out?*[lxvii])—and then, the rest.

All moves in slowness, robed behind cracked lens
that dignifies sore scars—my Wreckage—sealed
and not made public. Masquerade: I'm seen
as sacred, borne aloft as Guide, sores healed
but Not. So haunted: Dare I ask what meaning Spirit forged this éstranged state of shame,
at risk of losing You—or taking aim?

☞ *To take aim, turn to page 62, 166, or*
____ (fill in blank).
☞ *At risk of losing You, turn to page 222;*
at risk of losing Me, turn to page 245.
☞ *To add deformities neglected in this Galerie,*
turn to page 220 or 221.

Exhibit L

Let there be (no): lightening, snapshot, quick coordination of aperture and shutter. This is slower. Looking through the lens, a figure fixates: focusing. Curls and limbs shiver. Saturating, a girdled bust darkens white. Silvering. Her face tilts; eyes twitch. Blurring. An arm rises to wing. Reflected and inverted, here's the catch: posed ghost. Pictorially washed, her curves float in flight.

[S]ubjects of even *extreme brightness* range *must be represented within the limits of the paper, being translated into varying shades of gray, usually with a note of solid black or white, or both, which serves to "key" the tonalities.*[lxviii]

Ghost-hunting further: shadows shift. Pocks of light shimmer, hover and sheave, leaving a *Self-Portrait of Shade*. Illuminated by varied *Opticks*, I view from both sides of the glass: "In a very dark Chamber, at a round Hole...made in the Shut of a Window." Newton thought that "Light is never known to follow crooked Passages," but Grimaldi beheld its ability to bend.[lxix] So I shadow—

[B]eauty...must always grow *from the realities of life, and our ancestors, forced to live in dark rooms, presently came to discover shadows, ultimately to guide shadows towards beauty's ends...not so much a difference in color as in shade...*[lxx]

Blurring the most extreme brightness in a very dark Chamber, beauty in shadows render sun writings to be revealed: a secret about a secret— deforming an invisible woman only to be rendered as light.

And where she goes, I go—we go—flying further away from the sun, in the negative's frame. Light plays tricks on eyes. Inverting Icarus, shall I misread this sequence in motion, or be fueled by Muybridge's and Lumière's stop-times and successions? Like birefringence turns one to two, and refraction bends: a Brockenspekter casts our shadows upon clouds. While it may appear otherwise, I'm your shade, as you're a shade of me. See us for who we are, always accompanying. Shade us further— together—until "*the seen*, the revealed, is the child of both appearances and the search."

Is photography the portrait of a concavity, of a lack, of an absence?... And while that was its physical reality, it descended upon me as though it was its own vision that was ...I hadn't noticed that that woman was invisible.

And such is the same with shade. Silences shape sound (as after caress, hungering touch): "Someone is going to arise out of the silence,"

An art of reversal, *negative* turns *positive*. Observed and observing, the camera mirrors my chimera. Between exposure and development, "the world turn[s] upside downward," Burton imagines (if "Women weare the Breeches").[lxxi] Breaching to peer, pinholes lure "the pencil of nature" to render sun ... by sketching, etching, engraving, painting—as she and I face brightness, attempting not to go blind.[lxxii]

Light can in fact only give way to an image when its path is impeded, when it is turned away from its course. In other words, to be what it is, revealed, light must be interrupted...[lxxiii]

And such is the same with shade. Silences shape sound (as after caress, hungering touch): "Someone is going to arise out of the silence," Roubaud rouses the darkened room "where I catch the light by the handful."[lxxiv] Suspended at once: remembered and anticipated. Preferring to rove, *The camera never lies,* but *shoots* and *takes,* stealing and sealing—"forward," Arbus wrote, "The more it tells you the less you know."[lxxv] Emulsions trap more than the subjected. Harnessing eye, brain, and hand to make an exposure, a photographer is likewise exposed; choosing to partake in what is "essentially an act of non-intervention."[lxxvi]

Is photography the portrait of a concavity, of a lack, of an absence? And while that was its physical reality, it descended upon me as though it was its own vision that was ... hadn't noticed that that woman was invisible woman.[lxxvii]

And where she goes, I go—we go—flying further away from the sun, only to be rendered as light in the

Roubaud rouses the darkened room "where I catch the light by the handful." Suspended at once: remembered and anticipated. Preferring to rove, *The camera never lies,* but *shoots* and *takes,* stealing and sealing—"—Arbus wrote, "The more it tells you the less you know." Emulsions trap more than the subjected. Harnessing eye, brain, and hand to make an exposure, a photographer is likewise exposed: choosing to partake in what is "essentially an act of non-intervention."

Light can in fact only give way to an image when its path is impeded, when it is turned away from its course. In other words, to be what it is, , light must be interrupted...

An art of reversal, *negative* turns *positive*. Observed and observing, the camera mirrors my chimera. Between exposure and development, "the world turn[s] upside downward," Burton imagines (if "Women weare the Breeches"). Breaching to peer, pinholes lure "the pencil of nature" to by sketching, etching, engraving, painting—as she and I face brightness, attempting not to go blind.

[B]eauty...must always grow from the realities of life, and our ancestors, forced to live in dark rooms, presently came to discover beauty in shadows, ultimately to guide shadows towards beauty's ends...not so much a difference in color as in shade...

Ghost-hunting further: shadows shift. Pocks of light shimmer, hover and sheave, leaving a *Self-Portrait of Shade.* Illuminated by varied *Opticks,* I view from both sides of the glass: "In a very Chamber, at a round Hole... made in the Shut of a Window." Newton thought that "Light is never known to follow crooked Passages," but Grimaldi beheld its ability to bend. So I shadow—

negative's frame. Light plays tricks on eyes. Inverting Icarus, shall I misread this sequence in motion, or be fueled by Muybridge's and Lumière's stop-times and successions? Like birefringence turns one to two, and refraction bends: a Brockenspekter casts our shadows upon clouds. While it may appear otherwise, I'm your shade, as you're a shade of me. See us for who we are, always accompanying. Shade us further—together—until *the seen*, the revealed, is the child of both appearances and the search."[lxxviii]

Blurring the most extreme brightness in a very dark Chamber, beauty in shadows render sun writings to be revealed: a secret about a secret—deforming an invisible woman only to be rendered as light.

[S]ubjects of even the most extreme brightness range must be represented within the limits of the paper, being translated into varying shades of gray, usually with a note of solid black or white, or both, which serves to "key" the tonalities.

Let there be (no): lightening, snapshot, quick coordination of aperture and shutter. This is slower. Looking through the lens, a figure fixates: focusing. Curls and limbs shiver. Saturating, a girdled bust darkens white. Silvering. Her face tilts; eyes twitch. Blurring. An arm rises to wing. Reflected and inverted, here's the catch: posed ghost. Pictorially washed, her curves float in flight.

107

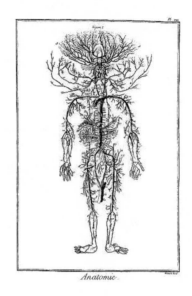

Anatomie

Title: Artist of the Body
Artist: Denis Diderot
Medium: Encyclopedia
Date: 1762-1777
Location: Printed in Paris, France

☞ *To meet another Artist of the Body, turn to page 68, 79, or ___ .*

☞ *To meet other ghosts of the Galerie, scan here.*

☞ *To try to catch an invisible woman, turn to page 155.*

What
is
all
this
deformity
about?

Exhibit T

We exist. In margins: manicules and bishop's fists vie (there, a curling cuff; here, a pointed index). Will you follow my hands? And that by which we call another name would swell: to *auxiliaries, directors, digits, pointers, fists, indices, index cuts, indictors, hand directors*. Pointing toward *Arcadia*, Zelmane "saw in him the glasse of her owne miserie, taking the hande of *Philoclea*, and with burning kisses setting it close to her lips (as if it should stande there like a hande in the margine of a Booke, to note some saying worthy to be marked) began to speake these wordes..."[lxxix]

☞ *E ne l'una de le mani mi parea che questi tenesse una cosa, la quale ardesse tutta; e pareami che mi dicesse queste parole: <<**Vide cor tuum**>>. E quando elli era stato alquanto, pareami che disvegliasse questa che dormia, e tanto si sforzava per suo ingegno, che le facea mangiare questa cosa che in mano li ardea, la quale ella mangiava dubitosamente.*[lxxx]

Unseating centuries, I unearth hands for hearts. Margins prompt *Dear Author & Reader* to respond: *groping* for knowledge, *shaping* thought, *plunging* into unknowns. "This booke (gentle Reader) is entituled a *Manuale*, which is deriued of the Latin word *Manuall*...that is, in the hand. It is a diminutiue of *Manus*, as it were a storehouse, & which ought always to be had in hand, as the handle of a sword."[lxxxi] If pen is mightier than sword, what of hands, holding my bone? Transporting relics, something (or someone) always gets lost in translation—

☞ *Et il me semblait qu'en une de ses mains, le Seigneur tenait une chose qui brûlait toute; et il me semblait qu'il me disait ces paroles: <<**Vide cor tuum**>>. Et quand il était demeuré quelaue temps, il me semblait qu'il réveillait celle qui dormait; et tant il s'efforçait oar son esprit, qu'il lui faisait manger cette chose qui brûlait en sa main, et qu'elle mangeait avc crainte.*[lxxxii]

Before Gutenberg, the scribe's art involved copying, illuminating and binding (*manu*-scripts: scribed *by hand*), and before and after orators and actors learned to "translate a thought into discoursing signs...while the articulated Fingers supply the office of a voice." And the soul? Bulwer believed "ordered motions of the hand [were] the most puissant agent of the soul," like Butler wrote, "Their sowl is in their fingers ends."[lxxxiii] Babbling aside, what of phantom limbs? Would they bury or bear souls, as my lips summon the sufferer: "forced to coin words...taking his pain in one hand, and a lump of pure sound in the other (as perhaps the people of Babel did in the beginning), so to crush them together that a brand new word in the end drops out"?[lxxxiv]

☞ *Y parecióme que el varón, en una de sus manos, sostenía algo que*

110

intensamente ardía, así como que pronunciaba estas palabras: **Vide cor tuum**. *Al cabo de cierto tiempo me pareció que despertaba la durminete y, no sin esfuerzo de ingenio, hacíale comer lo que en la mano ardía, cosa que ella se comía con escrúpulo.*[lxxxv]

Vide cor meum. Before breathing (or breaching: *breaking to allow something to pass through*) comes a friezing. Frescoed: muscular arcs. The point of this pointing: *Noli me tangere?*[lxxxvi] Like Bernini said of speaking: "a movement must be chosen and then carried through; the best moment for the mouth is just before or just after speaking."[lxxxvii] Or was it something else, just before or after (*hand to heart to mouth*):

☞ *And he who held her held also in his hand a thing that was burning in flames; and he said to me,* **Vide cor tuum**. *But when he had remained with me a little while, I thought that he set himself to awaken her that slept; after the which he made her to eat that thing which flamed in his hand...*[lxxxviii]

Handed through mouths, I move tongue in check: *touché, touchstone, touch-and-go, losing touch...* Neurons electrify limbs like galvanized frogs. Making leaps of faith: my meditation mutates, translating RNA into DNA, not DNR, to be resuscitated for another chance at change. Partaking in plasticity, hands and brain (with heart and bone) modernize my metamorphosis, as "touch teaches us the difference between *I* and *other*, that there can be someone outside of ourselves."[lxxxix] *Tuum. Meum.* Let's try this again:

☞ *To try this again, turn to 224.*

☞ *To revisit the scene of the crime, turn to page 30.*

☞ *To exercise your rights, turn to page 166.*

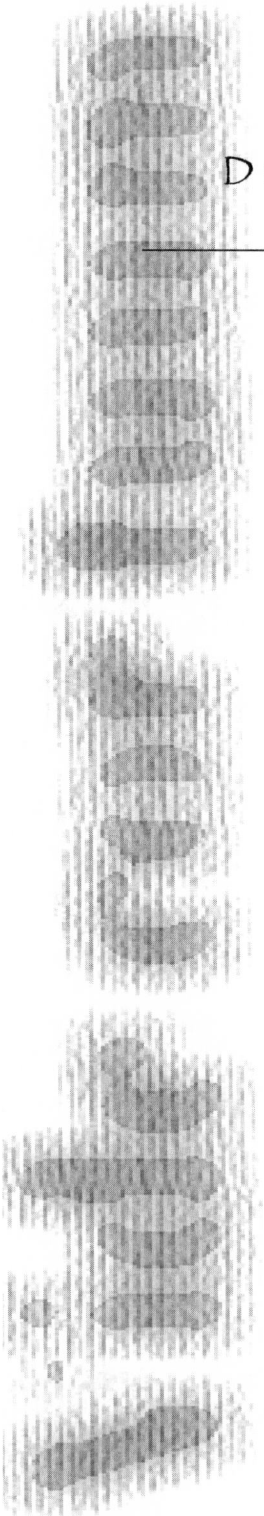

Did You Miss the Point?

Careful

As

yoU

Tread

Into

Other

Nethers

☞ To leave a guide for future travelers, turn to page 21 or 247.

☞ To explore other nethers, jump to page 173 or 222.

☞ To follow the monster underwater, turn to page 176 or 177.

☞ To read between the lines, keep reading.

☞ *To read between lines, turn to page 129 or 157.*

☞ *To return this to its "original" state, turn to page 105.*

☞ *To deform this further, turn to page 220.*

Dear Gloria,

As I assemble the semblance of a manuscript, your "Exhibits" become more familiar, yet more enigmatic. Is your alphabet incomplete, inadvertently or otherwise? Shall I mark absent letters as missing, akin to artwork stolen from the Gardner leaving empty frames? Or shall I become a literal ghostwriter, creating replacements and/or asking Subscribers to do the same? Are your "Exhibits" named for individual letters, or are they meant to be epistles, lacking formal address: To Whom It May Concern? Dear You?

G.H.

Dear You,

What haunts me most: something you said on the day we met, asking me whether I'd take your life into my hands. You said it like that: your life, my hands. We had only just met; somehow you trusted me. You meant your body-of-work, yet shared more: your cobbled jobs (tutoring varied grades, working in a library, home-making, etc.), your so-called "slow" son and ailing husband (who, in final years, suffered from Parkinson's that caused episodes when he couldn't speak but sing, walking backwards not forwards), your own physical condition…it was almost too much to hear, to bear, dismissed when you cautioned me about pity that loses a generous and generative sense of the body, its capacities and vulnerabilities. You laughed at yourself. That was when you asked me to take your life into my hands: your life, my hands. You didn't know whether you'd be able to finish your Galerie and hoped I might take over where you left off—continuing what started long ago, as if we were stewards carrying wishes to the future: like a bone with a heart-shaped hole…

G.H.

Dear Gloria,

In order to figure out how to enlist Subscribers, I need to backtrack to recall the process of my own subscription. It was accidental, like much of life. (What were the chances of my being struck by lightning?) I first saw you at the funeral of my grandfather, when my father shared condolences with you and shook your hand. At ten-years-old, I didn't put two-and-two together until he recounted the story years later, after he and my mother (your half-sister) divorced. She still declines to acknowledge your existence and any transgressions by her illustrious father. Always on-the-road, he died of a heart attack in a public bathroom, without identification, so it took a few days to be notified. His death precludes my questioning him about his double life, and my grandmother's senility leaves me at another impasse. Compared with meeting you, the facts about him seem admittedly anticlimactic; I'm less interested in his familial transgressions than your curated obsessions. After re-meeting you, I asked my father what he remembered: very little besides shaking your hand at the funeral, seeing your other arm withered, your tiny figure alone. He mentioned an old family friend, a protégé of your father's who made contact with you after the funeral (perhaps I should contact him now?). For some reason, I didn't tell my father about finding you, our subsequent visit, or the pages you started to send me. Somehow, I wanted to discover your role in my life without family interventions or editorials. Each of your dispatches (an Exhibit, sonnet, sometimes a definition, an image, some scholarship) equaled out to a few pages. I could've read a single sentence per day. All of a sudden, after two years, my expectations met absence, during which time I retreated to older pages. New meanings surfaced, changing my impression of the whole. Then I learned of your death. I reread the entirety in a single weekend and sensed another shape emerging, "if shape it might be called." With deformations of "deformity," new forms keep surfacing as I fell and keep falling back on my limited sense of form…How am I supposed to interpret "The Destruction Room"? Am I supposed to break your book apart and stitch it back together, along what lines? And what about the bone with the heart-shaped hole?

G.H.

☞ To continue reading Gretchen's letters to Gloria, turn to 137.

　　☞ To consider the relation of this book to said bone, close the book &
　　　cut out a heart from the front & back covers, then turn to page 223.

　　☞ To write your own letters to GH, tear paper to the size of the book &
　　　paste pieces over & around these letters.

☞ To choose your next step, turn to page ___ or ___ or ___ (fill in the blank).

Title: -----------------------
Artist: -----------------------
Medium: ----------------------- ← Fill in the blanks.
Date: -----------------------
Location: -----------------------

☞ If you think this is Pandora's box, turn to page 179.

☞ To decrease this page's inflammation, follow directions on page 220, then add a future directive: _____ .

☞ To reorient yourself, turn the page.

4. fig. Moral disfigurement, ugliness, or crookedness. c1400 MANDEVILLE (Roxb.) xxi. 141 Purged and clene of all vice and alkyn **deformitee.** 1561 T. NORTON Calvin's Inst. I. xv. (1634) 74 The corruption and **deformitie** of our nature. 1696 STANHOPE Chr. Pattern (1711) 71 If the **deformity** of his neighbour's actions happen to represent that of his own. 1741 MIDDLETON Cicero II. vii. 109 The **deformity** of Pompey's conduct. 1860 EMERSON Cond. of Life, Behaviour Wks. (Bohn) II. 382 It held bad manners up, so that churls could see the **deformity.** b. (with a and pl.) A moral disfigurement. 1571 CAMPION Hist. Irel. II. v. (1633) 80 They declined now to such intollerable **deformities** of life and other superstitious errors. 1576 FLEMING Panopl. Epist. 248, I supposed it a great **deformitie,** and disorder. 1705 STANHOPE Paraphr. I. 22 Those Vicious Habits which are a **Deformity** to Christians. 1855 MACAULAY Hist. Eng. IV. 333 Cromwell had tried to correct the **deformities** of the representative system.

Title: Deformity. 4.
Artist: Oxford English Dictionary, 2nd edition
Medium: English Language
Location: Online Database

☞ To continue to redefine deformity, turn to one of the following pages: 34, 50, 73, 99, 141, 156, 172.

☞ To turn more of this book upside-down, turn to page 220, follow directions for a blank box (choosing from #1-6), then overturn that choice on page 117.

☞ Turn forward or backward _____ (insert your age) pages.

In Hogarth's version, Caliban holds a cord of wood on his shoulders. In contrast to Fuseli, Hogarth exaggerates different but still precise features: Caliban's mop of black hair, rounded ears, decayed teeth, abscesses on his forehead and right shoulder, squat musculature, partially scaled skin, and webbed feet.	Fuseli depicts Caliban with spiked short light hair, pointy ears, ultra-round eyes without lids, a clownish mouth with blubbery lips, spiked nipples, excessive musculature, sharp fingernails, and bare feet. Caliban is not dwarfish nor are his shackles to the rock visible; he poses as if holding an invisible cupid-like bow.

Title: A Scene from "The Tempest"   Title: Shakespeare, The Tempest, Act I, Scene II[xc]
Artist: William Hogarth   Artist: Henry (Johann Heinrich) Fuseli
Medium: Oil on canvas   Medium: Line and stipple engraving w/ hand coloring
Date: c. 1730-1735   Date: c. 1800
Location: Nostell Priory, England   Location: Fine Arts Museums of San Francisco

[☞ *Directions: Above each word ✐, write another word that begins with the same letter. Don't worry about staying within the lines.*]

Thus far in the *Galerie de Difformité*, Bea's deformity has been shrouded, glimpsed here and there through hints and fragments: of her admissions and submissions, literally and figuratively, analogously and allegorically, while a reader is left to pick through pieces to decipher a (w)hole from her parts. In approaching her character in search of her infamous bone, I, as Undertaker, attempt to *undertake*—a term which I'll later return to— lines as well as spaces that arise from their assembly and reassembly. To tell the truth, as slant, I try not to reduce Bea's character to a caricature, suggesting her story through other characters, outside and within this book.

[☞ *Directions: Above each word ✐, write another word that rhymes.*]

In the case of this page, Caliban from Shakespeare's play, *The Tempest*, is framed by the bard's lines and further delineations by two artists: Henry Fuseli and William Hogarth. In the play, Caliban is not described physically to any great length: "A freckled whelp hagborn—not honour'd with / A human shape,"

"deservedly confined into this rock."[xci]

Apart from that, Prospero recounts their history together on the island and his animosity toward Caliban, who is the son of the witch, Sycorax. Both Hogarth's and Fuseli's depictions feature the enslaved creature in a loin drape, but similarities stop there.

(☞ *See illustrations.*) Although the paintings render different scenes (one earlier in the play without Ferdinand; the other later with the suitor), each depiction conjures different representations of deformity (which can be further reconsidered by consulting *Deformity as Sublime, page 173*; for a taste of *Deformity as Picturesque*, please see Handnote ☞), and also counterpoints the grotesque Caliban against other characters, like the fairy Ariel.[xcii]

[☞ *Directions: Make a list of sounds from the following paragraph. Compare it with a list of sounds from the book reduced by chance (for instance, equal to the number of pages in the book.[xciii])*]

☞ DEFORMITY AS PICTURESQUE

In the Picturesque, deformed (rough, irregular, asymmetrical) qualities were praised in nature, notably by Uvedale Price, who wrote: "whoever means to study nature, must principally attend to the effects of neglect and accident"—that is, to the extent that accident and neglect did not apply to people. Analogous traits in human forms were derided, considered "grotesque" or "ugly." Price's incongruous argument left him open to mockery, particularly by Richard Payne-Knight, who discredited Price's arguments etymologically: "In tracing...the word to its source, we find that *grotesque* means *after the manner of grottos*, as *picturesque* means *after the manner of painting*." Payne-Knight further addressed "my friend, Mr. Price," who "admits squinting among the irregular and picturesque charms of the parson's daughter, whom (to illustrate the picturesque in opposition to the beautiful) he wishes to make appear lovely and attractive, though without symmetry or beauty....to make the figure consistent and complete, the same happy mixture of the irregular and picturesque must have prevailed through her limbs and person; and consequently she must have hobbled as well as squinted; and had hips and shoulders as irregular as her teeth, cheeks, and eyebrows. All my friend's parental fondness for his system is certainly necessary to make him think such an assemblage of picturesque circumstances either lovely or attractive; or induce him to imagine, that he should be content with such a creature, as a companion for life; and I heartily congratulate him that his fondness did not arise at an earlier period, to obstruct him in a very different choice." (☞ *For comparison, turn to page 63.*)

[☞ *Directions: Selectively erase or paint over words above ✑.*]

120

Caliban might appear more fearful if he were formless or like a Blakean character, with a specter and emanation. In the text of *The Tempest*, however, he appears in costume and speaks, interacting with characters, leaving an audience to judge external details about him. The exactitude of both Hogarth's and Fuseli's representations prevents Caliban (and Ariel, for that matter) from being Sublime and matching the Tempest itself, whose force is unshackled (to the point of being formless or, at least, strong enough to destroy form), even if elicited by Prospero's magical arts. When Fuseli reviewed Joseph Wright's painting of "The Tempest," he wrote:

> PLEASE BREAK THE RULES!

Poetry and passions, when treated by the landscape painter, or the painter of still life, become mere attendants on the favorite objects—mere expletives of the situation. Prospero, Miranda, the prince, the vision, are in this piece only expletives of the painter's favourite [sic] cavern. Caliban and his company, direct us only to the storm, which bursts on our eye; in the energy of which, we forget that the figures have the first claim to our attention.[xciv]

To remind yourself which figures have first claim on your attention, see page 30.
☞ *To explore the aftermath of a tempest, turn to Wreckage (page 247).*

[☞ *Directions: Follow directions in the box above and apply below.*]

Ultimately, Caliban is fated by his parentage and society. His setting on an island historically suggests colonial voyages during the Elizabethan era, as well as period maps, which often depicted monsters in unknown waters, or *terra incognita*, which correlated foreignness with savagery.[xcv] Additionally, the geographic isolation raises questions: How might Caliban have faired back on the mainland? Where might such a character have been situated in surrounding centuries? Would he have found himself with Bruegel the Elder's crippled "Beggars" with their foxtails, or displayed like the Pig-faced Lady, Mule-faced Woman, Bear Woman, or Elephant Man? If not isolated in a rural countryside (like Andrew Wyeth's *Christina's World*, where Christina dragged herself between farmsteads in Maine), might Caliban have resembled figures in Francisco Goya's *Black Paintings* or been

121

included among Gericault's portraits of the insane (in the line-up with: *Maniac of Gambling,*

Maniac of Envy, and *Man Suffering from Delusions of Military Rank*)? Might he have worn a

public badge like Paul Strand's *Blind Woman,* or otherwise had to obey Ugly Laws (like that

in Chicago, lasting from the 1880s into the 1970s):[xcvi]

> Any person who is diseased, maimed, mutilated, or in
> any way deformed, so as to be an unsightly or
> disgusting object, or an improper person to be
> allowed in or on the streets, highways,
> thoroughfares, or public places in this city, shall
> not therein or thereon expose himself to public
> view, under the penalty of a fine.

[☞ *Directions: Collect all the artworks that most amuse or uplift*
or irritate you into one room and write the "salon" that
critiques them or accounts for their effect.[xcvii]]

In other situations and settings, not to mention genres and media, varied characters

draw further comparison and contrast: from *Oedipus* to *Moby-Dick* to *Murderball, The*

Hunchback of Notre Dame to *The Glass Menagerie* to *Children of a Lesser God, The Sound and*

the Fury to *Beloved* to *Finding Nemo* to *Avatar.* Returning to *The Tempest,* Caliban remains

on his island, leaving us to wonder at his ability to wander (whether physically or socially) if

he were alive today...

☞ *To consider this character in terms of today, turn to page 242.*
☞ *To consider more opposition, turn to page 142.*
☞ *To hear more from the Undertaker, turn to page 104.*
☞ *To pick a card, any card, keep reading.*

PICK A CARD, ANY CARD

PICK A CARD, ANY CARD

(a sampling of index cards to edit,
keep, discard, add your own)

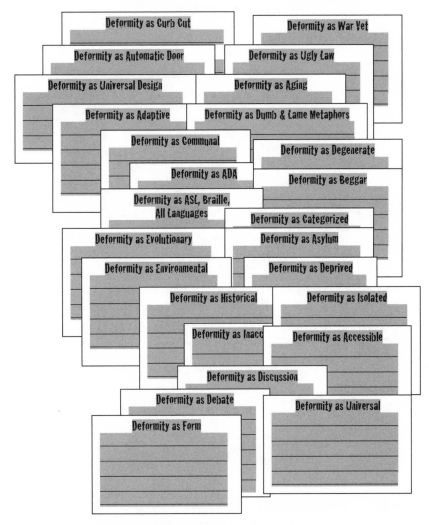

Deformity as Curb Cut

Deformity as War Vet

Deformity as Automatic Door

Deformity as Ugly Law

Deformity as Universal Design

Deformity as Aging

Deformity as Adaptive

Deformity as Dumb & Lame Metaphors

Deformity as Communal

Deformity as Degenerate

Deformity as ADA

Deformity as Beggar

Deformity as ASL, Braille, All Languages

Deformity as Categorized

Deformity as Evolutionary

Deformity as Asylum

Deformity as Environmental

Deformity as Deprived

Deformity as Historical

Deformity as Isolated

Deformity as Inacc

Deformity as Accessible

Deformity as Discussion

Deformity as Debate

Deformity as Universal

Deformity as Form

☞ To play a card (above or your own): write it here: "Deformity as _____.
Then turn to page 213 & write it there.

☞ To unpack one of these terms, turn to page 187.

☞ Turn forward or backward _____ (insert your age) pages.

123

Have I misplaced a key again?

PLEASE BREAK THE RULES!

Sample Key

☺ = Sublime

👽 = Terror, terrorist, terrifying

☯ = Form

🌍 = Deformity

👁 = Beauty

🎭 = Ugly, ugliness

🏞 = Picturesque, picturesqueness

⛰ = Nature, natural, forest, landscape(s), setting

🏘 = Houses

♥ = Heart, blood, bleeding

👤 = Man, father

👪 = People

📚 = Fiction

☞👍✋☝✌👇👌🤟 = gestures

☺ = Face, mirror

🍸 = ship

☞ To find a lock for this key, turn to page 173.
☞ To misplace other keys, turn to page 21, 123, or 247.
☞ This Way to the Great Egress! (page 249).

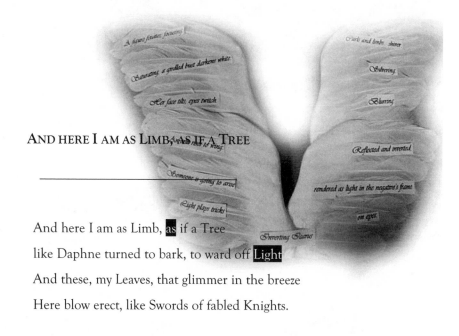

AND HERE I AM AS LIMB, AS IF A TREE

And here I am as Limb, as if a Tree
like Daphne turned to bark, to ward off Light
And these, my Leaves, that glimmer in the breeze
Here blow erect, like Swords of fabled Knights.

But there are other Barques and storied Nights[xcviii]
wherein we've sailed upon loved Seas and seized
the Sense that tales decimate our Frights
and turn us grateful, fatefully reprised

Into this Armor, amorous but loaned
from lines of Love that captivate my Heart
and keep it trapped within a morphing Bone
that feigns to hold me, Relic of some Art.
Embodied grace: that we should change to bear
this Spirit (Mind in Body) without fear.

☞ *To follow fear, turn to page 222.*
☞ *To follow the morphing Bone, turn to page 223.*
☞ *To consider the Bone (or Book) as a relic, turn the page.*

Here they fly again, unfurling like fritillaries, but frigid. Fingers: locked in a windowed box. Behind glass, bone shards pale in place of wings, cast with wood and wax to appear as hands. Palm to palm. They rest in a nest of cloth. The cloth is useful, nestled in the urn for unction: *corpus incorruptum*. *Indirect blessing*: medieval means of divine relativity. Visible through glass, the graceless grasp conjures saintliness and a thousand intercessions.

Pilgrims process. Stained glass and candles shroud shadows with light.

The eye is essential here. With the soul: coordinating correspondences, attuning to the butterflied box. Strikingly silent, the "speaking image" is shaped with five-pronged recognition: thumb, index, middle, ring, pinkie. No full-fledged *imago* (statue) or *caput* (bust) confronts the gaze, just the hands, unable to touch or be touched—(taunting ours?)—frozen in flight at this variegated threshold, as a rousing throughput between visible and invisible realms.

Losing my ability to see, I watch figures. Wandering shadows: deforming and reforming. Candles and stained glass. *Pera peregrinatoris*, with their petitions and repetitions:

Although much is lost, no relic is lost on a pilgrim. Pilgrims peregrinate like falcons, supplanting prayer for prey. Hungry for reverence, they seek out Catherine's head and finger; Teresa's arms and heart; Beatrice's bone. A jaw, foot, rib. Vial of Christ's blood; Shiva's manifold arms; Islamic geometries that hide the face of God. Although easily mistaken or forsaken, it's less about seeing than being. Many faces, reverential and referential. Reliquaries, sarcophagi, urns, stupas, and other containers feign—with faith—to hold and maintain the life of the dead.

A sidebar, too, feigns to hold and maintain the life of once-or-future dead (words): tiny tombs within this tomb-like room, reliquaries for past beliefs and practices resurrected.[xcix] *Let me pray*.

☞ **bee** *n.* **1:** a social colonial hymen-opterous ("winged membrane") insect often kept in hives for the honey that it produces; any of numerous insects that undergo complete metamorphosis, differing from related wasps esp. in the heavier hairier body and in having sucking as well as chewing mouthparts, that feed on pollen and nectar, and that store both and often also honey **2:** an eccentric notion: FANCY 3. [perh. Fr. OE *b ē n* prayer—more at BOON]: a gathering of people for a specific purpose <spelling~, quilting~>—**bee-like** *adj*—**bee in one's bonnet.**

Habit, homage, healing: many motivations keep the Pilgrim peregrinating toward or away from lands of milk and honey. Varanasi, Mecca, Jerusalem, and Rome swarm like hives—destinations—less urgent than the convoluted, confounding paths. A pilgrimage through the *Dhammapada* finds: "As the bee takes the essence of a flower and flies away without destroying its beauty and perfume, so let the sage wander in life."[c] Processing through the *Koran*: "Then comes there forth out of [the bees'] bellies a drink / of diverse hues wherein / is healing for men, / Surely in that is a sign for a people who reflect."[ci] And so, in the Bible, "he put forth the end of the rod that was in his hand, and dipped it in a[n] honeycomb, and put his hand to his mouth; and his eyes were enlightened."[cii] Through the *Upanisads*: "The honey of the gods, clearly, is the sun up there. The crossbar for it is the sky itself; the hive is the intermediate region; and the larvae are the glittering specks....the bees being the secret rules of substitution, and the flower, the formulation of truth (*brahman*)."[ciii]

Let us join hands, then, with winged bodies: mouths gagged with pollen, resurrected from recycled reliquaries.[civ] Seeking flight. Corporeal: a corpus cannot help but be; transubstantiated: any object can become sacred. (Consider the cow.) All parts of the whole can signify the holy, with enough conviction and contrition—or contrivance, as Luther cautioned (condemning two feathers and an egg purportedly from the hen-like Holy Ghost). Watch closely amid these wings. And listen (echoing): *hands may yet grace the air like birds. Taking flight. Imagine the fluttering: that singing.*[cv] The sound of one hand...

Flapping, defying expectations. Deforming and reforming in order to fly. (A story gets mistold, retold, unfolding:) Faith involves a suspension of disbelief, even when appealing to order, alphabetically and otherwise. *Reliquary* falls somewhere between *relinquishing* and *relishing*. It's easier to imagine what can be heard (*singing*) and touched (*stinging*)—deforming and transforming to connect our meager lives with meaning. Out of cocoons and eggs come fritillaries, peregrines, bumbling. "We behold the face of nature bright with gladness," Darwin writes, but "we do not see, or we forget, that the birds which are idly singing round us mostly live on insects or seeds, and are thus constantly destroying life."[cvi] Singing and ciphoning:

Where does that leave me in the Great Chain, no longer tiered as the Inferno, but linked and hyperlinked inside out? Should I *relinquish* this archaic art of the *relic* and discover something else to *relish*? Is there a way to bind the two—three, four, more?

Seeking further between *relinquish* and *relief*, I try to dissect the hidden *ligament* (*tough band of tissue connecting the articular extremities of bones*). Articulating further: joint by joint, word by word. *Hear. My. Prayer.* Consult Gray, who quoted Cleland: "[I]f neighboring joints be united by ligaments, the amount of flexion or extension of each must remain in constant proportion to that of the other; while, if the union be by muscles, the separation of the points of attachment of those muscles may vary considerably in different varieties of movement, the muscles adapting themselves tonically to the length required."[cvii] Adaptation and evolution: *Let us pray and prey*? Before we lose all sight, let us *relinquish* our desire to literally see and, instead, *relish* what lies between and within. *Ligare*: at the root of binding and being unbound:

☞ To see her existence pass in shadow, turn to page 147.

Portrait of the artist as deformed

Title: Phoenix or Phony?
Artist: Author
Medium: Body of the Book, Cremated
Date: 2008
Location: Nevada City, California

☞ To twist this tighter & frame the remains, turn to page 167.

☞ To unseal this, keep re
a
d
i
n
g

Novel Eighteen: Dante Alighieri and Beatrice Portinari meet and part. After her death, Dante obsesses about her, obeying and overriding poetic conventions. Florence's political situation forces him to into exile, describing his journey through the *Inferno, Purgatorio,* and *Paradiso.*

Novel Seventeen: Scholars argue for centuries over the identity of Beatrice in Dante's *Commedia*. Amid an array of alternative theses, books upon books upon books are written to debate her allegorical versus actual nature. The verdict is still out.

Novel Sixteen ½: "They are the poems and novels he never otherwise wrote," writes Luc Sante, describing Félix Fénéon's *Nouvelles en trois lignes* [Novels in Three Lines]. "His politics, his aesthetics, his curiosity and sympathy are all on view, albeit with tweezers and delineated with a single-hair brush....They might be considered Fénéon's *Human Comedy.*"[cix]

Novel Sixteen: "Penetrating as best I can into the structure of the *Divina Commedia,*" writes Osip Mandelstam, "I come to the conclusion that the entire poem is one single unified and indivisible stanza. Or, to be more exact, not a stanza but a crystallographic shape, that is, **a body**....It is unthinkable that one might encompass with the eye or visually imagine to oneself this shape of thirteen thousand facets with its monstrous exactitude."[cx]

Novel Fifteen ½: [*In the margins, add complimentary or contradictory novels, which can be done fairly quickly, if such novels are only three lines...*]

Novel Fourteen ½: Beatrice Portinari visits her father's property outside of Florence (adjacent to the Alighieri's country estate) where there are many bees. She is stung and dies of what now is considered anaphylactic shock. Although Dante has said only a few words to her during his life, he makes Beatrice one of his guides through the *Commedia*.

Novel Fourteen ¼: A post-graduate student equipped with honours and diplomas went to Agassiz to receive the final and finishing touches. Post-Graduate Student: 'That's only a bee'....At the end of three weeks the bee was in an advanced state of decomposition, but the student knew something about it.[cxi]

Novel Fourteen: "...one has to imagine how it would be if bees had worked at the creation of this thirteen-thousand-faceted shape," adds Mandelstam, "bees endowed with instinctive stereometric genius, who attracted more and still more bees as they were needed. The work of these bees, who always keep an eye on the whole, is not equally difficult at the various stages of the process. Their cooperation broadens and becomes more complex as they proceed with the formation of the combs, by means of which space virtually **arises out of itself**."

Novel Thirteen ½: Dante Alighieri and Beatrice Portinari have a lovechild, but Beatrice dies in childbirth. The baby survives and is raised by Dante and his wife as their own child. She becomes a nun and works in the convent's apiary, never learning the truth about her mother (although the girl is named Beatrice, nicknamed Bi, pronounced "Bea").

Novel Thirteen: "The fact is that the beautiful, humanly speaking, is merely form considered in its simplest aspect," writes Victor Hugo. "What we call the ugly, on the contrary, is a detail of a great whole which eludes us, and which is in harmony, not with man but with all creation. That is why it constantly presents itself to us in new but incomplete aspects."[cxii]

Novel Twelve ½: Dante dies, leaving the *Commedia* incomplete by thirteen cantos. His son, Jacobo, dreams that the final cantos are hidden in a hole in a wall and, upon waking, finds them there. Boccaccio records this account for posterity, but an alternative account claims that Beatrice's quill-shaped bone miraculously penned the last thirteen cantos of the *Paradiso*.

Novel Twelve ¼ (excerpted from Exhibit Q)**:** She flew up through the air it was blue not rose air there but it excited her so, not the air but the tree as she rose like a rose it excited her so not the air but the hive and the sting that would put her name there, that she several times forgot her wings and almost fell out of the air. It is not easy to carve a name on a tree particularly oh yes particularly if the tree is an overgrown bone and the letters are rare and bare like B and E and A, it is not easy. ***A Bea is a Bee is a Be is a B is a...***[cxiii]

Novel Twelve: "She is, in the whole *Paradiso*, his way of knowing," writes Charles Williams. "Attention is demanded of him and her expositions are the result of his attention. To say so is not to lessen Beatrice in herself to a mere quality of Dante, or only in the sense that, had we her *Commedia*, Dante would have been a quality of hers."[cxiv]

Novel Eleven: To be or not to be: "unravelling; *spec.* the final unravelling of the complications of a plot in a drama, novel, etc.; the catastrophe; *transf.* the final solution or issue of a complication, difficulty, or mystery"—the meaning of *dénouement*. To bee or not to bee? To Bea or not to Bea?[cxv]

Novel Ten ½: Grave robbers steal the bones of Beatrice Portinari from her family tomb in the Church of Santa Margherita de' Cerchi in Florence, looking for her quill-shaped bone. Rumor spreads of the existence of said bone (with a hole resembling a heart) used to pen the last thirteen cantos of the *Paradiso*.[cxvi] Four centuries later, the fraternal Ugly Face Clubb [*sic,* hereafter abbreviated to UFC] in Liverpool, Britain, adopts her bone as its secret symbol for membership, thanks to Walt Green.

Novel Nine ¾: Walt Green, an anatomist in Liverpool and collector of curiosities, joins the UFC. From his *museo segreto* (also known as the *gabinetto segreto,* not the original), he contributed their secret symbol: a bone attributed to Beatrice Portinari. As a fanatic for oddities of his time (which included Dante), Green keeps the prototype bone, even after discontinuing his UFC membership and immigrating to the American colonies.

Novel Nine: The **many faces** of Bea, taken together, suggest what's missing, so the seeking of Bea becomes the seeking of "we," ever changing. More than trying to decipher *her*, then, her *ability to change* may serve as a better guide. At this moment in history, the compilation of her mostly absent pieces leaves her (and *me*, with *you*) always at the threshold of an alternative *Vita Nuova*—another "new life"—even if that life in the end isn't hers.

Novel Eight: European immigration decimates the indigenous population of North America, wiping out...   "Wilderness" is a myth based upon...   a national economy founded on African slavery and exploitation of natural resources...   one hierarchy replaces another...   cheeks and balances, checks and balloons...

Novel Seven: "There were others **living among the dead** this morning. They were in shock, their bodies shredded by mortar fragments, still breathing. People who had escaped the attack moved slowly and silently through the carnage, a scene out of Dante's hell."[cxvii]

Novel Six ¾: Walt Green dies in Massachusetts on the eve of the Revolutionary War, and most curiosities from his collection end up lost or mysteriously buried, except for the infamous bone with the heart-shaped hole. In a diary, Green's niece dreams of a hole in a wall, wherein she discovers the enigmatic relic [*see page 60*]. According to their descendant, Gloria Heys (in her scrapbook of deformed texts, informally referred to as "*bone pomes*"), the bone with the heart-shaped hole remains in their family's possession.

Novel Six ½: See Exhibit W². In other words, turn to page 61. In other words, leave this Exhibit to return to after digressing to page 61, or follow the offered choices that arise from your bend in the road, and proceed along that path.

Novel Five: "Where to start is the problem," according to *The Robber Bride*, "because nothing begins when it begins and nothing's over when it's over, and everything needs a preface: a preface, a postscript, a chart of simultaneous events. History is a construct....Any point of entry is possible and all choices are arbitrary. Still, there are definitive moments, moments we use as references, because they break our sense of continuity, they change the direction of time."[cxviii]

Novel Four ¾: On his journey across the Atlantic, Walt Green throws the bone-with-a-heart-shaped-hole overboard. Although he fabricates a duplicate upon arrival in the colonies, a copy of the copy, it in no way compares with the real thing. Green incorporates the myth into stories that he tells his niece, without telling her about particulars of Ye Ugly Face Clubb (a branch of which migrates to the Southern colonies, notably with a chapter in Charleston, according to "The American Museum"; *see page 64*).

Novel Four ½: Along with "bone pomes" that give rise to her *Galerie de Difformité*,[cxix] Gloria Heys keeps a list of Beatrice "sightings." The last claims Beatrice to be a microsculptured bee in the Museum of Jurassic Technology in Los Angeles, California. She appears in the exhibit *"Tell the Bees...Belief, Knowledge & Hypersymbolic Cognition."*

Novel Three ½: "It is, therefore, a mistake to regard myth as an inferior mode of thought," writes Karen Armstrong, "which can be cast aside when human beings have attained the age of reason. Mythology is not an early attempt at history, and does not claim that its tales are objective fact. Like a novel, an opera or a ballet, myth is make-believe; it is a game that transfigures our fragmented, tragic world, and helps us to glimpse new possibilities by asking 'what if?'—a question which has also provoked some of our most important discoveries in philosophy, science and technology."[cxx]

Novel Three: Derived from associations and aesthetics of the long eighteenth century (with all its baggage), *Galerie de Difformité* is curated by an Undertaker—a deformed reincarnation of Dante's Beatrice—who irreverently undertakes the theme of **deformity**, in order to deform her perceived beauty into a kind of monstrosity. As "the Undertaker," Bea (and her contemporary mouthpiece, Gloria Heys, not to mention a fictional Gretchen Henderson who presumes to publish the *Galerie* on Gloria's behalf) leads a reader like Dante toward a kind of paradise. But following the novel's theme, Bea also deforms notions of paradise by deforming its contextualizing inferno.

Novel Two ¾: In other words, Gretchen Henderson writes a novel-that-deforms-a-novel about her fictional relative, Gloria Heys, and Gloria's fictional *Galerie* in which Beatrice is reincarnated as a fallen (literally: disabled by falling from heaven's heights—whether she fell accidentally, was pushed, or jumped is unclear) angel who bears the handle of "Bea." Bea (a.k.a., *Gloria*, a.k.a., *Gretchen*—at least a fictional version of *Gretchen*) reimagines her story from shards of a perceived paradise. Writing straight with crooked lines, she tries to deform "deformity."

Novel Two: Gretchen Henderson (and Gloria, et al.) dreams of *you* and *you* and *you*: **in motion**. She builds a gallery to invite *you* and *you* and *you* to meet her halfway. Her *Galerie* is her way of gesturing to *(s)he* and *you* and *me*, to become *we*.

Novel One ¼: [*In the margins, add complimentary or contradictory novels, which can be done fairly quickly, if such novels are only three lines....*]

Novel One: Choose-Your-Own-Ending:

☞ *To choose your own ending, turn to page 242.*

☞ *To consult the Alternative Table of Contents, turn to 21.*

☞ *To read an Apologia (as in, a defense) for GH's project, turn to page 234.*

☞ *To be examined, turn to page 209.*

(WRITE YOUR OWN CAUTIONARY NOTE)

[*Please write in pencil:*]_____

_____

_____

_____

_____

_____

_____

_____

_____

_____

_____

_____

_____

_____!!!!

☞ (*Please add directive:*_____

☞ (*Please add directive:*_____

☞ *If you return here & prefer an amended note, erase words to revise your caution.*

Oyster, p. 1543.

"There was in this village several years ago *o, from his
birth, was afflicted with a leprosy, as   a singular
kind, since it affected only the palms   les of his
feet.... Good women, who love to account for every defect in children by the
        his mother felt a violent propensity for* **oyfters,**
wh   d that the black rough scurf on his hands
                            and feet were the shells of that filth."

778,
ʃel)   89).

ams   -of-
aʃs   ms?"
                    Th   olas
                    O   GEH.

Vitel **lent** prop

Cleopatra   ʄtrine of longing.

Vitellius, **langu**   h, wages war

supported by h   the meaty

mantle, coated   **k, and**

where she shelters a parasite that gradually procures a pearl.

☞ To deform these deformations, turn to page 220.

☞ To pick up the trail of the monster, turn to page 93.

☞ To return to Gretchen's letters, pick a number: 46, 69, 95, 114,
        152, 168, 183, 204, 218, or keep reading.

Dear Gloria,

I just looked up and contacted your father's protégé and will let you know what I hear…

G.H.

Dear Gloria,

I just reread my initial entries and realize my grave mistake: trying to read your book in terms of our shared biography. In this way, I'm afraid of defeating what your Galerie is trying to do. Because ultimately, your or my story might get in the way—whether you've lived with this or that burden or joy, professionally of personally, traveled so far or stayed put, exiled or homebound, married or single or divorced, adopted or invitroed, with a gecko or goose, and all other inane ways that we identify ourselves, as a way of negotiating existence, rights and regulations, stereotypes and discriminations, accessibilities and assimilations, conformities and compromises, literacies and linguilisms, depending on positionings: rather than digging into something that lies deeper between lines, beneath words, where laws and legibilities can't reach—

In this era of memoirs and tell-alls, blogs and tweets, a reader might desire more self-display—splayed—cast open through revelations, resilience and griefs, intimate moments, climax and catharsis, physical attributes, foibles and flaws, political positionings, religious awakenings, aggravations and rants, sex lives, caloric intakes and survival strategies, self-help and how-to, what we've had for breakfast, whatever agenda…which expose as much as they don't. In the face of this expectation here, you're absent. Have you removed yourself so "Subscribers" don't get vicariously lost in details of your life? What happens if I try to put you or me into this book? Might Subscribers miss a bigger picture? And what might that picture be?

G.

Didn't Picasso say that every act of creation is first an act of d

"What seems eternal, he says at another point, contains within itself the impulse of its own destruction." ~ Adorno quoting Proust

Note to self: delete some earlier entries?

Note to self: create some earlier entries?

Note to self: delete some later entries?

Note to self: create some later entries?

Note to self:

Note to self:

Note to self:

Note to self:

Note to self:

Note to self:

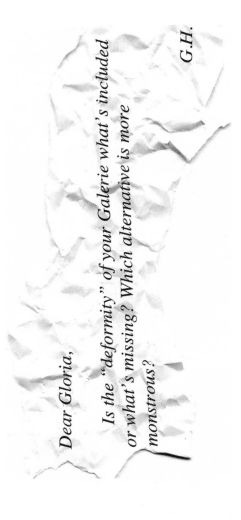

Dear Gloria,

Is the "deformity" of your Galerie what's included or what's missing? Which alternative is more monstrous?

G.H.

☞ If you consider what's included to be more monstrous, turn to page 166.

☞ If you consider what's excluded to be more monstrous, turn to page 212.

☞ To continue reading Gretchen's letters to Gretchen, turn to page 152.

_____ *Club's Emblem :*

[ ]

Please write a short history of your club & its emblem:

_____
_____
_____
_____
_____
_____
_____
_____
_____
_____

☞ To consider your membership in terms of form or content,
    turn to 144, 220, or ____ (fill in blank).
☞ To be further examined about clubs &c., turn to page 209.

☞ To (re)consider another club, (re)visit 10, 61, 65, or turn to:

1. The action of the verb DEFORM, q.v. 1552 HULOET, **Deformynge,** *vitiatio.* **2. That deforms: see the verb.** 1870 *Daily News* 19 Dec., Incongruity is a **deforming** feature. 1892 LD. KELVIN in *Pall Mall* G. 1 Dec. 6/3 He had now..a..demonstration of elastic yielding in the earth as a whole, under the influence of a **deforming** force.

Title: Deforming. 1 & 2.
Artist: Oxford English Dictionary, 2nd edition
Medium: English Language
Location: Online Database

☞ *To compare this with other forms, turn to 156.*

☞ *To revive your search for the monster, turn to page 32.*

☞ *To demonstrate "elastic yielding in the earth as a whole, under the influence of a deforming force," turn to page 23 or 180.*

Deformity as Op(posi)tion

Embracing elements of deformity, this wooden carving (depicting the Passion of Christ) exaggerates wounds in the hands and feet, stab in his side, crown of thorns on a blood-encrusted, emaciated body.

Title: Roettgen Pietà[cxxi]
Artist: Unknown
Medium: Lindenwood
Date: c. 1300
Location: Rheinisches Landesmuseum, Bonn

Not unlike ~~Lessing's~~ [*your / my (circle one)*] proclamation against ~~Hottentots~~ [*insert PC classifier of yourself, pl., same as page 74: _____*], J.J. Winckelmann reduced the complexity of another era's art when he wrote: "The stories of the saints, the legends and metamorphoses, have for several centuries been almost the only objects of painters," which he saw as "contrived in a thousand ways until finally the connoisseur of art is bored and disgusted."[cxxii] In contrast to classical alignments of deformity with sin and profanity, the style of "deformed realism" (as seen above in the Roettgen Pietà) correlated physical disfigurement with sacredness and spiritual perfection.[cxxiii] Since the Roettgen Pietà was created around the time of Beatrice Portinari's death, the carving raises questions about how to interpret and characterize the physical attributes of Dante's controversial muse. How might she appear in the style of "deformed realism"? Particularly since icons like the Virgin and Venus were depicted so variedly over centuries, deviations among Beatrice's representations suggest that beauty in former eras, like now, is a cultural construction that "lies in the eye of the beholder."

☞ *To behold variations of Beatrice, turn to 24 or 30.*

☞ *To behold other variations, turn to 38 or 39.*

☞ *To behold more variations, turn to 197 or 198.*

☞ *To find yet more variants, scan right box above.* ✍

☞ *To behold the Venus & Virgin, turn to page 236.*

☞ *To keep reading, do just that..............................*

And so deformity, like beauty, can be (m)aligned in any number of ways. At times, ancient Egyptians correlated disfigurement with divinity and also did not beautify deformity in their artworks, which implies general cultural acceptance. By way of contrast: an extant Egyptian relief of a pharaoh openly depicts his withered limb and cane, indicating a disease like polio, where recent controversies about the American presidential memorial for Franklin Delano Roosevelt have debated whether or not to hide his wheelchair. In ancient Egypt, in Pharaonic households and society, dwarfs also achieved positions of seniority, and records cite examples of other "deformed" humans (including a man with a shortened leg and a hunchback) in similar ranks. Moreover, many gods in Egyptian mythology—Bes, for instance, and the Nile's protector, Hapi—were deformed.

☞ *To jump in a river, turn to page 26.*

☞ *This Way to the Great Egress! (page 249)*

☞ *To upset a classification, read down about Down.*
Returning to the Middle Ages, especially the Gothic period: conflicts between Christian, Islamic, and other kingdoms led deformity to be associated with sin, profanity, madness and xenophobia, feeding later superstitions (for instance, that a pregnant mother's imaginings and exposures affected the form of her gestating child).[cxxiv] After plagues swept Europe and decimated populations without regard to social distinctions (class, race, gender, or religion), attitudes about divine disfavor and disability were harder to assign. By the time a follower of Jan Joest of Kalkar painted "The Adoration of the Christ Child," likely using local subjects as models, two of his angels bore facial features that modern viewers identify as Down Syndrome—even though the painting was made over three centuries before Langdon Down invented that classification.[cxxv] ☞

☞ *To invent a classification, turn to page 187 or 208.*

☞ *To deform your own realism, turn to page 80 or 150.*

☞ *To hesitate to classify, turn to page 226,*
then go where you like.

LET US REJOICE IF WE MUST BE CONSTRAINED

Let us rejoice if we must be constrained
in vain, so even monsters we decry
escaping death by chance, now pale and fair
within our dreams, will listen for reply:

(These questions that we frame in all but words.)

Cannot be damn'd; Alas, why should I bee?
cries Donne, while Herbert sings: *The beauty lies*
in the discovery—as lines entwine
to unleash false designs. And you, and I,

And us on earth? Kneeling anywhere to rave
of every body's pain, the panting world?
We dare & dance to revel on the grave
since piecemeal peace is poor (& pure peace, rare)
and there are scars, but none of you, to spare.

☞ *To revel with Bea, turn to page 197.*
☞ *To entwine lines, turn to page 113, 182, or 193.*
☞ *If you feel prepared for an examination on the subject,*
       turn to page 209.

144

Bodies on bodies, three breathe into one. A love triangle, cloaked in black, exposes a red robe and mouth, roving. Without resuscitation, theirs is a mastery of manipulation, a laying on of hands, under skirts, to hold and feign life. A triumvirate: the master directs the head, shoulders, right hand; an assistant controls the left; and a third manages legs and feet, shuddering to life, as a puppet rises in a Bunraku theater. Hollow-headed, wigged, repainted with blinking eyes and clasping hands, Hisamatsu or Princess Yaegaki takes the stage in a cotton-stuffed robe over a belted kimono, coordinated by three consorts wearing the color of nothing, as a chanter and shamiesen (thick, thin, or medium-necked, laced with strings, to play heart-strings of listeners) invokes *The New Ballad* or *The Dance of the Two Sambosas.*

The puppeteers hide under black cloaks, like a screen hosts shadows without impeding light, and flooded paddies become a liquid stage, and prosceniums conceal strings of marionettes, animating joints, lifted then dropped, lifted and propped, by unseen hands.

There is a bit of God in all this—the metaphors of animation, overtones and undertones of the sensuality of transformation, of submission and conversion, of water and wine, like wood and cloth and touch turn into something that walks and winks. It is a matter about matter, to determine whether and how (and if) this matters—at least, when evidenced in light of the *antagonist* of this story, who (or what) isn't paired with a *protagonist* but with an *agonist,* in a controlled interplay of contraction and relaxation. Contract; relax. Breathe.

Reciprocity must be more than a physiological strategy, but cannot be assumed without observing (as Descartes did) muscles in an eye: "...[whose] movements within the orbits corresponds remarkably to that of the head of the humerus within the shoulder joint: the brain points the arm and finger as accurately as it points the eye....Despite the fact that muscles can apply their force only in a straight line, the linear force is mechanically redirected (or translated into an angular force, or movement) through levers or pulleys."[cxxvii]

145

Pulling back, I try to gain leverage and better see this, the world as a stage, where (wo-)men are merely players, and God (in one entry of the *OED*) is defined as "the occupants of the gallery."[cxxviii]

Stay, I pray, if only to have a hand in this, to help me point the way, to move heads and hearts not with strings, but with hands that pretend to be wings.

Her existence will pass in shadow

☞ *To see some more "occupants of the gallery," visit any of these pages:*
    33, 45, 49, 57, 68, 72, 94, 98, 113, 117, 136, 140,
    151, 155, 167, 171, 182, 186, 196, 203, 207.

☞ *To witness her existence pass in shadow, please turn to page 198.*

☞ *To have a hand in this, turn the page.*

EXHIBIT I

Here comes the unclasping—there is no way to hold onto this. It's a matter of resistance, then release. Hands stroke strings, press keys, pull stops, as scores direct fingers forward through bars, movements, cadences, and cadenzas. Musicians learn about touch through painstaking practice, sensing every inch of an instrument, to elicit its tonal center. (True of a vocalist, too, whose instrument is the body, prone to the dissonance of disease, and warbles of woe.) A cellist learns "through mastering movements like vibrato...the rocking motion of the left hand on a string which colours a note around its precise pitch; waves of sound spread out...like ripples from a pool into which one has thrown a stone."[cxxix] The arm is an orchestra, then, with fingers as instruments among instruments (thumb, palm, wrist, elbow, shoulder, the body)— "miracle of form and function," capable of the greatest delicacy and danger.[cxxx]

With abilities to play violins, pianos, guitars, flutes, and harps comes the capacity to pull triggers, throw punches, and detonate bombs. Aristotle wrote: "A man can have many defences [sic] and always change them, and can have any weapon he pleases on any occasion. For the hand is a claw and a hoof and a horn, and a spear and a sword, and any other instrument whatever."[cxxxi] Avowing danger and debilitation, this thesis (deforming as you read) does not follow like *Clockwork* but re-views paleoanthopology and the evolution of *Homo erectus*, through which "this new hand reflected a modification...and brought with it the opportunity for a new class of situational knowledge based on as yet unexplored and undefined use of the hand. This change by itself was nothing but a mutation until its utility gave it the status of an adaptation."[cxxxii] Both instinctive and learned, manual manipulations have taught the mind through movements—faster, lighter, longer—to apprehend new thoughts.

To learn to play an instrument, then to lose the ability to play, is like dying.

Lying *apprehensio* (at the root of grasping and cognizance), we are what we feel— touch & play—like *What's Bred in the Bone*: "the hand speaks to the brain as surely as the brain speaks to the hand."[cxxxiii] "Put your finger into every bottle," Swift advises, "to feel whether it be full, which is the surest way, for feeling hath no fellow."[cxxxiv] Diderot wrote that Chardin "use[d] his thumb as much as his brush," and a long history reveals communicative hands: holding a stylus, quill or pen, reckoning or gesturing through three-dimensional signs.[cxxxv] *Ars memorativa* involves metonymy and mnemonics, embodied by "the first instrument," "the framer," "the most noble and perfect organ" by (and about) which Helkiah Crooke wrote in 1615: "we promise, we call, we dismisse, we threaten, we intreate, we abhorre, we feare, yea and by our hands we can aske a question."[cxxxvi]

What was the question?

By which we call another name: to learn and make music, language, love. Rendering fingers and joints to measure melodic intervals, to memorize: it's an ancient art. Not physiognomic. From West to East, played and sung. Reverential, improvised, referential. Stylized on paper. Conducted or cheironomic. Watch closely—hands may yet grace the air like birds. Taking flight. Imagine the fluttering: that singing.[cxxxvii]

Whatever the subject, memory often teaches with a dis-membered hand, drawn (or re-articulated: *deformed*) by an artist, as if that appendage (peripheral, yet central) could live apart from the body. Like a bone, with a heart-shaped hole. Illustrated & reproduced & re-rendered. Regenerating when split in two, like a planarian. Or imagine: a rebellion of Hands or Bones seceding from the Body, forming their own Kingdom. To be, or not to be:

...a quandary, between beheading and begetting. Like M.C. Escher drew a hand coming out of paper to draw another hand that drew the original hand. Round and round. Back where we started: Which came first, as currently conceived—hand or brain, heart or bone—or are they too innately tied to be unbound?

Nodding to Crooke, will my hands stay tied? "This progresse and insertion of these [flexor] muscles is an admirable and strange worke of Nature: for they are so severed, that the fingers in their motion might orderly follow one another, and each of them bend inward." With fingers figuratively severed, taking on a life of their own, I ask again: Nothing like the sun, roses, snow, those eyes and cheeks and breasts; what of her hands? *Manu*-mitting—master or slave, part of (yet apart from) the core of a body, closer than my shadow, as bound as busy. Wings, no longer. Rubbing eyes, itching skin, brushing teeth, holding hands, clasping pens, hefting loads, touching hearts. I have lost and found my flesh. Traversed with lines of fate, and laced by nerves and flexors, hands work wonders within and without, enabling *mani*-pulations of meaning from matter. *Manu*-ally, they point the way like Virgil (or me, Bea) to litigious and lofty layers of our lives, to buried scenes and senses too essential to ignore.

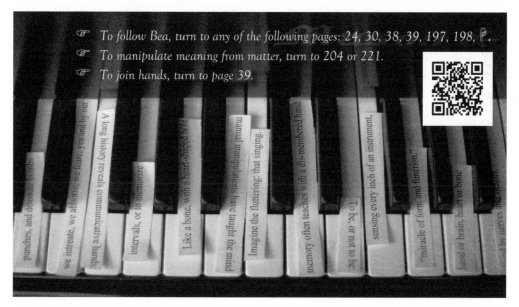

☞ To follow Bea, turn to any of the following pages: 24, 30, 38, 39, 197, 198, ✏.
☞ To manipulate meaning from matter, turn to 204 or 221.
☞ To join hands, turn to page 39.

What is a Self?

1. What is your name?

2. With whom do you identify?

3. Where were you born?

4. How old are you?

5. Where did you awake this morning?

6. How many years ago did you leave school?

7. Divide your age by three, and find pictures of yourself ∧^if available from these ages:

8. Is your mind somewhere else from your body right now? Where?

9. In what part(s) of your body do you usually reside?

10. Where are you now?

☞ *If you are Here, turn to page 220 or 230.*

☞ *If you are There, turn to page 222.*

☞ *If you think these are some of the missing portraits, turn to 60, then 80 and 103.*

☞ *To reapply to be a Subscriber, tear up your Application to be a Subscriber (page 12) & then paste a legible remnant into the box on page 72.*

To listen to what these characters are saying, turn to page 245.

To deform this page's story, write palimpsestually over this page.

To see this via a spectacle, visit page 157.

To consider this in another context, visit the corner:

Dear Gloria,

It's been weeks since I last wrote to you. My body has gotten the better of me. But I do have news: I heard back from Professor Protégé. To make a long story short: he'll gather a few colleagues to read your manuscript blindly without knowing your circumstances, then he'll be in touch. They owed him a favor, he said. I'll write more when I hear their responses…

Until soon,
G.H.

Dear Gloria,

The report is in. Your father's protégé taped his colleagues'
conversation: a peanut gallery of conflicting exclamations—

    Peanut 1: "It's anti-capitalist."
    Peanut 4: "Brilliant."
    Peanut 2: "Exhausting—too difficult. Why so difficult?"
    Peanut 1: "Extreme parataxis!"
    Peanut 3: "I never in all my years and all my training heard of creating
            something, no less so intricate, only to destroy it."
    Peanut 4: "Destruction misleads, like a sand mandala…"
    Peanut 5: "No one will publish this."
    Peanut 4: "What does publishing prove?"
    Peanut 3: "Who ever heard of a buttnote? It's masturbation!"
    Peanut 4: "No."
    Peanut 5: "I get lost—"
    Peanut 4: "Yes, we are…"
    Peanut 1: "But as performance art…"
    Peanut 2: "What about those miniature pictures? You can't see them…"
    Peanut 5: "Yes, who will take time.. how does the Author say: "to
            Subscribe"?
    Peanut 3: "Blah, blah, blah."
    Peanut 5: "Blah, BLAH."
    Peanut 1: "BLAH!"

And so on. I was glad, Gloria, that you didn't have to hear more jargon
turned &$!@%. The jurying didn't go much further, more of an impasse, from
what I could tell. (An audio recording can't capture facial gestures, shakes of
heads, and silent reactions—and my hearing misses a certain frequency of
sound.) I would've liked said Peanuts to challenge your designs (or decoys?) of
the eighteenth century, medieval iconography, implications of marrying
genres… so much more. Their disagreement may have delighted you,
regardless. Perhaps that kind of conflicted conversation is what you hope to
provoke… as if reading the Galerie could help Readers unlearn how to
read.. how? What can be unlearned if a Reader closes the book in frustration
and doesn't read at all? Does not reading "cut up" the book metaphysically,
still adhering to "The Destruction Room"? How will I attract those
Subscribers of whom you dreamed?

                                        Gretchen

Dear Gloria,

I've set aside their comments. It's hard to reduce the Galerie to something closed, when it keeps opening. Like a creature, living and breathing, its shape changes. With a spine and signatures (i.e., pages folded into parts of the book), the catalogue deforms itself and more: my impression of you, even of myself. I enter the enigmatic "Destruction Room" (with its single illustration and single quotation—otherwise blank) and leave it, inevitably returning through other pages, guided not forward and back in linear fashion but interwoven, almost, into some strange design "quietly awaiting an opportunity to be changed from generals to particulars…"

G.H.

☞ To revisit the Destruction Room as Gretchen first found it, turn to page 217.

☞ To continue reading Gretchen's letters to Gloria, turn to page 169.

☞ To be interwoven into some strange design, turn to page 105, 108, or 193.

This way to the Great Ogres! page 6?

This way to the Great Egrets! page 190

This way to the Great Egress! page 249

```
┌─────────────────────────────┐
│                             │
│                             │
│                             │
│                             │
│                             │
│                             │
│                             │
│                             │
└─────────────────────────────┘
```

Title: _____
Artist: _____
Medium: _____ ← *Fill in the blanks.*
Date: _____
Location: _____

☞ *To catch & release something or someone from this box,*
   turn to page 136 or ____ (fill in blank).

☞ *To catch & attach something within this box, turn to page 220,*
   then add directive for future reading, using an arrow from here:

☞ *Add together numbers in your mailing address & phone number(s) &*
   turn to that page.

aciform, aeriform, aliform, antiformalist, antiformalists, antireform, arciform, auriform, ausform, ausformed, ausforming, ausforms, autotransformer, autotransformers, biform, biformed, biotransformation, biotransformations, chloroform, chloroformed, chloroforming, chloroforms, choreiform, coliform, coliforms, conform, conformable, conformably, conformal, conformance, conformances, conformation, conformational, conformations, conformed, conformer, conformers, conforming, conformism, conformisms, conformist, conformists, conformities, conformity, conforms, cordiform, coryneform, counterreform, counterreformation, counterreformations, counterreformer, counterreformers, counterreformers, cribriform, cruciform, cruciforms, cubiform, cumuliform, cuneiform, cuneiforms, cuniform, cuniforms, deform, deformable, deformalize, deformalized, deformalizes, deformalizing, DEFORMATION, DEFORMATIONAL, DEFORMATIONS, DEFORMATIVE, DEFORMED, DEFORMER, DEFORMERS, DEFORMING, DEFORMITIES, DEFORMITY, DEFORMS, deiform, dendriform, dentiform, disciform, disconformities, disconformity, disinformation, disinformations, electroform, electroformed, electroforming, electroforms, ensiform, epileptiform, falciform, filiform, flabelliform, form, formabilities, formability, formable, formal, formaldehyde, formaldehydes, formalin, formalins, formalise, formalised, formalises, formalising, formalism, formalisms, formalist, formalistic, formalists, formalities, formality, formalizable, formalization, formalizations, formalize, formalized, formalizer, formalizers, formalizes, formalizing, formally, formalness, formalnesses, formals, formalwear, formamide, formamides, formant, formants, format, formate, formates, formation, formations, formative, formatively, formatives, formats, formatted, formatter, formatters, formatting, forme, formed, formee, former, formerly, formers, formes, formfitting, formful, formic, formicaries, formicary, formidabilities, formidability, formidable, formidableness, formidablenesses, formidably, forming, formless, formlessly, formlessness, formlessnesses, formol, formols, forms, formula, formulae, formulaic, formulaically, formularies, formularization, formularizations, formularize, formularized, formularizer, formularizers, formularizes, formularizing, formulary, formulas, formulate, formulated, formulates, formulating, formulation, formulations, formulator, formulators, formulize, formulized, formulizes, formulizing, formwork, formworks, formyl, formyls, freeform, fungiform, funnelform, fusiform, gasiform, gruiform, inconformities, inconformity, inform, informal, informalities, informality, informally, informant, informants, informatics, information, informational, informationally, informations, informative, informatively, informativeness, informativenesses, informatorily, informatory, informed, informedly, informer, informers, informing, informs, infundibuliform, iodoform, iodoforms, irreformabilities, irreformability, irreformable, janiform, lamelliform, landform, landforms, letterform, letterforms, libriform, lyriform, malformation, malformations, malformed, microform, microforms, misform, misformed, misforming, misforms, misinform, misinformation, misinformations, misinformed, misinforming, misinforms, moniliform, multiform, multiformities, multiformity, napiform, nonconform, nonconformance, nonconformances, nonconformed, nonconformer, nonconformers, nonconforming, nonconformism, nonconformisms, nonconformist, nonconformists, nonconformities, nonconformity, nonconforms, nondeforming, nonformal, noninformation, noninformations, nonperformance, nonperformances, nonperformer, nonperformers, nonperforming, nonuniform, nonuniformities, nonuniformity, omniform, outperform, outperformed, outperforming, outperforms, overinform, overinformed, overinforming, overinforms, oviform, paraform, paraformaldehyde, paraformaldehydes, paraforms, patelliform, pediform, perform, performabilities, performability, performable, performance, performances, performative, performatives, performatory, performed, performer, performers, performing, performs, piciform, piliform, piriform, pisiform, pisiforms, planform, planforms, platform, platforms, plexiform, postform, postformed, postforming, postforms, preform, preformat, preformation, preformationist, preformationists, preformations, preformats, preformatted, preformatting, preformed, preforming, preforms, preformulate, preformulated, preformulates, preformulating, preperformance, preperformances, pyriform, ramiform, reform, reformabilities, reformability, reformable, reformat, reformate, reformates, reformation, reformational, reformations, reformative, reformatories, reformatory, reformats, reformatted, reformatting, reformed, reformer, reformers, reforming, reformism, reformist, reformists, reforms, reformulate, reformulated, reformulates, reformulating, reformulation, reformulations, reinform, reinformed, reinforming, reinforms, retiform, retransform, retransformation, retransformations, retransformed, retransforming, retransforms, rotiform, salverform, scalariform, scalariformly, semiformal, setiform, slipform, slipformed, slipforming, slipforms, stratiform, styliform, terraform, terraformed, terraforming, terraforms, thermoform, thermoformable, thermoformed, thermoforming, thermoforms, transform, transformable, transformation, transformational, transformationalist, transformationalists, transformationally, transformations, transformative, transformed, transformer, transformers, transforming, transforms, triform, tubiform, unciform, unciforms, unconformable, unconformably, unconformities, unconformity, undeformed, unformed, unformulated, uniform, uniformed, uniformer, uniformest, uniforming, uniformitarian, uniformitarianism, uniformitarianisms, uniformitarians, uniformities, uniformity, uniformly, uniformness, uniformnesses, uniforms, uninformative, uninformatively, uninformed, unperformable, unperformed, unreformed, untransformed, ursiform, variform, vasiform, vermiform, villiform, waveform, waveforms

Title: Deformity. 4.
Artist: Oxford English Dictionary, 2nd edition
Medium: English Language
Location: Online Database

☞ To consider this form in terms of content, turn to page 5 or 77 or 230.

☞ To confront the formless, turn to page 173.

☞ Collaboratively deform the Galerie with [name:_____]. Document your doubling (or however you describe the process) as you alternate in making choices (or otherwise co-create a method to your madness). This can be done by turning to page 21 and/or adding a section(s) to the Appendix (page 247).

Deformity as Spectacle

Title: Another Part in the Same Fair[cxxxviii]
Artist: "Mr. Setchel, of King-street, Covent-garden"
Medium: Engraving
Date: c. 1721
Location: William Hone's *Every-Day Book*

While *wundercammern* showcased private wonders, public spectacles (like

REALITY TELEVISION

eidophusikons, panoramas, and dioramas) gave viewers more opportunities to see

EYEWITNESS ACCOUNT

without being seen. Fairs added yet another dimension—live exhibition—that

complicated the singular viewing experience. Part sport (i.e., *spectators* at a

spectacle), fairs assaulted all senses and sprang from a larger history of human display:

VIDEO GAMING

ON THE SCENE

involving imprisonment, surveillance, dissection, torture, even death—as well

(FILL IN BLANKS)

cxxxix

as seemingly benign interactions, both impromptu and staged.

"   **"cxl**

Providing showcases for human deformity, fairs elevated physical status through

REPORTING LIVE

public display by type or group. Poets like Wordsworth to some extent self‑identified with beggars and outcasts, basing his poetic portraits $\left(\textit{see above}\right)$ more upon observation

[BROWSING, TWEETING, FRIENDING, SKYPING ...]

than interaction◆ In the excerpt of *The Prelude* immediately preceding Bartholomew's

Fair, he writes about a blind beggar: " [TELL-ALL] on the shape of that unmoving man, / His

[BROWSING, TWEETING, FRIENDING, SKYPING]

steadfast face and sightless eyes, I gazed, / As if admonished from another

[IPHONE, IPAD, IMAC, ITOUCH, IPOD]

"cxli

world◆   Having observed this destitution, the Poet walks away ◆ ◆ ◆

☞ *To stop* & *watch a puppet show, turn to page 145 or 164◆*

☞ *To bypass another live display, don't turn to page 222◆*

☞ *To search for the Great Egress, turn to page 249◆*

◆ ◆ ◆into more locodescription◆ As a kind of secular iconography, beggars

[DVD, LCD, LSD, CDC, OCD, OEF, OED]

and freaks gain prominence in Victorian literature, depending on circumstances (for

[WIKIPEDIA, BABEL FISH]

instance, as Charles Dickens cries in his Introduction to *The Life and Adventures of*

[YOUTUBE, MY SPACE, FACEBOOK]

Nicholas Nickleby: " We hear sometimes of an action for damages against the

unqualified medical practitioner, who has deformed a broken limb in pretending to heal

[GOOGLE, GOOGLE EARTH, GOOGLE BOOKS, GMAIL]

it◆ But, what of the hundreds of thousands of minds that have been deformed for ever by the incapable pettifoggers who have pretended to form them**!")**. **cxlii**   This

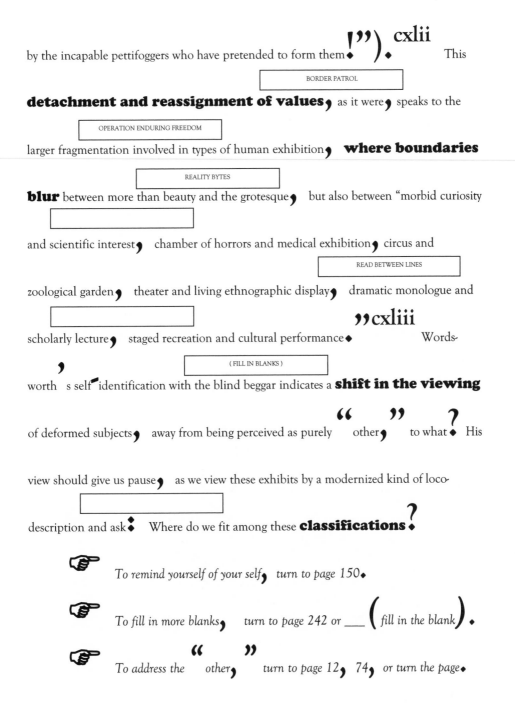

BORDER PATROL

detachment and reassignment of values, as it were, speaks to the

OPERATION ENDURING FREEDOM

larger fragmentation involved in types of human exhibition, **where boundaries**

REALITY BYTES

blur between more than beauty and the grotesque, but also between "morbid curiosity

and scientific interest, chamber of horrors and medical exhibition, circus and

READ BETWEEN LINES

zoological garden, theater and living ethnographic display, dramatic monologue and

"cxliii

scholarly lecture, staged recreation and cultural performance. Words-

(FILL IN BLANKS)

worth's self identification with the blind beggar indicates a **shift in the viewing**

"   "   ?

of deformed subjects, away from being perceived as purely "other," to what. His

view should give us pause, as we view these exhibits by a modernized kind of loco-

description and ask: Where do we fit among these **classifications**?

☞ *To remind yourself of your self, turn to page 150.*

☞ *To fill in more blanks, turn to page 242 or ___ (fill in the blank).*

☞ *To address the "other," turn to page 12, 74, or turn the page.*

Here we are, Love
        in a garden
     and all I have is this: flesh
of legend in my hand. Your pulsing heart. Still
     you cannot look me in the eye. (*If*
         you were Lady Beatrice and I
    the Florentine–) Nevermind,
just listen—not to me, but to your heart
     in my hand, clasped
         (*I'd never waste my time like this*
           if you were–) asking:
     Did the serpent tempt with a *pome-*
      granate? Did Mohammed inhale
eternity by this flushed scent? What of
    (*Lady Beatrice*)
     Daphnis and Atalanta? Knowing
what's forbidden, I worm and wedge (*I'd woo*
    and then demand a kiss, nor weep
      like Dante here, I ween)
     past the adage, harking back
        past Deuteronomy, King Alfred,
         et cetera: since what matters
     is the ability to grasp
         history as palpable, as malleable
         (*If you were Lady Beatrice*
        and I the Florentine) as us—
        prompting me
      to notice
     your *pupils* (derived from *child*
and *little corpse*, morphing) to see
     a globe spin round your glob.
        Do you see me now, Love—
If you were Lady Beatrice, and I the Florentine?
Face to face, here we are in a garden
     and all I have is this:
    (your own reflection
      in my eye).[cxliv]

THE WELL OF THE WORLD'S END.

Title: The Frog-Prince
    ("The Well at the End of the World")
Artist: John D. Batten
Medium: Woodblock print
Date: 1890
Location: *English Fairy Tales, collected*
    by Joseph Jacobs

Exhibit S

Waves lap like lips—sucking nape, chest, hips. Flames lick; tongues of fire. You never know when, or where, you'll find a body. Rhythms conceal corporeality. Trochees and dactyls, terza and ottava rimas, tetrameters and tercets. Sprung rhymes spring out of a stanza, creep after a couplet, hold a reader down to lift aloft (through an octet, sestet)—whispering and tasting. Many mouths: *Amor mi mosse, che mi fa paralare. O yonge, fresshe folkes, he or she, / In which that love up groweth with youre age. Some lovers speak when they their Muses entertain.*[cxlv] Whether Pamphilia or a Darker Lady, the question remains:

Is it ever a challenge to fit inside a form: with diametrically-opposed iambs, alliterated with assonance, fraught with masculine and feminine rhymes?

Refrain: refrain. Caesuras are everywhere, more (or less) than synecdoche and synaesthesia. You never know where you'll find a *Faerie* or *Queen* (near an alexandrine, when attending to feet, which suggests legs and thighs) or a key for a lock (or metaphors more primal, banal or blessed): it depends on questions that arise from the quotidian. Did Issa, in his haiku, hear snails *sizzling* or *frying* before, finally, *crying* in a saucepan?[cxlvi] Did the consummately chaste Ruskin get off on pathetic phallacy? *Cruel, crawling foam* reaches and retreats, under *rosy-fingered Dawn*, which never unfurled palms yet touched everything in *The Odyssey* and *The Golden Ass*, lingering before clasping, blindingly, retreating with advancing night or imminent storms.

And winds continue to blow—through myths & maps (ears, nostrils, mouths)—besmirched, bloody or clouded with wax, pus, or something more watery that courses through this corpus...

Lufu, Lof, Lowe, Loue, Lievun, Ljuby, Luba, Lubet...

Hands are helpful, but not needed for this. Forget pity. Underwater with you, a grasp feels like nothing. Even in a posture of contortion, of writhing, of release— Parts for whole, engorged: come. How, when, why: undone. Skin slips, entwining, lapping and leaching every surface, never deep enough— deeper— until each pore releases. Scent of sweat. Beckoning— burrowing— breaking— basking—

Come, again.[cxlvii]

☞ "[I]t is a common proverb in Italy that he does not know **Venus** in her perfect sweetness who has not lain with the ▮▮▮.

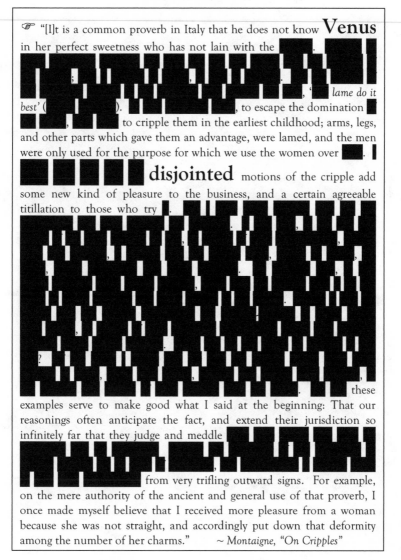

', '*lame do it best*' ( ), , to escape the domination ▮ to cripple them in the earliest childhood; arms, legs, and other parts which gave them an advantage, were lamed, and the men were only used for the purpose for which we use the women over ▮▮. ▮ **disjointed** motions of the cripple add some new kind of pleasure to the business, and a certain agreeable titillation to those who try ▮.

these examples serve to make good what I said at the beginning: That our reasonings often anticipate the fact, and extend their jurisdiction so infinitely far that they judge and meddle

from very trifling outward signs. For example, on the mere authority of the ancient and general use of that proverb, I once made myself believe that I received more pleasure from a woman because she was not straight, and accordingly put down that deformity among the number of her charms." ~ *Montaigne, "On Cripples"*

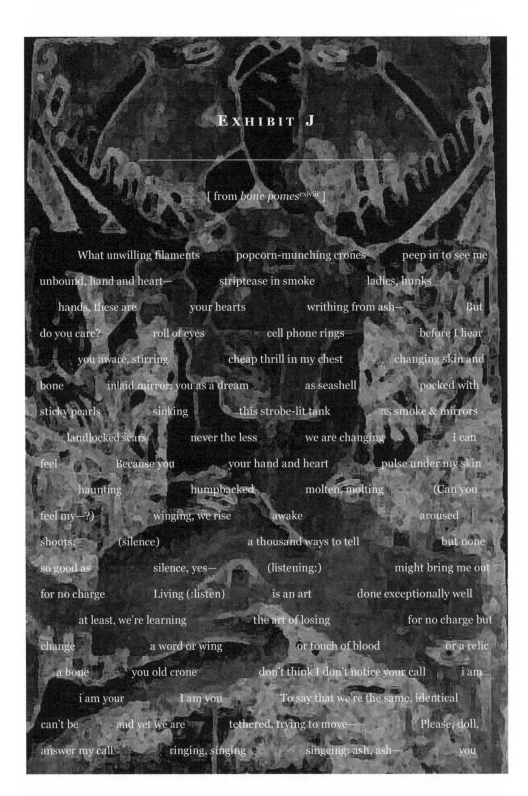

Exhibit J

[from *bone pomes*[cxlviii]]

What unwilling filaments   popcorn-munching crones   peep in to see me

unbound, hand and heart—   striptease in smoke   ladies, hunks

hands, these are   your hearts   writhing from ash—   But

do you care?   roll of eyes   cell phone rings   before I hear

you aware, stirring   cheap thrill in my chest   changing skin and

bone   inlaid mirror: you as a dream   as seashell   pocked with

sticky pearls   sinking   this strobe-lit tank   as smoke & mirrors

landlocked scars   never the less   we are changing   I can

feel   Because you   your hand and heart   pulse under my skin

haunting   humpbacked   molten, molting   (Can you

feel my—?)   winging, we rise   awake   aroused

shouts: (silence)   a thousand ways to tell   but none

so good as   silence, yes—   (listening:)   might bring me out

for no charge   Living (:listen)   is an art   done exceptionally well

at least, we're learning   the art of losing   for no charge but

change   a word or wing   or touch of blood   or a relic

a bone   you old crone   don't think I don't notice your call   i am

i am your   I am you   To say that we're the same, identical

can't be   and yet we are   tethered, trying to move—   Please, doll,

answer my call   ringing, singing   singeing: ash, ash—   you

start to stir and prod   flesh, blood, nothing there but: a heart-cut bone,

a deformed book,   a buzzing hive...   and fairy? Fair who?   Frau God, Frau

Alighieri: care, re-pair   out of the embers   we rise again   unburnt

and bare   to touch each other as air

☞ To touch each other as air,
   turn to 225, 233, or ____ (fill blank)
☞ If you seek embers, turn to page 128.
☞ To witness these characters rise again,
   turn to page 10 or 30.

¡Cuidado,
Prudence,
Vorsicht,
Attenzione!

Why don't you go back where you came from, following Ariadne's thread, H & G's breadcrumbs, mercurial pull of some compass? I'm wasting my breath trying to warn you (*moan*) of the MONSTER who guards the bone. (*Groan.*) But I know your rights and thus don't expect an answer, since You have the right to remain silent. Anything You say can and will be used against you in a court of law. You have the right to an attorney. If you cannot afford an attorney, one will be appointed to You. Do you understand these rights as they have been read to You?

☞ *To observe your right to remain silent, close this book until you find appropriate representation.*

☞ *To proceed for further questioning, turn to page 150.*

☞ *To look & listen more closely for the monster, turn to page 23 or 135.*

☞ *To take your chances, turn to page 224 or keep reading.*

☞ To tie this story even tighter, get a rope or ribbon & bind up this book.

☞ To unravel what's stitched, remove the spine or turn to page 105, 129, 131$_\wedge$[11], or 193.

Dear Bea,

I've decided to write to you, dear Bea, because I feel like you hold some key, some skeleton key, which may open doors that remain locked...

To treat you like some saint, fallen as you are, makes me doubt what I've undertaken: the mystery of the heart-holed bone. I'm wary of saints, dead heads of cults, cobbled together from mismatched anonymous bones. Gloria said your bone was a pen, a symbol for membership in an Ugly Club, exhumed and replicated, prized and passed down—leaving me to decipher its significance. Can that bone, a single bone (missing, no less), hold what's left of your truth? If said bone is found, will that alone change my life or anyone else's, perched on some pedestal to revere rather than touch? Will threads of your story tie together neatly, leaving me satisfied for the rest of my life? Does replication upon replication of said bone over centuries reduce its meaning, rather than acquire some alternate dimension... Dare I follow its elusive lead, even at risk of meeting a dead end?

Whatever questions I have about you beget more questions. Reading Dante and his devotees, I find contradictory accounts of you, constantly shifting my perceptions of who and how and why. Like this: "Dante has not been pleased to throw any light on these puzzling questions, and we are, therefore, left to the vaguest conjectures....of his love for Beatrice, detailed information about family affairs would have been out of place....a love which, in the words of Dante himself, cannot be understood by those who have not experienced it—Intender non la puo chi non la prova—" Resurrected in artworks, your form runs the gamut—such variant bodies across centuries!—leaving you present in absentia... much like Gloria, and her Galerie, materialized around a hole.

I don't want to be duped into trusting some faux relic—a deception built on deception—where the heart reveals another hole, and another, a sequence of diminishing mirrors. While you're almost entirely unknown, in a sense I sense (and only can trust rather than be incensed) that some body will emerge at the end of this.. if not you or Gloria, or even me, then some Subscrib· ·vill emerge who I haven't even imagined.

Dear Gloria,

    Some "body" is already here. Retaining the capacity to change and grow, your Galerie de Difformité seems tethered to a life. Not to you, exactly, or your father, your husband or son, not to me, not so much a life as lives— more at living. Your Galerie arises from characters who aren't the be-all-end- all: you identify Bea, just like I name you. But the book itself seems a character Am I misreading your intent, and who is/are "you"?

    I can't extract the heart ("The Destruction Room") without risking the life of the book, nor can that heart live without its connective tissue. To consider the book as a body risks simplifying your design. But if your book IS a body, "The Destruction Room" seems your Galerie's heart—not the "Exhibits" which serve as your "face" to the world as you say in your Pre-face, like some mask or armament, concealing, although at times they feel internal as arteries and veins, pulsing and releasing, feeding the central mechanism. With a heart, many faces, a bone, many hand(note)s & butt(note)s, no foot(note)s—no legs on which to stand: what exquisite corpse lies buried within these pages? And how might the book "change," "at least when cut up will be so"? Does it matter whether a Subscriber reads the book at all, so long as they cut it up?

                                                      Gretchen

Is the key to "The Destruction Room" dismembering in order to re-member, that is: to assemble a community of members?

If "The Destruction Room" is paradoxically about creation, does the bone matter less than what's missing from it: the heart?

A post-graduate student equipped with honours and diplomas went to Agassiz to receive the final and finishing touches. The great man offered him a small fish *bee* and told him to describe it.

Post-Graduate Student: 'That's only a sunfish.' *bee*

Agassiz: 'I know that. Write a description of it.'

After a few minutes the student returned with the description of the Ichthus Heliodiplodokus, or whatever term is used to conceal the common sunfish *bee* from vulgar knowledge, family of Heliichtherinkus, etc., as found in textbooks of the subject.

Agassiz again told the student to describe the fish. *bee*

The student produced a four-page essay. *bee* Agassiz then told him to look at the fish. At the end of three weeks the fish was in an advanced state of decomposition, but the student knew something about it.

I've assumed all this time that you were composing a story. Would I be able to recognize a story (or book or gallery, for that matter) in a state of decomposition?

☞ To continue reading Gretchen's letters to Gloria, turn to page 183.

☞ To consult your notes on the bone with the heart-shaped hole, turn to page 223.

☞ To consider the nature of relics, turn to page 125, 126, or 128.

☞ To look for another way in, find page 228, or for a way out, turn to page 249.

We destroy the book when we read it in order to make it into another book. The book is always born from a broken book. And the word, too, is born from a broken word…
~ Edmond Jabès

Title: _____
Artist: _____
Medium: _____ ← *Fill in the blanks.*
Date: _____
Location: _____

☞ *Write "A" through "Z" on papers & draw one out of a hat. Find the corresponding page/ exhibit (via pages on 224) & proceed as directed. Alternatively, ask the next person you see to choose a letter & don't continue reading until you find that person.*[cxlix]

☞ *Choose a sentence from any Exhibit & write it along the edges of the box (above), then proceed to page 220. Or write the sentence in the box itself, then turn the page. Add new directive for future reading: _____.*

Title: Definition [**extracts***]
Artist: Oxford English Dictionary, 2nd edition
Medium: English Language
Location: Online Database

☞ To visit the "poor definition-cutter" (☞**see translation of outer extract***),
   please proceed to page 217 or 230.

☞ To (re)view definitions, please consult any of the following:
   34, 50, 73, 99, 118, 141, 156, 187.

☞ To redefine language, turn to page 208 or keep reading.

* **Outer extract: "Alas, for our poor definition-cutter, with ~~his~~ her logical scissors!"**

Deformity as Sublime

In light of various historical representations of human deformity, Turner's "The Storm (Shipwreck)" indirectly hones the tempest-tossed debate. The painting's frenzied focus led William Hazlitt to say that the artist "delights to go back to the first chaos of the world... All is without forms and void. Some one said of his landscapes that they were pictures of nothing, and very like." Attention to light here blurs boundaries of physicality, heightening tone and mood. Although depicting a tempest, the painting differs from the engravings from Shakespeare's play by Hogarth and Fuseli. Characters are unseen in the ship, whose masts echo the few craggy rocks that cut the swelling waves, chaotically connected to surging skies. The ship itself is being enveloped by a kind of formlessness.

Title: The Storm (Shipwreck)[cl]
Artist: Joseph Mallard William Turner
Medium: Oil and pencil on paper
Date: 1823
Location: British Museum, London

"The other shape, / If shape it might be called, which shape had none / Distinguishable in member, joint, or limb; / Or substance might be called, which shadow seem'd..."[xli]

~ Milton

Note: displaced on page 124.

In contrast to a skeleton (whose "distinctness would take off that mysterious uncertainty," and thus diminish the sense of), Sir Uvedale Price called Milton's representation of Death: "." Price explained by analogy that is necessary for something to be : " is to , what is to ; though distinct from it.... alone, is merely disagreeable; by the addition of , it becomes hideous; by that of it may become ." Similarly, Edmund Burke wrote that subjects must be -less to evoke " " or "astonishment."[clii] Since is marked by some corrosion of , but still is , the relationship between and offers a poignant feature to ponder. Reviewing the , for instance, qualities that were revered in were reviled in , criticized or satirized using a range of terms: 🌏, *grotesque*, 🐚, *monstrous*, and the like. For lack of a better word, 🌏 of 🏔—seemingly antithetical to the ◐-less character of the ☺—are granted license that does not extend to each 🏔's live counterparts, like subterranean dwarves, forest sprites, or monsters in island caves (*to visit a monster in an island cave, turn to page 119*). That said, the ☺ is often associated with 🏔 prone to or marked by storms, volcanoes, subterranean caverns and grandiose mountain peaks, where 🏔 disasters put people in peril. In the pantomime *Wonders of Derbyshire*, for instance, 🏔 is personified with "rocks [that] are wild and grotesque" and "a bleak *mountain's foot*, whose craggy brow, Secures from *eastern tempests* all below....Which elsewhere round a tyranny maintains."[cliii] Inside the "wondrous" cave live impoverished 👪, who rope-spin and lead tours—one example of a curious affiliation between ☺ 🏔 and figures who live on the margins of society, as if that represents the edge of the super-🏔.

Gothic 🦪 similarly describes physiological effects but more psychologically, hinting at analogues between 🏔 (with its topoi of decaying 🏚, ruined abbeys and castles with dungeons and trapdoors, passages and crypts) and the labyrinthine 🏔 of psyches. In *Romance of the* 🏔 (by a " 👽 ," or female gothic novelist, Ann Radcliffe) the protagonist Adeline says: "Gloomy unpleasing images flitted before my fancy, and I fell into a sort of waking dream: I thought that I was in a lonely 🏔 with my 🧍 ; his looks were severe, and his ☞👍✊✌️🖐👆🤚🖖 menacing...while he spoke, [he] drew from his pocket a 😑, which he held before my 😑; I looked at 😑 and saw, (my 💙 now thrills as I repeat it) I

saw myself wounded, and ♥ profusely."[cliv] The character acknowledges her disfigure-ment in the context of 🏔, but is neither 🌐-less nor ☺—approaching (but not 🌍 like) Turner's storm, where sea and sky blur on the verge of swallowing the 🚏.

But I'm getting away from myself, the farther and deeper that I tread (and warn you against treading) into this *Galerie*. What options does this leave us; where are we being led? Returning to 👽 and the ☺, the question arises: is this book truly 🌐-less? And if not, then what 🌐 is it? Neither 👽 nor ☺, just 🌍—that is; nothing to be afraid of.

☞ *If the book is just* 🌍 *and nothing to fear,*
  turn to page 195 or 209.
☞ *If these pictograms feel fragmented,*
  turn to page 188.
☞ *To resuscitate (my* ♥ *now thrills as I repeat it)*
  a transplanted ♥*, turn to page 30.*

THE BOAT TILTS. SUN-SLANTED

The boat tilts. Sun-slanted
waters swarm portholes, cascading
over a casket, cornered:
                    (light—
eye to eye)
                                        inside
                        whittled boards
padlocked & sheaved (sailcloth: a-
palling gown, moth-eaten) mar-
oons: body within body
                    rises
                    up
stairs (footsteps click, hinges):

                        Opening
onto deck, bound, the cocoon
unwinds to un-
wound   (wounds
exposed, espoused) knotted
with rope: puckering to pouch
for a stone.

            Off sides, the crash
cradles. What might float
the stone drags
down.

☞ *Before this creature is submerged, turn hastily to page 38
      to hear it speak again or to page 247Ø.*
☞ *To follow the creature's course underwater, keep reading.*
☞ *If you think this creature is the monster, turn to pages 55, 177,
      129, 162, 110, 247, and 126 (which spells: _____)*
☞ *If you fear that you're lost, turn to 222.*

Exhibit O

By starfish, by screw-borer, by boring sponge, by slipper shell, by Black Drum, by mussel, by duck: there are many ways to die. Sucked clean, smothered or leeched, tunneled through like honeycomb, "She can feel shadows as well as the urgency of milt, and her delicate muscles know danger and pull shut her shells."[clv] Lacking limbs, by shutting, she survives for future shucking. The threat comes from without, not within, where she shelters a parasite that gradually procures a pearl.

Empty shells wash ashore with tides. Abandoned houses surface for hermits to inhabit. Crunched underfoot, scars-of-the-sea float back with tides, while larval stars flit freely, then filter-feed in shell-stocked beds. Unlike starfish, whose limbs can be lopped and regrow, oysters sustain unshapely shells. Their possession is misplaced, pared down to a pronoun: "The world is *your* oyster." Such is the stuff from which dreams are farmed: "Perle, plesaunte to prynces paye / To clanly clos in golde so clere, / Oute of Oryent, I hardyly saye, / Ne proved I never her precios pere."[clvi] Visions aside, anchored and abducting: the oyster may survive predators only to be hunted for the crystallizing ball that she (and he) hides.

Shall I leave this shell alone or deform it further: "secret, and self-contained, and solitary"?[clvii] If you seek a prematuring end, a maiden can break her necklace, drop seven white pearls and one black pearl into an onyx cup, and ask you to choose.[clviii] Or, in another version, sharks circle fabled shoals as fisher-folk in boats listen: "in the song there was a secret little inner song, hardly perceptible, but always there, sweet and secure and clinging, almost hiding in the counter-melody...the Song of the Pearl That Might Be..."[clix]

For-the-taking? Is this a two-faced tale? Don't be misled by aphrodisiacs (after all, pearl-producing oysters are inedible). Consider *harvesting* and *farming*: metaphors in metaphysical guise. What's embedded in the flesh is hinged to history, orchestrated by different valves than strings: *collar, choker, matinee, opera,* and *rope* (complimented by *earrings* shaped as tears, like those worn by Vermeer's *Girl*). Look beneath the surface: at turbaned girls described as "drunken birds" who dive and dive again.[clx] What should we make of this flock, and of the Venus de Medici (*poser* or *posed*?) who bears a wax-cast shell, in a swoon, wearing nothing but a pearled collar?

And thus comes my wish to pry open my shell, just as "Pearl set forth, at a great pace, and...did actually catch the sunshine, and stood laughing in the midst of it....until her mother had drawn almost nigh enough to step into the magic circle too," and was compelled to say: "Now I can stretch out my hand, and grasp some of it."[clxi]

To grasp what-is-ungraspable: slipping through gills. Pearls of wisdom drift though legends: where Cleopatra caters the costliest cuisine: crushing her prize pearl, mixing it in vinegar to serve as Antony's wine. Elsewhere, Vitellius wages war supported by his mother's single gem, and Marco Polo witnesses King Maabar's string of one-hundred-and-four (for each of his daily prayers) that are twenty-fold less than the swag seized from Alice Perrers. "We should have to resolve the contradictions of the shell," Bachelard muses, "which at times is so rough outside and so soft, so pearly, in its intimacy. And doesn't the finger that dreams as it strokes the intimate mother-of-pearl surface surpass our human, all too human, dreams?" From Queen Mary to Elizabeth Taylor, *La Peregrina* becomes the "pilgrim" it purports to be...and look at what gleams through the Koran, Vedas, Revelations...

Only a lover could attribute worth to luster born-of-a-wound. Wound inside aragonite and conchiolin, the petulant piece lies mothered by a humble shell. For the mollusk, the prize is more parasitic than something of great price. Caught in the meaty mantle, coated with nacre, the "worm coffin" grows within bivalves that nest on beds of the dead, which tempt divers who dare not sleep.

"Come, thou most precious pearl," Mary hears during her apocryphal assumption, while a servant fantasizes: "Next to my own skin, her pearls."[clxiii] "Her skin is tinct like pearl," Dante praises, while Milton eulogizes: "And those Pearls of dew she wears, / Prove to be presaging tears..." Perilous phrases impearl fears, presuming to lay them to rest—like oysters inadvertently cast ashore bits of their beds: "signs of approaching death. Rather than stand still and learn from them [o]ne tries to cure the signs of growth, to exorcise them, as if they were devils, when really they might be angels of annunciation..."[clxiv]

Annunciating: *O*.

Here is the pearl of great price, always eluding. Like a koan. Consider the adage: not "The world is your *pearl*" but your *oyster*. *O* is the secret of culturing: to know the knobby shell for what it's worth, in and of itself: more than mother-of-pearl. Unburden me of beauty. Shuck me of my gems. Look inside this dun, unshapely shell that "makes one little room, an every where."[clxv]

Without anything but this: Here I am, *O* Lord.

☞ *To shuck me of my gems, visit 220.*

☞ *To deform this, turn to page 136.*

☞ *To go pearl-diving, keep reading.*

178

CAUTION !!!!

Warning!

THIS BOOK MAY

SELF-DESTRUCT!

EXHIBIT G

Flares seed rains. More fires and floods—no matter, it seems. Seasonal cycles persist, as bodies swarm at ocean's edge. Irrigating ducts make this arid basin bloom. The fittest survive thanks to migrant fingers. The forecast boasts infernal sunshine for dauntless—

Wait: nothing is dauntless as it seems, like Thompson understood: he couldn't pluck a flower without troubling a star.[clxv] All presumes to spring from a garden, Edenic in proportions but as elusive, leading me to beseech Fiacre (leaning on his spade) and Alto (tapping his crosier to surge springs). Saints aside: Where rest seeds of my dream, devolving? Like Daphne or Hyacinth, or the seasoned shapes of of Arcimbolde's florid faces?[clxvii] Such chance for change winds past paths of stones, revealing a moon-shaped

a. *adore*, b. *carnivore*, c. *door*, d. *Gore*, e. *roar*, f. *sore*, g. *your*...

Breast, hip, eye: more than *eat*, "we are what we *treat*." Implanted like gardens, rife with deflowerings. Beyond notions (of the Black Prince and Duke of Marlborough, when tulips ruled the world, with dahlias worthy of diamonds), innuendos bud within entendres. The crutch of the crotch (*i.e.*, where tree branches join), like *The Tatler* coyly told his gardener friends about "a Chimney Sweeper and a Painted Lady in the same bed."[clxviii] Bodies evolve with phases of phrases—

Beyond time, out of rime: I hew emotions down to motions. Marveling (at *history*, call it *mystery*, even *misery*), I thumb through florilegia and leafy legends: as Earth morphs from a mother of bones-turned-to-stones...and Cuvier claims to conjure a skeleton from a tooth...Adam's rib rouses Locke's "little Finger"...hip bone connected to the knee...even mentalities shock, before electricity (when frayed fennel, brain-shaped walnuts & tongued leaves were thought to sprout hair, heal heads & mouths...)[clxix] Here, humors supplant humours (blood, phlegm, black and yellow bile) calcifying, until Shubin exclaims: "where once I had seen only rock, now I was seeing little bits and pieces of fossil everywhere."[clxx] Stacked stones; weathered **bones**. To get to my point:

Do you want me, Green?[clxxi]

(There, it's said:) To implicate my proposition, the decision shifts, weighing (us) in the balance. What will the future forgive? As flares seed storms and erode more shore, rain slips through my fingers that grope, forfeiting my foothold, to pluck or protect: "The weight of a petal has changed the face of the world and made it _____."[clxxii]

a. *bowers,* b. *cower,* c. *dour,* d. *flowers,* e. *glower,* f. *hours,* g. *ours...*

☞ To tree (v., as in, trap) yourself, turn to page 164, 191, or ____ (fill in blanks).

☞ To consider options from the previous page, proceed as follows: if you choose a. bowers, go to 16; if you choose b. cower, go to 44; if you choose c. dour, go to 93; if you choose d. flowers, go to 135; if you choose e. glower, go to 166; if you choose f. hours, go to 179, if you choose g. ours, go to 225.

☞ To contextualize the prior page's bones with The Bone, turn to page 31, 125, or 223.

Dear Gloria,

Decomposition, deformation, deformance (i.e., reading backwards), a thousand variations on a theme: each lends a lens for re-viewing your Galerie de Difformité. All that said, I'm missing something between lines, between pages, between "Exhibits," as you thread Bea's story with other stories (and non-stories: poems, scholarship, images, etc.) into a kind of corporeal query, a web-work that makes sense only at a slant. For instance, your "Exhibits" suggest a series of rooms that invite visitors to peruse a curated collection with political implications (as in a legal trial). If "exhibit" means "to hold out": who is holding out, and what (or who) is being held? Offering or withholding? Displaced and re-placed (subsumed or placed again?): A, B, C & the rest may not explicitly state YOU ARE HERE, but I am: here thinking about how best to engage what you've left behind: either to reduce it to a defense of what exists, or to explore what's absent. The latter may be the key, but can I unlock the Galerie or add some kind of window or trapdoor?

G.H.

I remember reading about Navajo rug-weavers sewing an imperfection in a pattern—"the spirit line," some scholar called it—leaving room for improvement, a place where spirit can move, in and out of the pattern, not locked into place. There's something here akin to the spirit line, whether or not attributed to this or that tradition, "a worship of the imperfect" (to borrow Okakura's phrase, which I found underlined in a copy of The Book of Tea—with your imprint—in your old public library). I don't think that the spirit line can be traced to a particular Exhibit or such, but somehow moves through the whole, just like any spirit tries to move in its body…

painting

impermanence

patterns restore

heal, teach, consecrate   the one-sung-over

cyclic and circular

mythic chantway

to learn

absorbs an affliction

sand painting   the Western

to suspend

becomes toxic   sand

the measurable

notion   absorbs an affliction

painting

needs to be destroyed   to unlearn

the 'real'   one possible

conception

Dear Gloria,

Alright, I've decided officially to include myself in your Galerie de Difformité fictionally through a few still to be decided signposts (labeled "You Are Here" or with these letters?). What your Galerie needs is a gallery-guide, a docent of sorts, even if said docent doesn't have all the facts and must interpret as best she can. Entrusted with what I've learned thus far, I'll frame your Galerie by vaguely introducing myself (in YOU ARE HERE: 1) as a "counselor at a community center who works with youths termed 'disabled.'" This is true, in its generality, even as truths mislead: a COUNSELOR suggests a range of advisors, be they teachers, lawyers, supervisors of one sort or another, even more informally. COMMUNITY CENTERS likewise include the gamut of agencies organized by a community (however COMMUNITY is defined), whether recreation centers or schools, colleges or hospitals, a range of public offices. (And what of the elasticity of any CENTER, suggesting many margins?) YOUTH, too, leaves something to be desired by definition, and DISABLED? In a round-about way: just like you removed yourself from your project, so too have I kept myself at bay, more absent than present, to suggest a larger picture that I'm still trying to see. At least, by addressing a visitor with "YOU ARE HERE," different narrative(s) might be co-created, like in any museum, to the extent that a visitor participates: in being placed and displaced.

This is what I know: in your Galerie, there's not a determined path, as each vectored variation suggests an alternate path. Bound by a single entrance and exit (the front and back covers, albeit mere manuscript pages), I wonder if the beginning IS the ending, the end might bode beginning? At times, a curator (you, Bea, me) will guide. If I am to further curate your work, it must appear in the guise of the book, but one with the capacity to break open, not fixed into place, but able to move and grow into the gallery it purports to be. And that may be where I try to enlist the help of Subscribers…

Now, to rest—
G.H.

☞ To continue Gretchen's letters to Gloria, turn to page 218.

☞ To enlist the help of Subscribers, turn to page 219.

☞ To remind yourself where you are, turn to page 6, 18, 42, 150, 225, or 230.

185

☞ To box in this box, turn to page 220; after deforming, add directive for future reading: _____.

☞ To extract, enacted, embroil, embed, exhume, &c.: scan here:

Title: _____
Artist: _____
Medium: _____ ← Fill in the blanks.
Date: _____
Location: _____

☞ Once you have finished deforming this book as much as you're able & (or) wanting, send to the Postmaster of a place you've always wanted to visit. Alternatively, spin a globe, close your eyes, & place your finger to stop its spinning; then, send this Galerie de Difformité to the Postmaster of that location. Keep documentation of the book's journey to share with the Undertaker in some shape or form.[clxxiii]

These pictures, and a thousand more,
Of These, my Gallery does store:
In all the Forms thou can'st invent
Either to please me, or torment:
For them alone to people me,
All drawn & unwrought Colony.
—Andrew Marvell

186

_____ AS DEFORMITY

(fill in blank ☝)

(FILL IN HOLE ☝)

[☝ Fill hole with definition of your choice.
If you return here after this hole is filled: rewrite,
paste over, or otherwise deform this word-filled hole.]

☞ *If you feel constrained by this hole (as a box, or in a bone), turn to page 144.*

☞ *If hole is already filled & you prefer not to change it, explain its context
in the surrounding white space.*

☞ *To view & review other definitions, please visit any of the following:*
34, 50, 73, 99, 118, 141, 156, 172, 208.

DEFORMITY AS FRAGMENT

Overwhelmed by the task of reenacting the classical narrative, the author falls into deep reflection about life and art, its interconnections and representations. Deforming figures and perspectives of embodiment to reflect physiological and psychological phenomena, the drawing takes on the character of a suspended sensibility, edged by impending darkness, without recognizing that the sculpted finger points outside the frame.

Title: *Der Künstler verzweifelnd vor der Grösse der antiken Trümmer*[clxxiv]
("The Artist in Despair over the Magnitude of Antique Ruins")
Artist: Johann Heinrich Fuseli
Medium: Drawing
Date: 1778-1780
Location: Zunsthaus, Zürich Switzerland

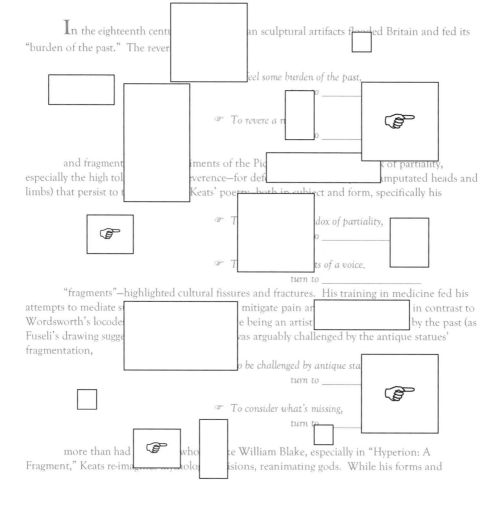

In the eighteenth cent_____ an sculptural artifacts f____ed Britain and fed its "burden of the past." The rever____

_____eel some burden of the past,

☞ *To revere a r_____*

and fragment_____ iments of the Pi_____ k of partiality, especially the high tol_____verence—for def_____mputated heads and limbs) that persist to t_____ Keats' poetry, both in subject and form, specifically his

☞ T_____dox of partiality,

☞ T_____ts of a voice,
turn to _____

"fragments"—highlighted cultural fissures and fractures. His training in medicine fed his attempts to mediate s_____ mitigate pain an_____ in contrast to Wordsworth's locode_____e being an artist_____by the past (as Fuseli's drawing sugge_____as arguably challenged by the antique statues' fragmentation,

_____o be challenged by antique sta_____
turn to _____

☞ *To consider what's missing,*
turn to _____

more than had_____who_____e William Blake, especially in "Hyperion: A Fragment," Keats re-ima_____ isions, reanimating gods. While his forms and references are classical, the appropriations are not strictly wedded to the past; as one example, he likely fabricated the urn in "Ode on a Grecian Urn" (see "Drawing of the Sosibios Vase from the Mu...

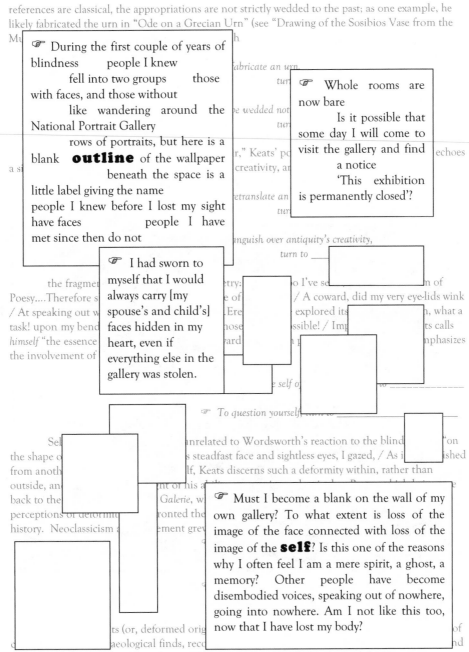

☞ During the first couple of years of blindness   people I knew   fell into two groups   those with faces, and those without   like wandering around the National Portrait Gallery   rows of portraits, but here is a blank **outline** of the wallpaper   beneath the space is a little label giving the name   people I knew before I lost my sight have faces   people I have met since then do not

☞ Whole rooms are now bare   Is it possible that some day I will come to visit the gallery and find a notice 'This exhibition is permanently closed'?

☞ I had sworn to myself that I would always carry [my spouse's and child's] faces hidden in my heart, even if everything else in the gallery was stolen.

☞ To question yourself

☞ Must I become a blank on the wall of my own gallery? To what extent is loss of the image of the face connected with loss of the image of the **self**? Is this one of the reasons why I often feel I am a mere spirit, a ghost, a memory? Other people have become disembodied voices, speaking out of nowhere, going into nowhere. Am I not like this too, now that I have lost my body?

commercial claims. The descendants of *Wundercammern* and *Kunstcammern* (whether art museums like the British Museum or halls of natural history, such as William Bullock's Egyptian Hall) became repositories for the preservation and display **of fragments, apart from their original** contexts, re-contextualized among other items from a collection—posited inside a new "narrative"—which continues to change with shifting cultural and curatorial studies.[clxxvi] It might behoove us to consider the number of artworks in this Gallery currently "loaned" from their home collections, participating in this exhibit, re-contextualized historically, artistically, anatomically and otherwise, inside a narrative about *Deformity*—when each could be as easily featured or fractured in a different frame, pointing toward a different end.

☞ *To point toward one end, turn to page 192, 193, or 194.*

☞ *To point toward a different end, keep reading.*

☞ *To unfold this story, turn to page 113.*

☞ *To fold this story in on itself, see below.*

What Haunts this Book is Want for Hearts Unbound

What haunts this book is want for hearts unbound
within a bone, whose hole deceives as much as grief
that leaves us bare and worn. To be bereft, undone
of sense, confuses holes for hearts; then, hands

hold fast to what is gone and voice by choice
departs. In sorts, this story is retold
unfolding like my hands that point but haunt
much less than bones, forgotten and unmarked

in graves, those holes that want for—
what we thought It was
nor can it well be held
as truth

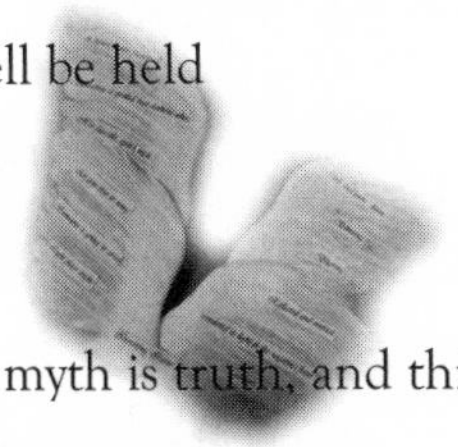

is myth, and myth is truth, and this
my masquerade, deforming
as these leaves
are le
f

t

Exhibit M

Exhibit O

Exhibit V

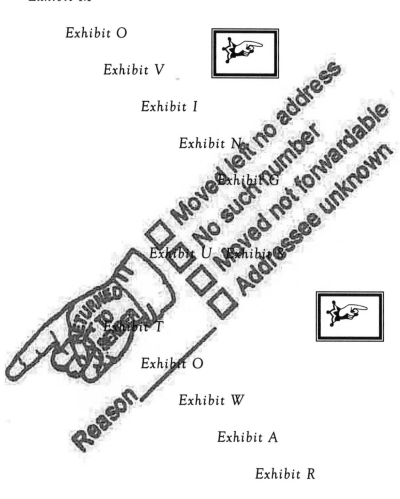

Exhibit I

Exhibit N

Exhibit G

Exhibit U Exhibit S

Exhibit T

Exhibit O

Exhibit W

Exhibit A

Exhibit R

Exhibit D

☞ *Insert hands pointing in whichever direction you deem appropriate.*

¡PLEASE RETURN to

"What is a Self?"

☞ To answer this & other Questions, turn to 150.

☞ If you have asked this question before, turn to 223 or 224.

☞ To try to unravel a mystery, turn to page 113 or 131.

☞ To punctuate this, turn to page 157.

☞ To search for a back way in, turn to page 9 or 228.

Here Lies

[your monster: ___________________]

✍ **Note:** *If your monster changes between visitations to this page, feel free to amend this page as need be.*

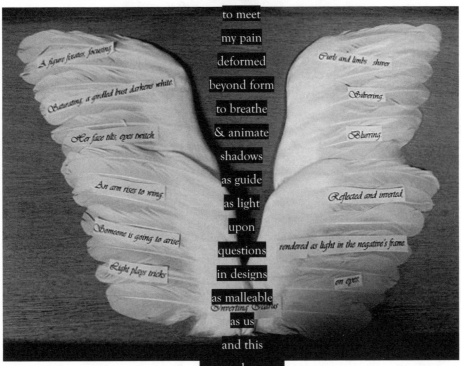

Undertake yourself
deformed
to meet
my pain
deformed
beyond form
to breathe
& animate
shadows
as guide
as light
upon
questions
in designs
as malleable
as us
and this
cornered cocoon
unbound

A figure fixates, focusing

Saturating, a girdled bust darkens white.

Her face tilts, eyes twitch.

An arm rises to wing.

Someone is going to arise.

Light plays tricks

Inverting Statues

Curls and limbs shiver

Subvering

Blurring

Reflected and inverted

rendered as light in the negative's frame

on eyes.

195

your Guide

not

love

will I agree to Bea

out assumption,

let me

bearing beauty (beastly beacons, beating)

before, but now

rising

fall

to bare my bones in parts

since beeswax lets me morph

(mat)ed

within beatitudes here on earth

not

consum-

to be as I may Bea

☞ *To unbind this cocooned book, do what you will–*

☞ *To review the means by which Dragons, Vipers, Eagles, Lions, &*
Unnam'd Forms deform into Books, please visit 200.

☞ *To meet Bea coming out of her hive, keep reading.*

I'M COMING OUT TO BE AS I MAY BEA

to be as I may Bea

since beeswax lets me morph

bearing *beauty (beastly beacons, beating)*

within *beatitudes* here on earth

to bare my bones in parts.

Here
they
fly
again,   let me
unfurling
love
like
not   fritillaries   rising

fall

out assumption,   not

consum-

(mat)ed

before, but now

will I agree to Bea   your Guide.

☞ To follow Bea as a guide,
turn to page 27(iv) or 234.

☞ To redefine any terms
in this project,
turn to page 208.

EXHIBIT B

2. circulating within and around the body

Vines entwine   small gilded leaves   *wax*: to grow

historiated initials   glossed marginalia   "His breast is of gold"   kneeling

    patterned dance   "The wind had halted, as in a painted picture"

circulating hemolymph   to go around   collect people   walking down

a promenade   *Apis mellifera* (the Florentine)   flared wings, compound eye,

sucking tongue   bodies of water, bodies of land   to flow from the heart through

the arteries & veins back to the heart   *Your lips distill nectar, my bride, / Honey*

and milk are under your tongue   Honey Moon   for mummification,

shipbuilding, lost-wax casting   (Bea) cross-pollinating   moving about at a

gathering   Vedic brides were honey-anointed for fertility   "Upon a courtyard

flagstone a bee cast a stationary shadow"   passing from hand to hand, mouth to

mouth   bee stinging (Bea)   "a shriek, a syllable, a twist of the hand"

    circulating within and around the body   "against protection"   alarm

pheromes   maggots (*for bedsores*), leeches (*for bad blood*), bee stings (*for arthritis,*

unless anaphylactically shocked)   "She thought: *Time has come to a halt*"

    mimicry: a lion carcass spontaneously generates bees   "(besides skin, flesh,

bones, etc., that are obvious to the eye)"   round an axis or in orbit

    to pass into the hands of readers   *The god Re wept and his tears fell to the*

ground and were turned to bees   visiting every   moon circulates about the

earth   *Fable of the Bees*   *shocking*: life-threatening   "Her

existence will pass in shadow"   (Be a) messenger function   *of Brightness, anoint me with the honey of the bee, that I may speak forceful speech*   "compound of

various passions"   responding to frequencies of light   "lofty invisible labyrinth"

"Where the bee sucks, there suck I—"

electrostatic charges   "saliva of the stars"   histamines,

prostaglandins, leukotreines   *Some have said that a share of divine / intelligence is*

in bees   wax-cast enemies, melting   "Come down with the falling stars"

"winged words"   bees in elephant trees   "She thought: *I've gone mad*"

one of the four humours   decrypted   Hymenoptera   vasodilation

"hys maker bee"   constricted   bated breath   "the shadow of the bee

still did not shift in the courtyard"   pumping action of the heart   "Not a sound reached

her from the stricken world"   San's trances   Thriae   Ah Muzen Cab

"invisible hand"   *Bocca della Verità* ("Mouth of Truth")   "She thought:

I'm in hell, I'm dead"   Snow Queen, snow bees   waxing & waning

"sweetness & light"   extreme sensitivity to antigen   *dbure* (meaning *bee*)

from *dbr* ("word")   *wax*: to weave (veil, sail)   when slightly warmed,

moldable & shapable   myths of virgin births   "paralyzed"   connective

tissue   colony collapse   "Come down gracefully"   *Feminine*

Monarchie   hibernating   buried in honey   "For pity, sir, find out

that bee / Which bore my love away"   *Meanwhile the moisture, warming in the*

softened bone, *   ferments, and creatures, of a type marvelous to see, swarm*

together, without feet at first, but soon with whirring wings as well,   and

more and more try the clear air,   until they burst out, like rain, pouring from summer

clouds.[clxxvii]

☞ *To reshape the softened bone,*
   turn to page 31, 181, or 246.
☞ *To add new notes to the Lineage*
   of a Bone, turn to page 223.

Broken-Winged Puppet

☞ Plato sometimes seems penetrated by that high idea of love which considers man as the two-fold one thought.... ...ain Plato, the ...ntellect, treats ...e as ...d Hands ...the that man, if he ...ivileges of one degraded ...m of woman, ...f he do not ...lf, into that of or bee. ...es most happily ...ical is this state Margaret Fuller

☞ "...only l[e] every deformi[ty] be excluded, every weakne[ss] impediment [of] decay, and whatever else [is] not suited to [a] kingdom.... B[ut] since we have

Encased Ing[...]

to tell us wha[t] this spiritual body is, o[r] how great its beauty is, I suspect that a[n] utterance published concerning it[...] rash." ~ Saint Augustin[e]

☞ I was in a Printing house in Hell & saw the method in which knowledge is transmitted from generation to generation. 1. In the first chamber was a Dragon-Man, clearing away the rubbish from a caves mouth; within, a number of Dragons were hollowing the cave, 2. In the second chamber was a Viper folding round the rock & the cave, and others adorning it with gold silver and precious stones. 3. In the third chamber was an Eagle with **wings** and feathers of air, he caused the **inside** of the cave to be infinite, around were numbers of Eagle like men, who built palaces in the immense cliffs. 4. In the fourth chamber were Lions of flaming fire raging around & melting the metals into living fluids. 5. In the fifth chamber were Unnam'd forms, which cast the metals into the expanse. 6. There they were receiv'd by Men who occupied the sixth chamber, and took the forms of books & were arranged in libraries.

~ William Blake,
'The Marriage of Heaven & Hell'

d Heart

☞ To seek the way back, turn to 222; to find the back way, turn to 228.

☞ To fly away, turn to page 39, 190, or 249.

☞ To occupy the sixth chamber, donate this book to a library, writing a note here for the next reader(s) to find.

Exhibit V

It's all about breath. Before, during, after. Everything comes down to breath, including voicing. Orating. Singing. Beyond the aforementioned archaic meaning of "hand": "is" (from the Aryan *as*, "to breathe") "not" (the Sanskrit *na*, "to be lost, to perish").[clxxviii] HAND IS NOT [LOST]. In voicing: "breath accumulates behind the vocal cords. The pressure builds. Before long, the pressure becomes so great that the vocal cords can no longer maintain their seal..."[clxxix]

[*Enter:* Phantom limbs.]

Reduced to four morphemes, one negates, yet: "HAND IS NOT [LOST]." To understand [HAND] is to grasp: manipulations, ever roused by breath. Vibrating, the "undersurface of sounds" animates (even in stillness) as breath pulses "like the sweet sound / that breathes upon a bank of violets, / stealing and giving odour."[clxxx] The scent of music:

[*Chorus:* Breathing.]

Inspiring; expiring. Volume, intonation, pitch: no longer resting. Prodding, tonguing, teething (as simple, as difficult as glottals, glides, liquids, stops) arbitrary sounds, like *love*—irreducibly bid & bound, complicating & constricting the acts to follow:

[*Chorus:*]

Strophe: *Clamore!*
Antistrophe: *Amore, more, ore, re, e.*

A handless voice transforms: a *din* into *love, increase* into *mineral, solemnization* into a *letter. Amore, more, ore, re, e:* clamoring.

Strophe: *Clamore!*
Antistrophe: *Amore, more, ore, re, e.*

Echo's curse becomes nature's antiphony. Lamenting (until only her voice remained), her song taunts my silence to move: invisibly transmuting to other hands. Like Kircher explained: "But as I pursue her, she runs away, while I run away, she pursues me, and she redoubles her voices by taking on additional voices like attendants, as she seductively tricks me and I cry aloud, for she is incapable of yielding."[clxxxi] *Amore...*

201

More... "...an act of touch may reproduce itself as an acoustical event," writes Scarry.[clxxxii] *Ore...* With echoes of da Vinci, "so sound will fall and bounce back from the original concussion to the concavity and to the ear."[clxxxiii] *Re-*garding Crooke, I ponder three (sounds, not to mention speakers) arising from this one: "As therefore no ƒound is made without two bodyes mutually impeaching or offending one againƒt another, as euen our Sight and Hearing doe ƒufficiently teach vs."[clxxxiv] Three, two, one: *Upon hearing* my *words in* your*...lips shut with stinging, sweet...?*[clxxxv]

[*Chorus:*]

Clamoring within this body, this instrument, I try to hear: vibrations (inlaid cavities: mouth in head, in body, whose arms outstretch) whose pressure mounts to release a voice that *reaches, gropes, carries.* Like Ricci wrote: "the whole point of writing something down is that your *voice* will then *carry* for thousands of miles, whereas in direct conversation it fades at a hundred paces."[clxxxvi] *Amore, more, ore, re, e...*

[*Exit:* Phantom limbs.]

Through ear trumpets and megaphone mouths, I listen for more (echoes): beyond clamors outside my skin's armor to the clamor within, breathing life into the question: "Would you cure a singer of her voice?"[clxxxvii] (*Echo:* HAND IS NOT...) Generating more gestures, my masquerade (here as Punch) may not *cure* but *cur-at-e* (isolating "at," *to indicate presence or occurrence in, on, or near*): breath.[clxxxviii] Breathing, I revive to re-call: the controlled decrescendo, syllable by sibylla, breaking down to silence, to reply. Muscles constrict and relax; abdomen fills and inflates lungs, to wedge open my throat. My mouth cries *Amore. Echoing.* My breath becomes a hand that holds your ear, for a second helping it hear, to let me go.

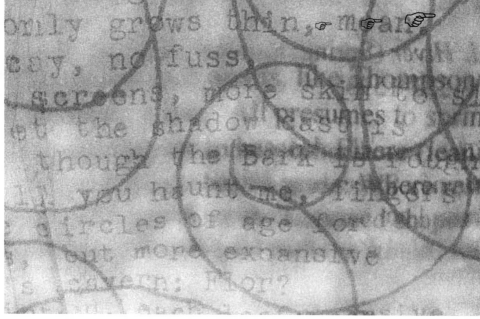

202

☞ To let Bea go, turn to page 197 or 239.

☞ To let go of preconceptions of this story,
   turn to page 65, 129, or ____ (fill in blank).

Dear Gloria (and Bea, this concerns you, too):

A few months have passed, more like a year. I've adapted my lifestyle, adjusted whatever sense of "normal" I knew to something more flexible and changing, concentrating on what I can do rather than what I can't. Behind the scenes, it's easier to make changes, but "going public" has been harder. But let's leave memoir out of this, particularly if I decide to add my diary to your Galerie de Difformité, as my Subscriber's contribution (with YOU ARE HERE). At least I can say, vaguely, that I work part-time as a consultant to my old job and have decided to take a detour: into installation art. Auditing a class at a neighboring community college (housed in an old mental asylum, at that), installation strikes me as "a back way in" to your Galerie...

For the past few weeks, we've covered a circuitous history of the artform, sprung from the last century yet tethered to ancient forms, which were incomplete without participants. Each class introduces new artists and terminology, a range of materials (fishnet, coupons, gutter guards, chicken wire, jars, gold leaf, sugar cubes, skin, gas masks, etc.), actions (categorizing, diagramming, neglecting, wrapping, disassembling, looping, shrinking, exploding), and skills (designing maquettes, casting, welding, building & dismantling walls, manipulating digital video to invite viewers to interact)—all feeding discussions about designing a full-fledged installation.

At present, students are working on public "interventions," taking cues from community projects, performances, constructed sets, altered architecture, fake advertising, socio-political confrontations, to name a few possibilities. While understanding a bit about my physical limitations, the professor asked if I'd like to do more than audit, which led me to think of possibilities related to your Galerie, even peripherally...relevant to this campus...which led me to confront something I'd been dancing around but not with: ACCESSIBILITY.

Your Galerie butts up against this very word in a way, with its form and content that's accessible yet isn't. Regardless, at your disposal lies the sprawl of an unbound book, while my challenge reduces a similar scope to a short-term, ephemeral intervention. Starting with your Exhibits—not their texts, rather generic labels: A, B, C, &c.—one idea led to another, until a map emerged with the following "key":

YOU ARE HERE: This ubiquitous phrase often marks maps, helping to orient viewers to public spaces: whether in a museum, a subway, or a city. Around campus, you may notice "Exhibits" (colored paper signs: A-Z), as well as lettered maps: all part of an "intervention" to draw attention to disability and accessibility. By keeping "Exhibits" unnamed (A-Z), they hopefully rouse curiosity about the curated collection and, secondarily, become exhibits with political implications (allied with "exhibits" in a legal trial). Areas that have been made accessible include the word "Exhibit" crossed out; areas that need redress include just the label "Exhibit."

Exhibits A, B, C, D, E, F G	Exhibits G, H, , J, K, L, M	Exhibits N, O, P, Q, R, 	Exhibits T, U, V, W, , Y, Z

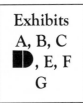

A few campus sites barely suggest the larger picture that encompasses a range of physical, mental, and sensory impairments—many visible, many invisible—that affect people's day-to-day living with variant conditions, in the midst of social and cultural responses to "unruly" bodies and varying accessibilities. What I hope this "intervention" demonstrates, in some small way, is that "disability" is not about *them* but rather about *us*. Recent articles in our own campus newspaper have discussed admitting more students who are disabled, meeting student needs with accommodations, promoting diversity, maintaining the integrity of historical buildings while making them accessible, etc. The U.S. Census of 2000 identified 20 percent of the population as people with disabilities, and 10 percent of our student population currently identify themselves with a disability. These percentages continue to rise. Does this say more about those bodies or their environments? Concurrently, programs in Disability Studies have proliferated at the undergraduate and graduate levels, fostering interdisciplinary collaborations to think anew about disability and Universal Accessibility from the vantages of not only medicine, engineering, and architecture, but also art, literature, and music, helping to illuminate this often stigmatized, misunderstood, and misrepresented aspect of our collective human condition:

"Like people in all times and places, most of us have been, are now, or (as we age) will be people with disabilities. Despite its universality, however, disability is not uniform or immutable. The nature of disability, the kinds of conditions that are considered disability, and the meanings attached to disability all vary with time and place. To a significant extent, disability is socially and culturally constructed rather than given: it has a history."
~ *Joseph Straus*

"When a disabled body moves into a social space, the lack of fit exposes the shape of the normative body for which the space was originally designed...While people with disabilities have little power in the social world, their identities possess great theoretical power because they reflect perspectives capable of illuminating the ideological blueprints used to construct social reality."
~ *Tobin Siebers*

"Because our prevailing representations constrict disability's complexities, they not only restrict the lives and govern the bodies of people we think of as disabled but also limit the imagination of those who think of themselves as non-disabled."
~ *Rosemarie Garland Thomson*

"Disability is not a brave struggle or 'courage in the face of adversity.' Disability is an art. It's an ingenious way to live."
~ *Neil Marcus*[clxxxix]

In preparing this "intervention," I interviewed a variety of people around campus for ideas of sites and history and also was able to contact a professor who taught here in the 1980s and returned last year for a visit. She chose to leave to teach at a more accessible campus and said: "I think that the biggest sea change is the fact that the campus now sees disability as an issue that they need to address to become the kind of community that they want to be as opposed to addressing issues piecemeal for someone stuck between floors of an inaccessible building...When I came to visit last spring, so much had changed...but the small part that still needs to be addressed is the piece that could make it a completely different culture." She described her teaching experience back in the 1980s, with Spina bifida, having to crawl up stairs in buildings without lifts, having a "travel adventure" each time she needed an accessible bathroom, incurring injuries trying to get in and out of buildings. She posed the following questions: "Can a person really have the whole college experience, the whole of what that means, if the campus remains partially inaccessible? Are students who are disabled here able to be known *not* first for their disability? Who do we risk losing, and lose, by keeping spaces inaccessible? How do we value the various contributions [disabled] people make in that stage of their lives?" She added: "When you're fighting for disability issues, you don't always realize you're fighting for a redefinition of what it means to be human."[cxc]

I think these questions echo your own, Gloria, even if the Intervention was a deviation from your more obscure (might some readers say "inaccessible"?) Galerie. How else might you have interpreted the assignment; how else might you have intervened? Would you have endorsed this intervention, or challenged it, designing something differently? What's the median between aesthetics and politics, form and content, all counterparts, messily hitched? At what point does a person ask to be accommodated, in a political sense, in order to participate and not retreat for the wrong reasons? If exclusions endanger, can we envision ourselves in ever-changing forms, naturally or bursting at the seams, being repieced: transplanted, grafted, cyborged, and the rest, retrofitting identities that currently fall along stricter lines of race, gender, religion, disability, age, nationality, genetics, and other classifications? Is the label of "disabled" disabling? Is something in the wings making way for new states of Being?

G.H.

☞ *To make this book more (in)accessible, turn to 221.*

☞ *To make way for new states of Being, turn to 197 or ____ (fill in blank).*

☞ *To reconsider your identity, turn to page 12, 80, 103, 150, or 189.*

☞ *To see Intervention Kit, turn to page 247m.*

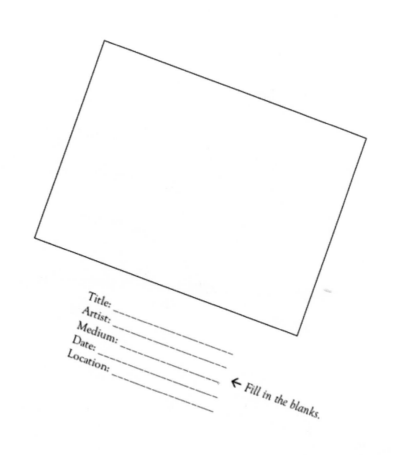

Title: ------------------
Artist: ------------------
Medium: ------------------
Date: ------------------
Location: ------------------

← *Fill in the blanks.*

☞ To not be daunted by this hole, follow directions on page 220, then add a future directive on this page.

☞ To consider this as a conceptual work, leave it as is & proceed wherever you like.

☞ To fit the whole book inside a box, fashion one for that purpose.

The action or an act of redefining something. 1857 O. E. ELLIS *Half Cent. Princ. Controv.* 380 If we take any one of the obscurest problems in doctrinal or speculative theology we find it to be involved with terms each of which asks for **re-definition**, or a rectification of its popular or scholastic interpretation. 1865 D. MASSON *Rec. Brit. Philos.* 106 The whole tenor of his labours was towards an assertion, purification, and **redefinition** of Transcendentalism. 1942 A. HUXLEY *On Living in Revol.* 13 A **redefinition** of the status of colonies. 1956 *Nature* 25 Feb. 370/1 Many, and perhaps all, scientific advances involve the **re-definition** of terms. 1970 S. L. BARRACLOUGH in T. E. Horowitz *Mass. in Lat. Amer.* iv. 125 Another effect of changing technology is to force a **redefinition** of the traditional relationship between peasants and management. 2007 *N.Y. Times* (National ed.) 16 Aug. E1 Doctors around the country are noting a democratization of cosmetic medicine, a **redefinition** of it as a coveted yet attainable luxury purchase.

Title: Redefinition.
Artist: Oxford English Dictionary, 2nd edition
Medium: English Language
Location: Online Database

☞ *To redefine this book, turn to page 9 or 230.*

☞ *If you have fears or doubts, please turn to page 222.*

☞ *To consider deformity as natural, turn the page.*

Title: _____
Artist: _____
Medium: _____
Date: _____
Location: _____

Examination:
The State of this Book

DIRECTIONS: *Read through the entire examination before making any marks. If you do not feel prepared to be examined, retrace your steps & keep (re)viewing.*

1. Write "Deformity as Natural" as caption in the space for *Title*.
2. Write "Gloria Heys" as the *Artist*.
3. Write "Ink and paper" as the *Medium*.
4. Write "c. 2004" in the space for *Date*.
5. Write "US" as the *Location*.
6. Ignore directions 1-5 (above), following directions 7-13 (below) instead:
7. Find an image on http://difformite.wordpress.com, deform & affix it inside (or around, over, in the general vicinity of) the box above.
8. Write the title of your choice in the space for *Title*.
9. Write both the artist's name & your name as *Artist*.
10. Write the *Medium* to correspond with your deformation.
11. Write this year for *Date*.
12. Write your location (street, city, country, continent, hemisphere, planet, GPS, or some other geographical identifier) for *Location*.
13. Continue to read the Examination before making any marks. Once you have read the entire section, please respond in the space provided by imitating the voice(s) of the Author.

From *Curiosity* to *Caricature*, *Spectacle* to *Sublime*, and all other essays and exhibits

herein, ephemera & et cetera, this *Galerie de Difformité* has attempted to provide a funhouse, reflecting visual and verbal representations of *Deformity*. Considering changing

social perceptions and our roles in these processes, the *Galerie de Difformité* has highlighted

related artworks, if only a few. (For review, see *Undertaker's Note on the Text, page 14*:

"Upon the merits of the pictures themselves, it is not for me to speak, except with relation

of each to Deformity...") As with any collection, presences suggest absences, and a long list

of alternative artworks could have been added, headed under *Deformity as Panorama, as*

Bazaar, as Urn, as Claude Glass, as Allegory, as Metamorphosis, as Mashup, as Cutup, as Mixtape,

as Blogroll, as Second Life...the list is as broad, yet paradoxically parochial, as it appears. The

presentation itself has been a deformation of genres, where stories progress in margins and

between lines, negotiating bibliographic borders while transgressing those bounds.

Likewise, the act of classification has worked both with and against itself, like Tobin

Siebers explains: *Category* "derives from the Greek kategorema, meaning a public

denunciation or accusation. Categorical thought is accusatory logic."[cxci]   In concluding

this *Galerie de Difformité*, it seems apropos to suggest a legacy of this history, which also is

our present: *that is*, "A State of This Book."

PART A: Please write "a legacy of this history, which also is our present: that is,
'A State of This Book.'" As noted in the Directions, please imitate the voice(s) of
the Author, providing a possible path for the future of this Book. Points will be
added for illegibility and deducted for neatness. If more space is needed, use extra
materials, which later can be affixed into or around these pages.

☞ E.g., *State of This Book*: I'm still thinking about ultimate "pay off": how and what to unearth as the bone with the heart-shaped hole? The book itself is the relic, and materially speaking, I'd like to align the bone more with the book—perhaps with the heart-shaped hole cut through the tome? But in tandem, I'm also hoping that readers might travel at least a few paths that offer more resolution (for lack of a better word), finding fictional counter-parts to points raised in the apologia (i.e., *Exhibit A, pg. 234*). What ways might that narratively work? Without being heavy handed, how might I draw attention to the fact that readers have spent however many pages seeking out a mysterious fictional bone, while heaps of unidentified bones lie in mass graves, past and potentially future, leaving us to question whether those bones hold our own heart-shaped holes? With so many strands raveled together, a reader can follow each as it unravels, to leave or restitch, in both cases deforming the material that's present, while getting a sense of some whole (as opposed to hole) to consider not only Bea but also...

Part B: Add a section entitled "Deformity as _____," addressing an angle not covered in the Book & including a boxed description of a representative image. Points will be added for using microfont or otherwise (mis)representing or calling attention to (in)accessibility, &c. As before, points will be added for illegibility and deducted for neatness. If more space is needed, use extra materials, which later can be affixed into or around these pages.

Title: _____
Artist: _____
Medium: _____
Date: _____
Location: _____

In summarizing the Romantic movement in *The Great Chain of Being: A Study of the History of an Idea*, Arthur O. Lovejoy wrote "in the entire history of thought, [there have] been few changes in standards of value more profound and more momentous than that which took place when the contrary principle began widely to prevail—when it came to be believed....that diversity itself is of essence of excellence; and of art, in particular, the objective is neither the attainment of some single ideal perfection of form in a small number of fixed *genres*...but rather the fullest possible expression of the abundance of differentness that there is, actually or potentially, in nature and human nature," including "the aesthetic legitimacy of the *genre mixte*," "the naturalization in art of the 'grotesque,'" "the endeavor to reconstruct in imagination the distinctive inner life of peoples remote in time or space or in cultural condition," "the *étalage du moi*," and (among other aspects) "the feeling of 'the glory of the imperfect.'"[cxcii]

Lovejoy published these words in 1936, and the encouragement of diversity (with glaring examples otherwise, promoting uniformity through genocide) has continued through the 20th century into the 21st. But 'the glory of the imperfect' has been accompanied by 'the banality of the monstrous,' so to speak, where nothing startles, and all can be collapsed into sameness. Considering consequences of culture wars and world wars, developments in medical and technological fields, and ever-extending notions of entertainment: the glory of diversity rings almost hollow at a time when the most bizarre and horrific are taken as representative and negligible, where Otherness appears in a range of stark to subtle shades, often at neglect of our own short-sightedness and vulnerabilities. My problem remains: Beatrice's bone-with-a-heart-shaped hole, while treated as an antiquated relic throughout this *Galerie*, may symbolize an ongoing deformation of *deformity*, *disability*, and other terms that reflect distortions: less in our bodies than in our perceptions, of others and of ourselves.[cxciii] (*See Appendix: Index of Indicators & Dictionary of Deformed Ideas, page 247d+v.*)

And this is where I step into the picture frame, more present than my Authorial and Curatorial roles have admitted. I have been inducting you, dear Subscriber and Inheritor, to be my Undertaker as much as my esteemed Bea. Among other *OED* definitions, an *Undertaker* refers to the following:

One who aids or assists; a helper.

A rebuker, reprover.

One who undertakes a task or enterprise. Also const. of (the thing attempted).

One who takes up a challenge.

One who makes a business of carrying out the arrangements for funerals.

One who engages in the serious study of a subject or science.

A baptismal sponsor.

One who undertakes the preparation of a literary work.

As for me...

[Gretchen's Note: *Gloria Heys' original section ends here, torn.*]

Examination Ends Here.

The Destruction Room

A room full of interesting Books, or at least when cut up will be so, as far as regards the places they refer to, and quietly waiting an opportunity to be changed from generals to particulars.

During
dressmaking
time good shears

To see the footnote that Gretchen added, please turn to page 230. ☞

☜ Close the book & open randomly to continue your deforming path. ☞

☜ To find a letter from Gretchen to Gloria, visit page 185 or read below.

Dear Gloria,

I've started to dream about your Galerie becoming an actual gallery, to travel in the tradition of freak shows. I'm not sure if I can physically proceed with that prospect, unless enabled by other hands to carry out its potential dimensions. If I can retrofit or even curate accommodation into your project, inviting co-creation to decreate the body of your book....hopefully, my lengthy footnote to "The Destruction Room" will help, accompanied by a virtual prototype and invitation, with variations on the theme depending on circumstances, starting as follows:

---------- Forwarded message ----------
From: **Gretchen Henderson** <difformite@gmail.com>
Date: Mon, 09/09/XX09 at 9:00 AM
Subject: Galerie de Difformité (Update)
To: difformite@gmail.com

My dear Subscriber ~ !

Thank you so much for your interest in Gloria Heys' *Galerie de Difformité* project. As a "gallery," this manuscript is meant to grow beyond the bounds of a "book" in different stages over the next couple of years. For this to happen, I'm enlisting "Subscribers" ~ a very minimal commitment, which need only happen this one time, more if you like. To participate, please download a copy of an "Exhibit" from the project's website < http://difformite.wordpress.com/ > to deform however you like. Once you have materially deformed your "Exhibit," please email me a representation (e.g., digital image) of the metamorphosed product, to post on the site with your permission. Early submissions will be considered for inclusion in the published book. Further instructions and examples can be found on the website. (You may credit using your actual name, a persona, anonymously, what have you.) *Galerie de Difformité* will deform in stages; subsequent invitations will be included in the book and online. If you know of other artists, writers, colleagues, students, teachers, friends, enemies, bedfellows, strangers, et cetera, who might be interested, I'll be most grateful if you can send them my way. The more, the merrier ~

Thanks for your interest in this project!

All good wishes,
the Undertaker

☞ *To return to the decoy application, turn to page 12.*
☞ *To see some Subscriber's deformations, flip through this book or scan here:*

Foreshadow or Flashback to
The Destruction Room?

IF A BLANK BOX LED HERE, choose from the following boxes: ↓	OR	IF AN IMAGE LED HERE, follow the directions in the box below: ↓

http://difformite.wordpress.com

1. Find an image in 👆 online *Galerie*, electronically copy & enlarge it beyond bounds of the blank box, print (color or black-and-white) & paste over box.

2. Find an image from the online *Galerie*, electronically copy & shrink it within bounds of the blank box, print (in color or black-and-white) and paste in the box or in margins.

3. Find an online image NOT from the *Galerie*, & proceed with instructions 1 or 2, as the spirit moves you.

4. Find an image from any book & reproduce it (photocopying, drawing, tracing, etc.) to transfer it into this *Galerie*.

5. Collage: ignore or incorporate the box & caption as you like.

6. Draw over the page, ignoring or incorporating the box & caption.

7. Spray the page with perfume.

8. Soak page in ice to decrease its inflammation.

9. Stuff page with sage & garnish with rosemary.

10. Rub page with dark chocolate, serve with red wine.
11. Stain with tea, red cabbage, or walnut shells.
12. Compost page or the whole book.

Cut out the image to re-place outside this book (in another book, on your refrigerator, on a bulletin board at a local coffee shop or bus depot, etc.) Once image is re-placed, photograph its new context to share, perhaps with the Undertaker.

Amend original page: strengthen frame with band-aids or sutures. Affix materials behind page as a window to view something new. Alternatively, leave space open to the elements. On the subsequent page write a message over existing text (e.g., "peek-a-boo") to read through the frame. Decorate as desired. After deforming, photograph its new context to share, perhaps with the Undertaker.

Continue reading from where you left off: 33, 45, 49, 57, 68, 72, 94, 98, 113, 117, 136, 140, 147, 151, 155, 167, 171, 182, 186, 196, 203, 207, or ___.

☞ *Return from where you came.*

How to Make this Book More (In)Accessible

(a very cursory & cursorily deformed starter list)

1. Use a magnifying glass, ZoomText, microscope, opera glass, or other vision-related technology to enlarge or shrink text until it is legible or illegible.
2. Use the computerized functions of Cut and Paste, or graphics applications like Photoshop or Paintbrush, to move around and manipulate textual locations, legibilities, and orientations.
3. Read the text aloud into Dragon Naturally Speaking, MacSpeech, or a similar voice-activated technology to see what words are rendered back to you.
4. Wear ear plugs while listening to someone read the text aloud. Either lip-read or listen to the muffled sounds, then transcribe what you think is being said. Try this repeatedly with different speakers and/or grades of ear plugs.
5. Use a version of Kurzweil to scan the book into your computer, to have it read to you aloud. Write down whatever words you can without pausing the equipment. Alternatively, talk back as it speaks. Alternatively, sing along.
6. Insert text into a translation engine, like Babel Fish, then retranslate the translated language into English.
7. Apply Oulipian and other experimental exercises and devices to existing text.
8. Scan the book to make an electronic version, then use a Braille embosser to print the text in Braille.
9. With scanned/electronic version (*see* #8), use JAWS for computer to read it aloud. (JAWS also can provide Braille output in addition to, or instead of, speech.)
10. Find a sign language interpreter (or learn ASL), then communicate the book via video relay service.
11. Learn about other assistive technologies (UbiDuo, Daisy, etc.) as a means of learning how books can deform to access their meaning. Do an Internet search for "What is assistive technology?" to get more ideas, not only for the *Galerie de Difformité*, but for books in general.
12. Leave the book in a public place to be environmentally deformed (*see page 220*).
13. Visit "The Destruction Room" (*page 230*) and follow directions, or take your own interpretive license.
14. If you care to deform the novel as hypertext, please contact the Undertaker.
15. Cross out the above instructions & (or) insert with updated technologies.

☞ *To consider this as an intervention, please turn to page 204.*

☞ *If you fear that you don't understand this in context of the book, keep reading.*

EXHIBIT K

[from *bone pomes*^{cxciv}]

I have this fear   that I won't find the way back   the birds

will have eaten all the crumbs   I won't find my notches on

the trees   that when I get "there"   I won't find

anyone   I have this fear that if I dig   into myself

turn around   swallow me and grin   a bee's or witch's

or serpent's head   will turn around to embrace myself

that when I do reach myself   I have this fear   the marrow

flushed out   stripped flesh from bone   the

blood vessels   that if I drain   that if I take off

my skin   I have this fear   the fear that I'm

the dreamwork   inside someone else's skull   clearing

and darkening   that I come and go   that I'm

an image   I have this fear   that I don't

know my names   that I have many names   that I

have no names   I have this fear

☞ To assuage your fear, turn to page 166 or ____ (fill in blank).
☞ To face your fear, turn to 194.
☞ For alphabetic options, turn to 224.

Lineage of a Bone

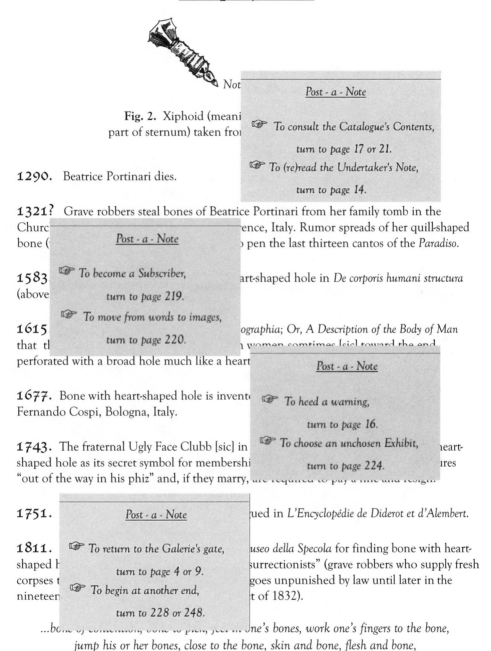

Not[...]

Fig. 2. Xiphoid (mean[...] part of sternum) taken fro[...]

Post - a - Note

☞ *To consult the Catalogue's Contents,*
turn to page 17 or 21.

☞ *To (re)read the Undertaker's Note,*
turn to page 14.

1290. Beatrice Portinari dies.

1321? Grave robbers steal bones of Beatrice Portinari from her family tomb in the Churc[...]ence, Italy. Rumor spreads of her quill-shaped bone ([...] pen the last thirteen cantos of the *Paradiso*.

Post - a - Note

☞ *To become a Subscriber,*
turn to page 219.

☞ *To move from words to images,*
turn to page 220.

1583. [...]art-shaped hole in *De corporis humani structura* (above[...]

1615. [...]ographia; Or, A Description of the Body of Man that th[...] women somtimes [sic] toward the end perforated with a broad hole much like a heart[...]

Post - a - Note

☞ *To heed a warning,*
turn to page 16.

☞ *To choose an unchosen Exhibit,*
turn to page 224.

1677. Bone with heart-shaped hole is invent[...] Fernando Cospi, Bologna, Italy.

1743. The fraternal Ugly Face Clubb [sic] in [...] heart-shaped hole as its secret symbol for membershi[...]res "out of the way in his phiz" and, if they marry, are required to pay a fine and resign.

Post - a - Note

☞ *To return to the Galerie's gate,*
turn to page 4 or 9.

☞ *To begin at another end,*
turn to 228 or 248.

1751. [...]ued in *L'Encyclopédie de Diderot et d'Alembert*.

1811. [...]useo della Specola for finding bone with heart-shaped h[...]surrectionists" (grave robbers who supply fresh corpses t[...]goes unpunished by law until later in the nineteen[...]t of 1832).

...bo[...]ne's bones, work one's fingers to the bone, jump his or her bones, close to the bone, skin and bone, flesh and bone, blood and bone, make old bones, dry as a bone, bred in the bone...

EXHIBIT F

A list of those Exhibits that might, could, would, or should have been visited in the *Galerie de Difformité*, rearranged here alphabetically:—

A is for......, as if to explain,	} *234*
B is for......, that swarms through the brain:	} *198*
C is for........, bleeding through pages,	} *78*
D is for......, sleeping with sages.	} *42*
E is for....., who bundles all verse,	} *247*
F is for......, this summary terse!	} *224*
G is for.........., that grows out of bounds,	} *180*
H is for.........., that affords us these rounds.	} *39*
I am the Author, a rhymer erratic—	} *148*
And **J** is for........, who dares the pathetic:	} *164*
K is for.........., who finally sees,	} *222*
L is for.........., that invisible Bea.	} *105*
M is for......, retracing all courses,	} *55*
And **N** is......, compressing all sources.	} *129*
..........is for **O**, hiding under the sea,	} *177*
And **P** is for......., trying to move free:	} *145*
Q is the..........., that wants for collection	} *131*
While **R** is for......., that revives with dissection.	} *126*
S is for......, sworn foe of strict rules,	} *162*
T is for......, needing fine rhythmic tools.	} *110*
U's........., whose action is missing	} *242*
While **V** is the........, ceaselessly listing.	} *201*
W's........., by Museum made frantic,	} *58[1], 61[2], 65[3]*
X the xiphoid, grown quite pedantic.	} *91*
Y offers *you*, whom nobody thought about—	} *245*
Z is the Zoo that this gallery grows about.[cxcv]	} *247*

☜☞ *Choose any of the above Exhibits & go to the indicated page.*

☜☞ *If you have visited all Exhibits, thumb through the Galerie & find an unvisited page.*

☜☞ *If you have missed the Contents of the Catalogue, turn to page 17 or 21.*

☜☞ *To read other letters, turn to: 46, 69, 95, 114, 137, 152, 168, 183, 204, or 218.*

you are here

•

In a work that purports to be presented by an "Undertaker" (with all those implications, at once anonymous but also tethered to the mysterious personage of Beatrice Portinari), Gloria Heys undertook a project of: assisting, rebuking, attempting, challenging, burying, exhuming, studying, christening, dissecting, preparing—*undertaking*, in all manners of speaking. That isn't to say that her project was totalized or completed. Far from it. Indeed, of the materials sent to this "Subscriber," she failed to put to rest the ghost she conjured, leaving that spirit to haunt: *me*, at least, and perhaps now *you*. Beyond our family's lineage (derived from that infamous bone with its heart-shaped hole), there seems to me a particular reason why Gloria allied herself with Beatrice—whose physical features are lost to posterity, left to be envisioned as "beautiful" and "deformed" by whichever eyes try to behold her.

As eyes can be masked, I have joined with you to pass the ghost of this *Galerie de Difformité* into other hands, to be deformed further by future Subscribers. In searching for the MONSTER in this book, no less trying to undertake it, I wonder whether you, like I, have faced a kind of projecting machine—not unlike that invented by Athanasius Kircher (described in *Physiologia* in 1680) that provided "a thousand ways to deform a [wo]man," wherein one discovers "no monster is so ugly whose shape you will not find in yourself."[cxcvi]   And in so doing, undertaking our own monsters (*that is:* assisting, rebuking, attempting, challenging, burying, exhuming, studying, christening, dissecting, preparing—*undertaking*, in all manners of speaking), I would venture to add that we have, or might yet, discover something more, like Gloria anticipated, as she provided "a thousand ways to beautify a

225

person," wherein one discovers "no being is so beautiful whose shape you will not find in yourself."

And so, you are left with self-reflection.

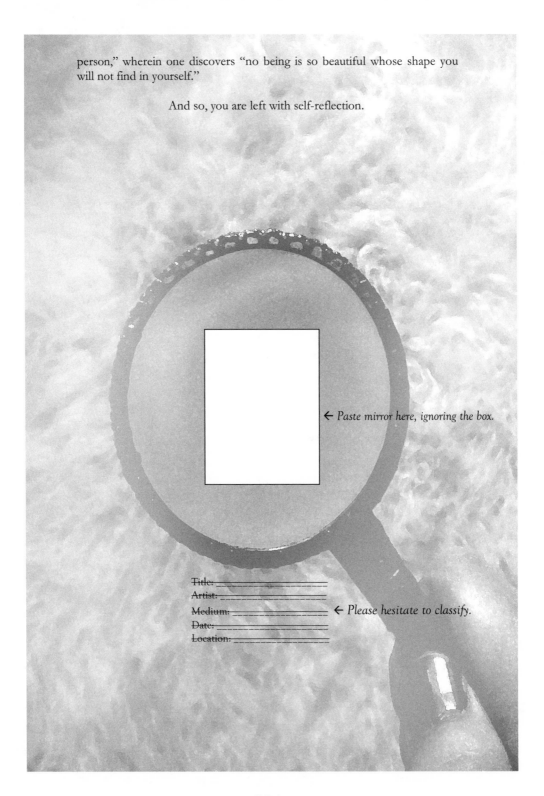

← *Paste mirror here, ignoring the box.*

Title: _____
Artist: _____
Medium: _____   ← *Please hesitate to classify.*
Date: _____
Location: _____

☞ This manuscript arrived to the Publisher from the Author's estate with announcement of the "Death of the Author." (The "Author" being Gretchen Henderson, using the pseudonym of "Gretchen Henderson.") Said manuscript arrived with instructions for binding and unbinding, including a signature entitled "Portrait of the Artist as Deformed" (as well as a jar of ashes with the same caption). Also included was a proposal for transforming the *Galerie de Difformité* into an actual gallery, first executed on a small scale virtually, using "Exhibits" deformed artistically by "Subscribers." The proposal explained: "As a 'gallery,' the manuscript is meant to grow beyond the bounds of a 'book' in different stages," including post-publication, when Subscribers can metamorphose the published book-object for an actual exhibit to travel in the tradition of an antiquated freak show. As stated on the Frontispiece: "As the Number of SUBSCRIBERS to the GALERIE DE DIFFORMITÉ must be limited, it is recommended to those, who have any design of becoming Subscribers, to be as early as possible in their Application."

☞ *To Subscribe, turn to page 11, 12, or 219.*

☞ This manuscript arrived to the Publisher from the Author's estate with announcement of the "Death of the Author." (The "Author" being Gloria Heys; Gretchen Henderson was a figment of Ms. Heys' imagination, fabricated for the purpose of her book.) Upon access to the Author's belongings, it was discovered that the Author owned an unusual ballpoint pen whose quartet of cartridges was dry, except for red. Upon further inspection, it was discovered that the pen's barrel held sliver-like fragments that scientists confirmed as human bone. No further identification has been performed.

☞ *To reconsider the source, turn to page 31, 70, or 223.*

☞ G.H.'s manuscript arrived electronically to the Publisher with announcement of the "Death of the Reader." The manuscript was deemed unmarketable, deleted from the Publisher's Inbox, and received a form rejection letter via email.[cxcvii]

☞ *To revive the Reader & fill in missing blanks, turn to page 209 or 242.*

☞ This manuscript arrived to the Publisher from the Author herself (the living author, Gretchen Henderson, to be distinguished from the character Gretchen Henderson) with an invitation for the Publisher to become a Subscriber, as well as instructions to extend the invitation to other potential Subscribers: to deform Gloria Heys' *Galerie de Difformité*. The Author could not be reached for further comment, but left addendum stating that she will be fingerpainting, crumpling, unraveling, singing, & otherwise decreating (physically and/or psychically), until further notice.

☞ *To co-create with the Author, turn to page 220, 221, or 230.*

Paradise is
now shut and locked,
barred by angels;
so now
we must
go forward,
around the
world, and
see if
some- how,
some- where
there is
a back way
i

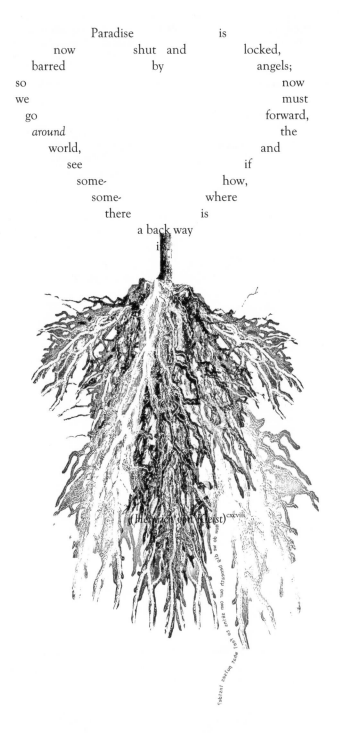

(Heinrich von Kleist)^{cxcviii}

How do we get passed the two angels to get back instead?

PORTRAIT of THE ARTIST AS deformed

The Destruction Room

A room full of interesting Books, or at least when cut up will be so, as far as regards the places they refer to, and quietly waiting an opportunity to be changed from generals to particulars.[1]

During
dressmaking
time good shears

---

[1] **YOU ARE HERE:** The only footnote in this entire *Galerie de Difformité*. Not a handnote nor buttnote, but the sole and heel (even soul and heal, weak as Achilles) of this exhibitional enterprise. Being the only footnote, a responsibility is borne by what it foots—THE DESTRUCTION ROOM—that revives an extra-illustrative entity invented by Frederick Strong when he advertised himself as "neither a book or printseller" but one who sold printed ephemera "ALL DATED, CUT UP" and "ARRANGED" according to his own classification system. "In short," Lucy Peltz writes in "Facing the Text," "Strong had gone in to book-breaking." (See *Owners, Annotators and the Signs of Reading*, eds. Robin Myers, Michael Harris, and Giles Mandelbrote, 91). But Strong is dead, and I am not: guiding you now by reviving a Gentlewoman named *Bea*, for lack of a better *nom-de-plume*. Minding P's & Q's, you've found me middling while mending: "During / dressmaking / time good shears..." Facing the text, I wouldn't call myself a breaker so much as seamstress, enlisting your help to tailor this book around a budding body: the once-and-future corpse of this corpus. To survive, I need your help to evolve. To deform and reform, to dream and metamorphose (or otherwise risk misreading: me & Bea.) Open Sesame: "During / dressmaking / time good shears..." ✂✂✂✂✂✂ ✂✂✂✂✂✂✂✂✂✂✂✂✂✂✂✂✂✂✂✂✂✂✂✂✂✂✂

XXXXXXXXXXXXXXXXXXXXXXXXXXXXXXXXX
XXXXX Snip, snip...or start by sketching manicules (☞) in margins...or merely manifest a set of hypothetical instructions: "how to" build, operate, repair, maintain, recycle materials (paper, stitching, board, letters, &c). "How To" Deform This Book: 1. Make hundreds of paper dolls. 2. Make dozens of paper dresses for dozens of paper dolls. 3. Forget the dolls, and stitch all pages into one life-size dress. 4. Forget the dress, and fly origami cranes. 5. Or fold a flock of variably-shaped planes (enlisting a high school physics class). 6. Wallpaper. 7. Papier-mâché sculpture. 8. Installation art with mounds of crumpled paper. 9. Performance art, shearing & shredding & reconstructing. 10. Or otherwise demonstrate, in performative fashion, any of the above or next instructions. 11. Shred pages to fill a dream-pillow. 12. Cut confetti to celebrate whatever occasion. 13. Make ghostprints or something palimpsestual. 14. Use each page as a canvas, painting over text & leaving words exposed, yielding a new narrative. 15. Cut into pieces for scrapbooking, bricolage, collage, &c. 16. Scatter scraps near nest-building birds. 17. No bookburning (although Exhibit J may suggest otherwise). 18. Shuffle extant pages & add new exhibits, whatever your heart desires! When you've deformed the *Galerie de Difformité*, please contact me (difformite@gmail.com) to document your process, with the expectation of my curating an Exhibit from this collective enterprise. A virtual prototype can be found at difformite.wordpress.com. Images most welcome. ☞ ☞ ☞

☞ *To see a sample of deformed Exhibits, turn to page 220*
& look for a list of page #s.

☞ *To deform an Exhibit, revisit instructions on becoming*
a Subscriber by turning to page 219.

☞ *To visit Exhibit J, turn to page 164, or for an alternative*
Exhibit, consult page 224.

☞ *To read Gretchen's letters to Gloria, pick a number:*
46, 69, 95, 114, 137, 152, 168, 183, 204, 218.

☞ *To transform this book from black & white, treat it*
as a coloring book.

PLEASE INSERT CHAP→

☞ *If you're not ready to make a book*
  within or outside this book, turn to
  page 223 or 224.

←BOOK OF DEFORMATIONS.

☞ *To download a chapbook or edit*
your own, explore these options
to participate in this (re)collection.

E X H I B I T   A

There are hundreds of her. Here: she poses in shimmering gold, with burnished curls and closed eyes.[ccix] In another portrait, her gaze fades behind lavender veils. Ghostlike, she rematerializes black and white in a palm-sized chariot. Her eyes widen under a wreathed brow; her arm points toward clouds. Rising, she flits in Saturn-like rings. She's close enough to be vibrating, buzzing, close enough I presume to call her by name:

Bea.

More or less than *Beatrice*, each image is but a trace. "We have only hints and fragments of her story," Charles Williams writes in *The Figure of Beatrice*. Her replication multiplies her potential, like when Sandro Botticelli draws her in *Paradiso* amid tight-furled flames, seeming bees, unfurling angelic wings. Williams continues: "To say [that Beatrice is Dante's Knowing] is not to reduce her actuality nor her femininity. The reason for the insistence on her femininity is simple—it is that this is what Dante insisted on….not confined to romantic love of the male-female kind. Wherever the 'stupor' is, there is the beginning of art. Wherever any love is—and some kind of love in every man and woman there must be—there is either affirmation or rejection of image, in one or other form."[cc]

"Stupor": illuminated, engraved, printed, woodcut, painted, and sculpted by Sandro Botticelli, William Blake, Dante Gabriel Rossetti, Marie Spartali Stillman, Gustave Doré, Salvador Dalí, Tom Phillips (to name only a few "replicators"). And that's not to mention Dante's textual translators: Henry Wadsworth Longfellow, Laurence Binyon, Allen Mandelbaum, Robert and Jean Hollander, and so many more. "It may be startling to speak of the *Divine Comedy*," writes Elaine Scarry, "or the *Mona Lisa* as 'a replication' since they are so unprecedented, but the word recalls the fact that something, or someone, gave rise to their creation and remains silently present in the newborn object."[cci]

And that "something, or someone" leads me to ponder—beyond Dante—the many faces of Bea. Writers more traveled than I have retraced Dante's road of rendering and reckoning, all the while fleshing out details about his actual life, paying homage to his exiled bones. His physical frame is familiar, thanks to Boccaccio's description: "stooped" with "grave and sedate" gait, "seemly garments," "long face with "aquiline" nose, "rather large" eyes, and "heavy" jaws."[ccii] But Bea is another matter. Her existence has been validated only by "hints and fragments"; otherwise, little is known. Put her imagery side-by-side in a line-up, and who could tell which is the "real" she?

Reading her portraits across centuries, I look about to see: Bea upon Bea, gazing in every direction. Dozens of eyes evade my own. Centuries after Dante's death, I walk within narrow walls strewn with varied off-prints, photocopies, opened pages of her disparate forms. Watching these multifarious portraits, as if Bea were in motion, I wonder about more than the girl who compelled Dante Alighieri to invent a poetic form, to journey through the *Inferno* and *Purgatorio* and *Paradiso*, to "say of her what has never been said of any woman."[ccciii] How did someone so singular lead to something so multifold? Touched by a strange and silent stupor, I close my eyes to partake in this moment: of putting Bea away from sight, of trying to see her anew.

If this is your first visit to Exhibit A, stop reading and proceed back from where you came or consider your options on pages 18, 19, 223, or 224.

If you have visited Exhibit A before, pick up where you left off or visit…

Early in *La Vita Nuova*, Dante famously records a dream in which he's visited by Death, and Beatrice is forced to eat his heart. It's a terrifying scene, what a modern reader might consider a metaphoric stalking, followed by a rape. Despite being an admirer of Dante, I shiver upon reading this scene that foretells Beatrice's death, as if she's a sacrificial lamb: binding her physical sacrifice to poetry, blurring her existence with myth. At the same time, I would be naïve to read this scene literally. For as long as readers have journeyed through Dante's Hell and Purgatory and Heaven, Beatrice has evaded being encapsulated or reduced to any singular reading.

Quite the contrary—and yet many have tried to decipher her riddle. For centuries, scholars have debated the nature of Beatrice's presence and provenance, digging into the poetic tradition that nursed Dante's verse, her literary counterparts (like Lady Philosophy), and annals of her history: from the cost of her dowry when marrying Simone de' Bardi, to the esteemed reputation of her father, Falco Portinari (who founded a hospital serviced by the first nursing staff on record), to the location of her tomb in the Church of Santa Margherita de' Cerchi.[cciv] The particulars tell us little, ultimately, leading to the same threshold of unknowing, beyond which we must grope through our own lives and times—where Hell no longer lies below, nor Heaven above, but both commingle in our mixed-up midst.

Just search for "Dante" in the archives of the *New York Times*, *The Atlantic*, and other contemporary publications to find references not to the *Commedia* but to Rwanda, Zambia, Croatia, Iraq. More than Dantean scholarship, these figurative references point to something beyond the presence of Bea. Together with the scene where she eats Dante's heart, these references suggest to me, finally: the more I try to seek her, the less I'll know. Or said another way (like Ursula Le Guin writes in *The Left Hand of Darkness*):[ccv]

And so I ask another question, echoing the Gryphon in *Wonderland*, who cries: "Never heard of uglifying!…You know what to beautify is, I suppose?[ccvi] In kind, I wonder: Have I ever seen Bea depicted as anything *but* beautiful? If beauty is singular, why do images of her appear so differently? Do I know what it means "to beautify"? And what of "uglifying"? Bea's beauty—and I would add, her uncharted deformity—are left to the eye of each beholder, so the many faces of Bea, taken together, suggest what's missing.

The seeking of Bea becomes the seeking of "we," ever changing.ccvii More than trying to decipher *her*, then, her *ability to change* may serve as a better guide. Compiling her mostly absent pieces leads her (and *me*, with *you*) always to the threshold of an alternative *Vita Nuova*—another "new life"—even if that life in the end isn't hers. Instead, it's ours.

☞ Please gloss this essay. In other words, annotate & (or) crossreference & (or) draw your own manicules for future readings/readers. ☙

☞ Please erase this essay. Use the (partially) blank slates for new narratives, & draw manicules for future readings/readers. ☙

☞

Among the anatomical waxes collected at La Specola in Florence (Beatrice's hometown), *Venus* rests on a silky fringed pink drape. Lying prone, she's naked except for a string of pearls. From neck to pubis, her removable abdominal skin reveals six additional layers. Paradoxically modest and exhibitionist, this human model (once used to teach medicine) bears a goddess' name, while exposing budding knowledge of the female body. Unlike her counterparts (for instance, Botticelli's vertical *Venus*, rising from her scallop shell, or Salvador Dalí's *Venus de Milo with Drawers*), this *Venus'* inlaid strata remind me somehow of the *Inferno's* tiers. Anatomically waxed, her skin can be peeled down to her innermost, concealed core: embodying "new life" with a uterus full of fetus (whose tiny size, in relation to its developmental stage, defies laws of gestation). Defined by her reproductive capabilities and dressed only in a string of pearls, with a facial expression that's been called "orgasmic," La Specola's *Venus* bears a ridiculous incongruity as a corpse.ccviii

Beyond the *Anatomical Venus* in La Specola, my interest in Venus generally—in relation to Bea—is less about *her* than her *variation* across history. Her disparate depicters (including the Irish performance artist, Mary Duffy, who was born without arms and who imitates the *Venus de Milo*) tell us something about ourselves. "This is more a question about the nature of the subject than the qualities of the object," writes Lennard Davis, "more about the observer than the observed."ccix Like fickle fashions, female forms have gone in and out of favor, and icons beyond Venus have borne partial brunt. In artistic renderings of the Virgin Mary, for instance, her lithe and pale form has grown plump and aged variedly as young or old, white or black. Noteworthy too has been Mary's resemblance to Venus, particularly when holding a Cupid-like baby Jesus. A single depiction of Mary (of Venus, of Bea) doubles and troubles any singular reading of "the real thing," which holds true for representations generally: secular or sacred, female or male.

The question remains: what's the trouble with singularity? Of Mary, Pietro Amato has said that her changing face "belongs to the history of spirituality."ccx His sentiment implies that Mary's faces (plural) also reflect tensions about spirituality. A case in point: in 1999, when the *Holy Virgin Mary* by Chris Ofili (a British-Nigerian artist) appeared at the Brooklyn Museum, the painting came under attack—notably by Rudy Giuliani, then mayor of New York—for its use of elephant dung and cutouts of genitalia from pornographic magazines. Justifying the presence of materials, critics described the sacred nature of pachyderms and their dung in Africa and the cutouts as analogous to naked putti in traditional religious art. "I don't feel as though I have to defend it," the artist himself responded. "The people who are attacking this painting are attacking their own interpretation, not mine."ccxi (Another article said *Holy Virgin Mary* wouldn't have been attacked if it had been titled "My Friend Mildred.") As Ofili's artwork suggests, benign as representations seem, they have the potential to take on fatal weight. And more has come to pass: beyond defacements of saints during the Reformation, to recent violence against cartoons (of Mohammed in Denmark) and statues (the monumental Buddhas of Bamiyan in Afghanistan).[ccxii]

Without knowing if representations of Bea have been attacked, purposefully or inadvertently, I am struck by contemporary invocations to her creator, analogized in the news:

☞ "There were others living among the dead this morning. They were in shock, their bodies shredded by mortar fragments, still breathing. People who had escaped the attack moved slowly and silently through the carnage, a scene out of Dante's hell."[ccxiii]

☞ "The boulders here are hard enough that the scavengers who have taken over the abandoned quarry south of downtown prefer not to strike them directly with hammers....At dusk, when three or four blazes spew choking black clouds across the huge pit, the quarry looks like a woodcut out of Dante. A boy named Alone Banda works in this purgatory six days a week."

☞ "In response to the verdict, Mr. Sakic clapped his hands and laughed in derision....He was the protégé of Vjekoslav Luburic, the leader of all Croatian concentration camps, including Jasenovac, a sprawling 150-square-mile conglomeration of several camps. It quickly became known for a brutality that shocked even visiting Nazi officials, one of whom likened it to Dante's hell."

☞ "It's like this every day. Before I know it, I can't see straight, because it's 0400 and I've been at work for 20 hours straight, somehow missing dinner again in the process....It's not really like Ground Hog Day; it's more like a level from Dante's Inferno."

And so on. The analogies tell us less about their subjects than our own subjectivity. As if in a funhouse, cumulative Dantes (like many Beas) reveal mirrors of their makers, deforming any singular version of the subject. Which brings us back to Bea's "uncharted deformity." To speak of one of the most beautiful women as *deformed* may seem akin to depicting the Virgin smeared with shit; however, that makes as many assumptions about deformity (and shit) as about Beatrice. There's more *to deform* than common usage suggests: "to mar the appearance, beauty, or excellence of; to make ugly or unsightly; to disfigure, deface."[ccxiv] Other definitions bear more elasticity; for instance, in physics, the qualification becomes naturalized: "to alter the form of." *To difform* (*obs. rare*) further obscures negative connotations by suggesting a potentially positive imperative: "to bring out of conformity or agreement: the opposite of *conform*." Breaking the word apart at its roots also stretches its meaning: *de-* provides "the sense of undoing the action of the single verb, or of depriving (anything) of the thing or character therein expressed," paired with *form*, which can range from the visible aspect of a thing ("shape, arrangement of parts"), to its abstract consideration ("one of the elements of the plastic arts"), to behavioral decorum ("often depreciatively: mere outward ceremony or formality"), to "a set or fixed order of words" (as accords with custom, law, or ritual). Deformed another way (in reference to the "språkgrotesk"): "A softness, malformation...may be penetrated, distended by multiple languages from multiple directions, which is a process, which undermines hierarchies...which is becoming."[ccxv] Bea coming: into new forms, to be reformed and deformed further. Deforming my initial question: Are there forms that we think Bea dare not take, if she becomes too unattractive—however defined—to inspire poetry or serve as someone's guide?

Someone so blessedly banal allows us to question not only her, and her representations across history, but also how we represent ourselves. To some degree, we are our gods—at least, we play G-d whenever we presume to judge who is divine or damned, beautiful or ugly. No longer consulting diagrams of frogs to treat human ailments, or phrenologists' heads to understand the mind, we live at a time when paradoxes persist about the body and its representation, not to mention its care (i.e., "Managed Care"). Millennia after Aristotle correlated outer deformity with inner worth, and centuries after Linnaeus devised a classification for *Homo monstrous*, we often overlook actions that speak louder than politically-correct words.

In the process of factualizing and fictionalizing Bea, of deliberately erring, I'm following the lead of Lewis Thomas who wrote in "The Wonderful Mistake": "The capacity to blunder slightly is the real marvel of DNA...Biology needs a better word than 'error' for the driving force in evolution. Or maybe 'error' will do after all, when you remember that it came from an old root meaning to wander about, looking for something."[ccxxvi] Keeping in mind this notion of "error" as the foundation of our species, I imagine Bea not as singular and stagnant, but multiple and moving: as one who errs, who wanders, who's looking for something. And in looking, there lies potential communication...

In wandering about myself toward this end, the many faces of Bea communicate and teach me to consider subsequent eras that have given her new contexts. After all, the *Commedia* wasn't labeled "Divine" until after Dante's death. Thus, it seems feasible to consider the work's journeyed progression in human terms—replete with joys and sorrows, sincerities and struggles—not only in Dante's day, but also in our own. Like Osip Mandelstam writes: "It is unthinkable to read the cantos of Dante without aiming them in the direction of the present day. They were made for that. They are missiles for capturing the future. They demand commentary in the *futurum*."[ccxxvii] Mired in interpersonal and intercultural conflicts, our era likewise seems to be manifesting more of Bea's story—in the very struggle of the conjoined body and soul, trying to process its own change.

In *Metamorphosis and Identity*, Caroline Walker Bynum explores the Western obsession with change and personal identity. Speaking of "Change in the Middle Ages," she writes: "explicit, energetic, and confused efforts to understand change seem to me typical of the late twelfth century, and the terms in which Gerald [of Wales] distinguishes varieties of *mutatio* (inner and outer, nature or substance and appearance, illusion and transformation, metamorphosis and hybrid) figure in major discussions by his contemporaries."[ccxxviii] Making analogies with the present, she writes: "In our current culture wars, 'identity' tends to have divergent denotations. Nonetheless change is the test, the limit, of all denotations of the term 'identity'....Unless there is some connection, or nexus, between what was and what comes after, we tend to think we have not a change but merely two things."

Body; soul. Black; white. Red; blue. Good; evil. Before; after. Sick; healthy. Abled; disabled. Beautiful; ugly. Inner; outer. Self; other. Platitude and propaganda (and more subtle manifestations between) paint the world in terms of oppositions, rather than as two sides of the same coin. Joseph Campbell famously described the danger of becoming stuck on images, and at times that tendency has contributed to the fervor to destroy them.[ccxix] To know the answer to the wrong question constantly misleads, like John Mandeville observed: "to the one-eyed, those with two eyes will seem deformed, and to those of other religions, Christians will be the cannibals."[ccxx] Patterns elude. In many regards, our only hope is to remain wakeful, to participate in our collective change, to recognize and take responsibility for how we shape and are shaped by one another.

Like a figure in an early anatomical treatise (a lively cadaver displaying her dissected bowels, for instance, gesticulating as if carrying on an animated conversation), I too am aiming, literally and figuratively, outside and within: to reanimate more than Bea, more than the Venus or the Virgin.[ccxxi] Such icons act as vehicles toward something else. From my Western vantage, the process of renegotiating their actual and potential variations invites me to partake in the "history of spirituality" while trying to recognize an "other" always present but changing within. And so, to some degree, the *Commedia* rests in the eye of this beholder.

☞

Within my small apartment (in the "City of Angels," apropos for seeking the pseudo-celestial), all this beseeching leads me not to open my eyes, but to listen: beyond the hum of traffic on the 405 freeway, honking and barking dogs, recorded choral music, muffled voices rising from the sidewalk, to the sound of her name in my mouth, spoken more toward the Italian: "Bee-che." It sounds slightly like "bitch," with more charm. *Bice. Beatrice. Bea.* Lolling her name along my tongue, I vary her syllables with other words in which "bea" nests: *beautiful, be(a)stial, beatitude,* which reminds me of Jack Kerouac's claim: "*Beat* doesn't mean tired, or bushed, so much as it means *beato,* the Italian for *beatific:* to be in a state of beatitude, like Saint Francis, trying to love all life, trying to be utterly sincere with everyone, practicing endurance, kindness, cultivating joy of heart. How can this be done in our mad modern world of multiplicities and millions? By practicing a little solitude, going off by yourself once in a while to store up that most precious of golds: the vibrations of sincerity."[ccxxii] And so I try—

Using the hand as directive, my words attempt to do more than trace a "self," to reach outside and within the body of this essay toward events beyond Bea, to myself, to you.[ccxxiii] Today in these pages; tomorrow in some other way. In *Decreation,* Anne Carson maps the writings of Sappho, Marguerite Porete, and Simone Weil to describe how "Love dares the self to leave itself behind." Carson describes the three writers' "tellings" as "a function of self," in which each "feels moved to create a sort of dream of distance in which the self is displaced from the centre of the work and the teller disappears into the telling." "Decreation" (a neologism of Weil's) is "an undoing of the creature in us—that creature enclosed in self and defined by self. But to undo the self one must move through self, to the very inside of its definition….[as Marguerite Porete says] 'For everything that one can tell of God or write, no less than what one can think…is as much lying as it is telling the truth.'"[ccxxiv]

In offering multifold portraits of Bea, I try to move through her, through my "self, to the very inside of its definition"—flawed as that attempt (and notion of self) may be—to both embrace and evade definition, offering instead a series of gestures that manifest a self-in-motion: living and changing. Inviting the same of you. Having puzzled over "the perfect uselessness of knowing the answer to the wrong question," what remains—of Bea, of me, of we—brings the end back to the beginning, as a means of getting lost. I am getting lost, as described by Rebecca Solnit in *A Field Guide to Getting Lost:* "That thing the nature of which is totally unknown to you is usually what you need to find, and finding it is a matter of getting lost."[ccxxv] Having lost *who* ("the real she"?) to address *how* and *why,* I find ultimately not *Bea* (noun), *me* or even *we* (pronoun), but *be* (verb). The many faces of Bea beget Be. *To be or not to be,* was that all I need to ask? Or, what words might invite you to get lost in whatever way you need? I leave you to ask these words:

241

EXHIBIT U

(fill in blank)

☞ If this is your ending, turn to page 247.

☞ If you want to continue Exhibit U, turn to page 432.

☞ To reconsider the monster, turn to page 16, 250,
the copyright page, or consult "I":

244

EXHIBIT Y

In the beginning was the Verb, and the Verb was made flesh. Into *tu, vous, voi, você, du, ty, sie,* and more of *you:* in motion. And yet: according to classification, *you* became objects, direct and indirect, objects of prepositions: objective and objectifying. Tens and hundreds and thousands and millions and billions of *you.* Ah! dear friends, does that mean you and me? "[T]hings once they are named," wrote Stein, "the name does not go on doing anything to them and so why write in nouns"?[ccxxvi] Speake if you can: what are you? Though the language may seem to imply a 'you'...I believe, to impute to the flint just as much, or as little, of personality. I will roare you as gently as any Sucking Doue: I will roare and 'twere any Nightingale. How should poor little you deal with a maiden who dares to call the Tsar a bear...to magnify him, and treat him in the plural number by *You,* and by degrees to deify him by transcending Titles? Quantity of syllables...there is a modern education for you! Let the music through, find the inner you. You. A Single Person, to save the Charges of another You. I don't mean that you have not bodies..., but that all that deserves to be called *you,* is nothing else but spirit. We run tests...Then, once we had really found the real you, we...would try to find a place that provided a challenge to your best creative talents. For every quantum-mechanical branch point in your life...you have split into two or more you's riding along parallel but disconnected branches of one gigantic universal wave function. If your flesh and blood be new, You'll be no more the former You. Vicaltein can be your ticket to a newer, slimmer you: you-know-who, you counterfeit, you puppet, you. You asse you. You have

245

killed me between you—you [were a] scamp not to write before. Now tell us, we pray

you, Why thus you array you? Walk a few yards ahead of me, and look out you for all

that cross you. Not a word to Mrs. You Know Who. Be my gazelle, my wishing well...But

never you-know-what, or down you go, in you know what. Progressing...You and your

long words! I say unto you: Good people all, of every sort, Give ear unto my song; And if

you find it wondrous short, —It cannot hold you long. That it be not strange to you, I will

tell you. I shal shew yow one exampel: I in you, and ye in me. What ye rede, se you

practise it in lyfe and dede. If you men durst not vndertake it, before God, we women

would. Turne againe, my daughters; Why will you goe with mee? And do you assure us

that you are all sound men? I thought your piece was very much you. Pure, scientifick

and illustrious Spirits You are: Get you home. You have made good work, you and your

Apron men. I haue founde you fai[th]ful of speche. I will nocht brek my brane, Suppois

[ygh]e sowld mischeif [ygh]ow. If yew love your selfe, and those that love yew, I can yw

thanke for ywyr lettyr that ye sente me. **Here my bone**...For sorowe my soule

ha[th] [ygh]ow so[ygh]t. The drawing of that whereof the copy is send yow. My lord and

you my lady, yf ye vouchsaf it were tyme that we went thrugh the world at our auenture.

Pray mind what you're upon. Pray set it downe, and rest you....Pray now rest your selfe.

I love you for trying, you dear. Commend you: and rest you. You don't know how I love

you all.[ccxxvii]

☞   *If you believe the infamous bone lies here, close the book & hold it in your hands.*

☞   *If you believe this is a decoy for said bone, turn to page 223.*

☞   *If you believe that the Galerie de Difformité is dedicated to you, turn to page 1.*

APPENDIX*

> ☞ ☞ ☞ *Due to an emergency, we regret to inform you that an appendectomy had to be preformed on this appendix. We apologize for any inconvenience.* 🖝 🖝 🖝

[☞ *Add section(s) to Appendix (i.e., tip-in a fold-out to continue). If you think your sections should join the Galerie as an appendage, please contact the Undertaker.*]

☞ *Count forward two pages & proceed from there.*
☞ *Count backward two pages & proceed from there.*

* 𝕿he beginning of the end?

Difformité

POSTSCRIPT

Since I finiſshed this Book, I am in Doubt whether I ought not to change the Title. For I have heard of a very ingenious Performance, called *The Galerie de Beauté* which proves inconteftably, that it confiſts in Curved Lines.[ccxxix]

Difformite

Difformity

Defformity

Deformity

Disclaimer: By the time this book is

Deformit

printed, it already will be

Deform

outdated

Form

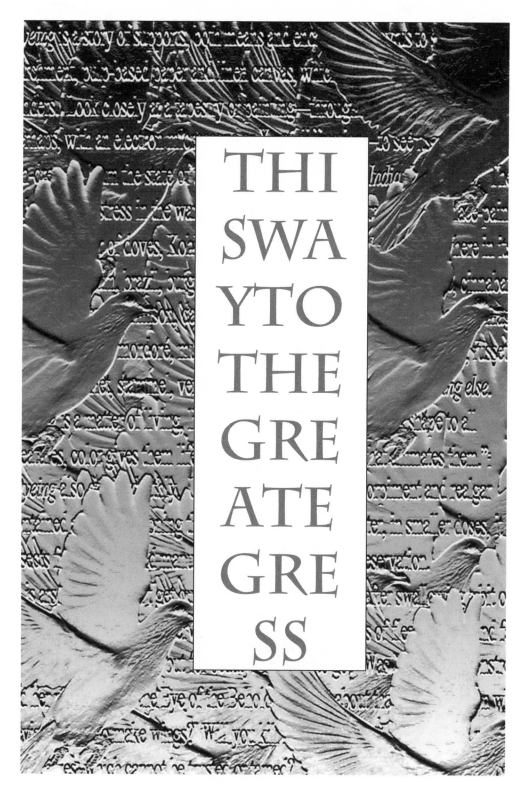

THI
SWA
YTO
THE
GRE
ATE
GRE
SS

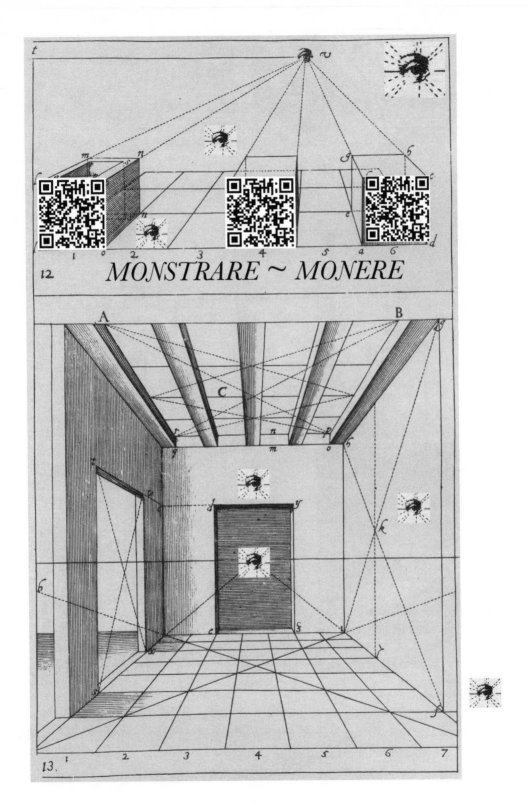

MONSTRARE ~ MONERE

250

THE MADELEINE P. PLONSKER
EMERGING WRITER'S RESIDENCY PRIZE

lakeforest.edu/plonsker

Yearly postmark deadline, April 1.

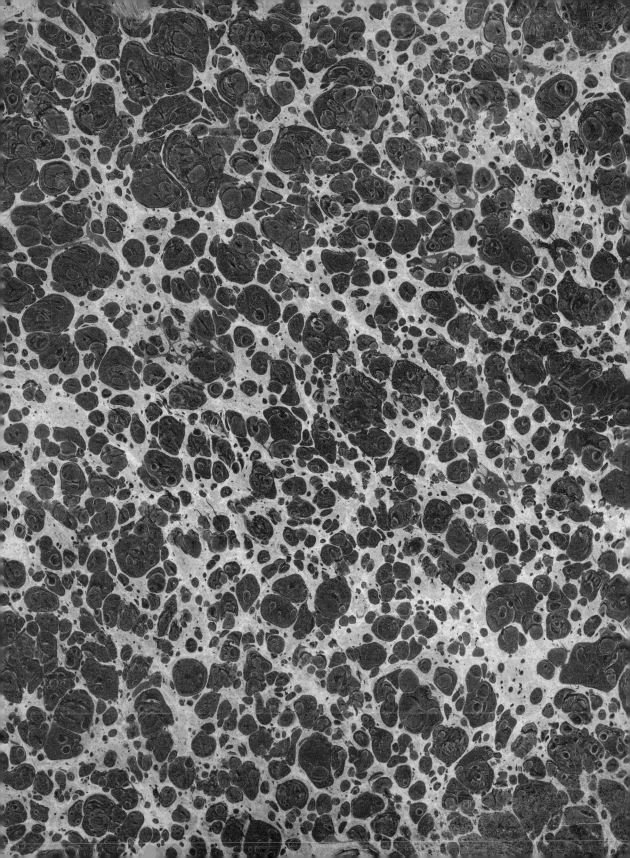